RECYCLING HUMANITY

By
Jackie Griffey

Bookman LLC
Publishing & Marketing

Providing Quality, Professional
Author Services

www.bookmanmarketing.com

"In this humorous and upbeat story, two escapes from an old folks' home use their skills and financial assets to help others. Guaranteed to make you smile!"
Pat Browning, author of FULL CIRCLE

"Jackie Griffey breathes life into the pages of her book, she writes with a poignant flare that is sure to captivate readers' hearts."
Suzie Housley, MyShelf.com

"Two friends battle retirement, a greedy daughter-in-law and a conglomerate, with determination and humor."
Debbie C. Lincoln, The Penpoint Group

"Imagination and knowledge of some medicine make for easy reading."
Betty Magie, Magie Newspapers, Cabot, Arkansas

"A New York adventure with humor and suspense."
M. L. Holland, The North Shelby Times, Memphis, Tennessee

"RECYCLING HUMANITY is just the breath of fresh air and humor needed in a good fiction novel. It's fun to read about 'the little guy" making a difference and sending a message to the world."
Melissa Parcel, In The Library Reviews

ISBN: 1-59453-364-4

DEDICATION

To true friendships which having been forged strong and beautiful above the rainbows in Heaven, laugh at mortal rules and simply love, heart to heart.

Heartfelt thanks to fellow writers who answered my questions or pointed out where I could find needed information; to my sibs on the net and local who listened, critiqued, and gave me hope; to my family who ate all those crockpot dinners so I could work; and to three beautiful and capable ladies in white for their input, Nurses Brenda Kittrell, Jackie Keltner, and Marita Upton.

CHAPTER ONE

RATS!

The sun glistened on the lures fastened to Aaron's hat as he turned to look toward the sound intruding on his privacy. The gleam of irritation in his eyes was enough to put at least a mild curse on anyone but Blanche, his self centered daughter-in-law and her coven of friends.

Aaron was as healthy in his sixties as he was in his thirties. The only time he had trouble moving was when his body didn't agree with his brain and he didn't want to move. This was one of those times.

Delaying moving as long as he safely could, he reeled his line in from the swimming pool. The sound of the approaching cars grew louder, they would clear the curve around the house in seconds. He shot a last venomous look toward the sound and scuttled like a burdened down pack rat to the pool house.

Drat! That's the end of my fly casting today. Where's that other lure? He found it caught on the hinge of his gear box and slammed the door shut behind him. *Wouldn't want to embarrass Blanche and her airhead friends,* he told the scarred up treasure box.

He kicked off his slippers and plopped down on the sofa as if it were somehow to blame for the unwanted interruption. He stuffed a pillow under his head, still grumbling.

The heck I wouldn't! I just don't want to listen to her gripe about it. Comfort won out over temper and he closed his eyes with a sigh. *Might be a good idea to plan a trip for myself next time Alton has a business trip to make. The way she's been acting and trying to get information out of my secretary, she's up to something, and it's something that's going to cost me money, from the questions she's been asking. I'm prepared, but being braced for whatever she's up to is hard on the nerves.*

His thoughts were interrupted by a rap on his door. His daughter-in-law's voice floated in the window.

"Aaron?"

Humpf! Sounds almost cheerful. I wonder who died?

"Aaron!" She banged with both hands on the innocent door that separated them.

Aaron smiled to himself, wondering if woodwork could cringe.

"You come open this door!"

That's more like it. She must want something important. She's not big on family visits. Aaron went to open the door, taking his time about it. He turned the knob and let the door swing open on its own. The first thing that was obvious, other than the bad temper, was Blanche was not alone.

"This is Aaron Willoughby," Blanche introduced him to the two men in white uniforms who stood there with her.

It was only half an introduction and Aaron didn't acknowledge it, eyeing Blanche.

"We've come to take you for a ride," she announced assuming an unbecoming false brightness.

Aaron stood there, silent and suspicious. *You look like a high fashion cat that's swallowed some kind of designer canary, that's for sure, I'll give you that,* was his grudging appraisal. *But nothing you could come up with, including this, would surprise me.*

Blanche's mask of pleasantness began to crack like a faulty wax museum figure as the silence got embarrassing. She turned to the two men and motioned toward him. The two men took hold of Aaron's arms, gently urging him toward the door. Aaron ignored them, refusing to budge.

"A ride? Where to? He addressed Blanche as if they were alone.

"To somewhere nice," she put her pleasant expression back on. "It's a very nice place, you will like it there."

Aaron glanced down at the hands on his arms. "Yeah, it must be a barrel of laughs if they have to send two guys after you."

"Don't give us any trouble," Blanche's voice hardened, "You're going."

"What makes you think I'm going? I never did take kindly to being ordered around."

Both white clad attendants had dropped their hands from his arms and stood looking for instructions from Blanche.

Aaron broke the silence, "You're wondering if you can get me out of here without getting hurt." His eyes locked on the eyes of the tallest attendant who was closest to him. "Truth is, you can't. I'm bigger than you."

Aaron grinned in an anticipation which was almost diabolic. "And I could use the exercise!" He put up his fists.

"This is futile, Aaron. Are we going to have to give you a tranquilizer or something to get any cooperation?" Blanche drew herself up, her back stiff and her face grim. She showed no signs of backing down. Aaron could see he had about as much chance as the designer canary.

"I'm not going anywhere without my car coat and my fishing hat."

"All right, that's fine. I'll get them for you while you put on your shoes."

Blanche pushed past him and he turned his attention to the two attendants. "So," he asked, "How's the forced travel business," he imitated Blanche's phony brightness. As he spoke, he looked down the drive, weighing his chances of escape. Without moving his eyes, he used one foot to scoot his slippers closer.

"We're only doing our jobs, sir."

Then Blanche was back. "Here you are."

Aaron got his slippers on as Blance returned and took his hat and coat from her. He put them both on before accepting the small shaving kit she handed him. He studied the little kit in his big hands, feeling like a bear with a peanut, and the determination hardened to put as many problems as possible in the way of Blanche's plans, no matter what they were.

He held the kit up as if weighing it. "The execution must be tomorrow."

"Don't be sarcastic. I'll bring you some more clothes in a couple of days when your laundry comes back. You'll make it all right."

Aaron felt comforted as well as protected in his old coat. He reached up and adjusted his fishing hat to a jaunty angle before stepping outside.

Might as well enjoy the human comedy, up to a point, that is. He looked happier at the moment than the two attendants, who watched him closely as they moved toward the van. He noted there was no name or logo painted on it. *They're right to be ashamed of themselves,* he mumbled to himself.

This is it, the waiting's over. I'm about to find out what she's up to and how far she'll go. Look at her, locking the door to the pool house like she's in charge of everything including me with Alton gone on his business trip. Yeah, she's been planning this, all right. But she's dead wrong if she's thinking she's going to make all the rules in this little game of wits. Aaron's jaw set as one of the men took his arm, supposedly to help him into the van.

"Sit right here, sir, watch your head there." The attendant was polite, but he held onto Aaron's arm like it was his last chance at salvation.

Blanche got into her car and Aaron waited as the van driver got in. He saw what seemed to be some sort of restraints as he sat down.

"Should we," the younger attendant spoke softly to his partner, following Aaron's gaze.

"Not unless you want to wear them back," his partner answered with a knowing glance at Aaron. "Shut the door."

The drive was not a long one. They turned into a drive just past a sign that said Pleasant Hill, and Aaron noted the name. The street sign was too far away to read. They stopped, letting Blanche pass then followed her car to park behind it. Aaron wondered briefly if parking was allowed at the entrance, not that Blanche would care about anyone's rules but her own. She waited until the attendants made a show of assisting him out of the van, and they walked into the building together in a tight little knot.

Blanche and the two attendants stopped before a combination nurses' station and admittance desk. Aaron stood between them, doing a good job of pretending he was not a member of their party, and wasn't interested in anything they did or said.

They waited in silence as the woman behind the desk shuffled papers, then gave them a brief smile. "Here we are, sir. You must be Aaron Willoughby." Willoughby tilted up at the end like a polite question as he examined his surroundings, ignoring her.

His wandering attention was caught by a granite faced man in an office across a hall behind the desk. *Looks like a ferret,* he decided, then amended the thought with an apology to all the ferrets in the world both wild and in captivity, as he was soon to be.

The ferret got up and closed the door.

"That's right," Blanche chirped, answering the woman. She had her phony brightness back, nodding to the woman like a bright kindergartner with the right answer to something the teacher asked.

"Is he—ah," the woman paused and gave an imperceptible nod in his direction.

"Yes, he's all right. He's fine. Just having an attack of stubbornness, is all, he's all right," Blanche hastily explained. "I'll give you any information you need."

Blanche answered the questions and the woman made notes before looking up again. "That's all I need for now. Just sign right here at the bottom, please."

Blanche took the sheet and read it quickly before signing it.

Aaron didn't let his amusement show. *She's anxious to get rid of me, but not reckless enough to take any chances.* He squelched the chuckle that rose in his throat and looked away at a potted plant.

The woman behind the desk took the paper back and darted a quick look at Aaron before addressing Blanche again. "I'm assigning him a room. There's a twenty-five hundred dollar payment due now, which waives the entrance fee and pays the first month in advance exclusive of any extra supplies or medications he may need. The monthly bill is always to be paid a month in advance."

No one moved. The woman looked at Blanche, then at Aaron, who was still examining the foyer and the general decor.

I gave at the office, Aaron retorted mentally, eyeing the woman vacantly as if she hadn't spoken English.

"Aaron," Blanche prodded.

Aaron moved nothing but his eyes, giving Blanche a look that would have stunned an army mule. *Don't see any reason to start talking now,* he reasoned with himself, *It would be downright hazardous to my bank balance. Let her figure it out. Maybe they'll give her a discount on looks, since that's all she's got.* He went back to studying the potted plant to keep from laughing in their faces. Parting with money was painful for Blanche.

Figuring it out didn't take Blanche long. She fumed. Her high bosom heaving with frustration and aggravation, she fumbled in her oversized purse for her check book.

Thank you, Fredericks of Hollywood, Aaron sneered mentally.

Without a word or another look at Aaron, she hastily wrote a check and handed it to the woman behind the desk. She turned and left, her high heels sounding like staccato gunfire on the tile floor. She was still shaking with anger when she got back to her car.

Miserable old wart! Pure anger nearly choked her, she had fled like a demented escapee, fighting tears of rage. *I should have thought of a way to tie this in with fishing. That and aggravating me are the only things he enjoys!* She dashed hot tears of rage away and ground her teeth as she stomped the last few feet, threw herself into the driver's seat and slammed the door. The tires screeched as she called Pleasant Hill's one speed bump everything but helpful. She took a deep breath and pulled her BMW out into the stream of traffic, glad to be leaving Pleasant Hill and Aaron behind.

***

Martin stirred on the narrow bed. His eyes fluttered open briefly, then squeezed shut hard enough to make his worry lines hurt.

Lord! I must have been partying with a bunch of vampires and joined the club last night, the way the light hurts my eyes. Maybe I'm dead...

Throwing off the thin blanket brought on more discomfort from every system in his waking body. Martin groaned, trying not to move anything that might generate any more aching.

Well, dead's out. I couldn't feel this bad if I were dead.

He carefully put both legs over the side of the bed and stood up. He felt briefly proud of the accomplishment, even though he was none too steady. He swayed, and ran his tongue over his teeth. *My mouth tastes like something crawled in there and died, and my feet are cold.* He wiggled his toes and opened his eyes just wide enough to look down at them.

The carpet's gone! And where's the bathroom? His insides began some kind of rebellion and his hands flew up to cover his mouth. *First things first!* He ran toward the white fixtures he'd spotted and bent over the toilet.

He wiped his mouth on a hand towel beside the sink, taking in his surroundings. Balancing like an ungainly stork, he warmed one foot on the other, squinting at the black lettering on the towel. *Pleasant Hill, that must be this cage I'm in.* He took the terry robe hanging on the back of the door and went back to the bedroom, looking around.

This must be the standard drying out place or nursing home set up. Well, there goes any hope for some Hair of the Dog for my condition. What's that?

A manila envelope on the dresser caught his eye. It had his name on it, Martin Hammond, in big print. He made a successful grab at it, and since he was planning on sitting down anyway, it was a simple act to let gravity do its thing over the narrow bed.

He opened the brad, *Looks like I'm going to get my education broadened, at least on the point of how I got here.* He dropped the towel over his cold feet and began to read. It took a while. His features ran the gamut from indignation to surprised amusement.

Incredible! This fairy tale would put the Brothers Grimm to shame. It must have been that weasel who brought me here. I must have let him in, I know I had gone home, and I dimly remember his face, unless it was a nightmare, it's hard to remember. He frowned with the effort. *It was that runty little weasel all right, had to be. Who else would have done this? He's the 'consorting with the enemy' type if I ever saw one. And here's these termination papers. It was that prize jerk all right, and some partner in crime from the hospital that helped set me up for this. Those boys from the conglomerate play hardball—dirty hardball! No doubt the weasel enjoyed this, he's too dumb to see how he's being used, not that I'm going to waste any sympathy on his sorry plight.*

Martin rose and tossed the papers back on the dresser, kicking the towel in the direction of the tiny bathroom.

Maybe I can catch one of the inmates here to fill me in on a few things. He tightened the sash on his robe and stepped out into the hall.

Hey, I'm in luck! He waved to attract attention and a young woman in a white uniform came toward him.

"I'm Martin Hammond," he gestured at the door behind him. "Were you here when I came in last night? I guess it was last night," he added uncertainly.

"You were here when I came on duty, Mr. Hammond. You may ask at the nurses' station if you want to know exactly when you came in. It's down that hall and to your right." She paused just long enough for Martin to notice it.

"It's okay," he assured her pleasantly, "I still know my left from my right."

***

Dusk fell on Pleasant Hill, dark and the plots within its walls deepening fast. One of the plotters stood regarding himself in the mirror of a small dresser. He had to stoop a little to inspect all of himself. *Hum, fortunately, being six feet three inches tall and a black man too, that usually discourages any negative comments about how I look. Out loud, anyway.*

Aaron made a frightening face, his arms up in a threatening pose, then smiled at his reflection. He went to the door of the room and peered out, his eye at a narrow crack between the door and the facing.

Not a soul in the hall. Quiet as a tomb, and damn near as much fun from what I've seen.

He glanced back at his reflection across the room. *Distance doesn't help,* he observed realistically. *I look so round in this car coat, if I fall down trying to get out of here I could not only get caught, I'd rock myself to death like a terrapin. I'll watch it, wouldn't want to do something to cause Blanche any joy if I can help it.*

He felt the outside pockets and the padded lining of the coat. *I've got everything I'm going to need with me, stowed away like a winterized squirrel, good thing I was prepared for this.*

Looking back once more he considered the empty shaving kit on the bed. *Don't guess it will hurt Blanche's feelings to leave that thing here, even if it was a Christmas present. Must have spent as much thought and time shopping as she did money. She could have done better shop lifting at Wal-Mart as tight as she is.*

He took a deep breath before quietly stepping out into the hall and went directly to the window at the end of it.

Everything's some shade of gray, he muttered nervously to himself. *Carpet, walls, everything. Color it quiet, the man with the money must have said. Well, let's see here.*

He glanced back. The hall was still deserted. He lifted his foot to the window sill, holding onto the facing and balancing himself.

Ah, good. Sill's not too high to step through, I figured I could make it.

He put his foot down and concentrated on opening the window. He worked at the lock to no avail.

Dang stubborn lock, the dratted thing won't budge. He stopped to peer out into the darkness. *Wonder how many alarms it would set off if I just broke the thing and ran like hell?*

Before he could decide whether or not to live dangerously, a hand descended on his shoulder. He spun around, fists up, ready to defend himself if he had to.

"Take it easy," the stranger hissed, apprehensively glancing over his shoulder.

Aaron looked him over, sizing him up quickly. *Skinny white man, about five eleven, no threat. I could throw him out the window.* He relaxed, but only a little. *And he must be one of the inmates here, why else would he be wearing that robe over street clothes?* He was still wondering when the man spoke.

"What are you doing here?"

"Why do you ask," Aaron countered cautiously.

The stranger frowned, losing patience. "Because it looks like you're bailing out of here the same as I am, and you're in my way."

"Humpf, that's what I had in mind, all right," Aaron spoke in a stage whisper, "But the lock's stuck. The morons must have shellacked over it."

"Let me see what I can do." The stranger reached into the pocket of his robe.

"Hey, you've got tools," Aaron remarked, admiring them as he leaned closer. "Pliers and a little rubber hammer."

"It's for testing reflexes," the stranger confided with a smile. "I looked around here today and helped myself to them. Let's see what a few well placed taps will do to loosen this thing."

The stranger worked while Aaron kept watch, listening and glancing up the hall behind them for unwanted company.

"That's got it." The stranger straightened up and put the tools in the pocket of his suit. "Help me raise this window."

Aaron put his six foot three frame to work and they soon had the stubborn window up high enough for them to crawl through. Outside, they landed in a mulched bed a few feet below the window.

"Damned holly bushes," Aaron swore with feeling, jerking around like a puppet on a set of strings to free the loose threads of his beat up car coat.

The stranger tossed his terry robe over another holly bush and poked him sharply in the ribs, "Shut up and get moving!"

"Used to giving orders," Aaron grumbled as he hurried after him.

They made grotesque shadows in the light from the building, moving quickly and close together, like night predators on the prowl.

They made it to the street and the stranger stopped under the light at the corner, "That's better," he panted, "We made it."

"Yeah, I think we're home free, thanks to your little rubber hammer. I don't see or hear anyone looking for us yet." Aaron stuck out his hand, "My name's Aaron Willoughby, but that's privileged information." He paused, again sizing up the man before him. "There may be people looking for me that I don't want to find me, you understand?"

"I understand," the stranger shook hands. "I doubt there will be anyone looking for me, or much concerned I'm gone. My name is Martin Hammond, Dr. Martin Hammond."

"Dr. Martin Hammond," Aaron's eyebrows went up in recognition, "The surgeon at St. Josephs Hospital?"

"Right now, that seems like another life, but that's right." As he spoke, he gazed in fascination at the light dancing on the fishing lures on Aaron's hat, then watched as Aaron broke off a few dangling threads the holly bushes had pulled loose on his coat.

He glanced back across the dark lawn, "Listen, I've got enough money with me to put us up for one night, and I certainly could use someone to go with me, being a strong believer in the buddy system. I've got enough to put us up for a night, maybe two, depending on how lucky we get, but that's about all I can do until I can get back and at least get my checkbook, I'm not going home now either. I don't want to be found by the wrong people any more than you do, and the kind of shelter I can afford right now, it would be safer to have company. I'm going to get as cheap a place as I can find that has a lock on the door," he added hopefully, "If you'd care to join me?"

"Thanks for the offer," Aaron smiled, turning from the dark behind them, "But I think I can beat it. I know a safe place we can go, and it won't cost you anything. I may need you too, since I'm going to be keeping a low profile, all you have to do is be around if I want a message or papers sent, maybe not even that, just be there in case do I need you. And as I said, it won't cost you anything, if you're interested?"

Martin studied Aaron's face before answering carefully, "I am, certainly." He grinned, "Sure can't beat the price, but are you sure I'll be welcome?"

Aaron tilted his head, his white teeth showing in amusement. "That was about as subtle as a kick in the shins, but," he shrugged, "I've had to consider the color I am and where I was a few times myself. To answer your questions, you will be among black people, but you will be with me and you will be welcome."

"Then it's my turn to be grateful." Martin looked down the dark street. "I wonder if the public transportation is still running, never thought much about it before." He rubbed his wrist with his fingers. "They took my watch, for safe keeping, they said."

Aaron's face twisted in derision, "Believe that if you want to. If that jerk I saw overseeing things when I came in had shook my hand, I'd be counting my fingers now."

An approaching car cut off his comments. It was a cab and Aaron stepped into the street, whistling and waving his arms. He motioned to Martin when it pulled over, "You coming?"

Martin got in with mixed feelings, wondering if he was facing as much welcome as Aaron thought, and knowing at the same time he hadn't much choice. *Until I can get back and get some money, I'm too broke to pay attention. I've got to see about getting back to work somehow, too.* Aloud he asked, "You sure about this?"

"Sure as I am about anything else at this point," Aaron leaned forward to give the driver an address before turning back to Martin. "We've got too far to go to take a bus anyway."

Martin grabbed the arm rest as they took a corner too fast. "Good thing there's no traffic, this feels like a cruise in the Batmobile!"

"Guess it's one of the hazards of life in the city, most cabbies drive like they're running for their lives. Some of them probably are—or should be." He felt around between him and the door, "This thing's probably too old to sport seatbelts."

"Or they got worn out defying gravity and bouncing bodies," Martin grabbed the armrest again. "Don't know why I'm so concerned with his driving, I don't know where we're going anyway."

"Right," Aaron laughed, "I see you're a philosopher with a practical approach. I never would find this place without a cab, but I know the address is right. He looked out the window, "Hey, we're slowing down, and there's not a cop behind us."

"Always a good sign," Martin nodded amiably.

The cab had eaten up the darkened city miles quickly, passing areas that were strange to both of them.

"The only thing we have to worry about is if my friend is still there, but I'm pretty sure she is," Aaron sounded confident.

Martin noted the female pronoun as the cab crawled past an Italian market place, the driver with his head out the window, looking at the street addresses he could find. He pulled to the curb in front of a large and well built but slightly shabby apartment building.

Aaron got out and talked to the driver as he eyed the building. "I'm going to pay you now, but wait for us, in case my friend isn't here. I'll wave if it's all right to leave."

Martin waited, wondering if there was a plan B.

Aaron took several bills from his pocket and handed them to the driver, who stuck his hand in his pocket looking worried.

"That's all right, keep it," Aaron told him, "But wait till I wave to leave."

"Yes, sir, I will," the driver's smile showed a gold tooth and a renewed faith in human nature.

He's well aware money talks, Martin commended him, *I hope to God he's got some more with him.*

Martin continued to worry as he went up the steps and entered the building behind his new found friend. He looked back out the window as Aaron studied the names by the intercom, hoping again he was right about his being welcome. He turned to look at Aaron's broad back and felt better. *Whatever's waiting for us, he's a good one to have on my side if we have to fight our way out of this place.*

After a brief conversation on the intercom, Aaron stopped to flash a grin at Martin before waving the cab away. A few seconds later, a buzzer sounded.

"I told her to count to fifteen and a half and then buzz, but I guess the cabby saw me all right."

"Yes, he's gone and he's happy." Martin surreptitiously examined the list of names as they passed by the intercom, even more uncertain of his welcome since he hadn't been able to hear the conversation. The name where Aaron's finger had stopped was a woman's name.

Aaron didn't miss the look. "She's an old friend of mine. Been knowing her a long time. Here's the elevator."

They stepped in and Aaron pushed a button. The elevator jolted to a start and rattled as it slowly rose upward. Martin put a hand against the wall.

"This thing sounds as bad as it smells." He looked around, "Clean, though."

"Yeah, I could have done without the el cheapo spray. Just be glad it works. Must be an antique like the tenants here."

"Fine," Martin loosened up, "We'll fit right in. Did you tell her you're bringing a friend?"

"I did. She's got a guest room we can use. And since we'll need to be here a while, I'm going to pay her for the room—"

Martin reached into his pocket, but a gesture from Aaron stopped him. "No, no. Don't worry about it, you're my guest. She can use the money and I've got it, it's that simple, so there will be no further discussion." With an air of having settled things, Aaron carefully removed his fishing hat and took off his car coat.

Martin eyed the coat shrewdly, "Our cab ride alone must have cost a bundle. If that old coat is stuffed with money, I'll take back what I thought about it the first time I saw it."

"As a matter of fact, if it will ease your suspicious pain, it is. I was expecting something like this Pleasant Hill thing and made sure I wouldn't be caught unprepared."

He gave the coat pat, "I know it looks like a fugitive from skid row." He looked at the floor indicator as he spoke.

"What floor is she on?"

"Three. And we'll be there in a few seconds, even at this rate."

"Yeah, we're moving along like a herd of turtles."

"Maybe it's just as well to have a little time. I could tell you were wondering about this lady. I met her a long time ago, on a business trip. She's a good friend and a good person. When we met, I was married to a fine woman I loved and we had a son I was proud of, still am. My wife is gone now, and I've kept up with my friend through the years without her knowing. That's how I knew where to come tonight."

God! Martin panicked mentally, *I'm not even sure if he's welcome, much less an uninvited guest.* He was too surprised to comment aloud and the elevator saved him the embarrassment of saying the wrong thing.

It ground slowly to a stop with a long, metallic sigh of relief. It shuddered slightly as Aaron got out. He checked numbers on the doors along the hall as they walked.

"She's in three-oh-three." He stopped. "Here it is."

He rapped lightly. A panel about three by five inches slid back and framed a pair of large, brown eyes which looked into Aaron's.

"Let me in, I'm not selling anything," Aaron chuckled, his voice low.

The door was flung wide and a slender woman who appeared to be ten or twelve years younger than Aaron crossed the threshold and threw her arms around him. Martin watched as he enfolded her in his arms. Touched by their expressions of affection, Martin stood back a little, trying to place the pleasant scent she was wearing.

The woman drew back, looking up at Aaron as if he were some Prince Charming, or at least a matinee idol. She didn't notice the old car coat over his arm. "Aaron, it's been so long! How did you ever find me?"

"It's a long story," Aaron hedged, "We've got a lot of catching up to do." He reached out to Martin, drawing him closer. "This is the friend I told you about."

Martin smiled, letting his admiration show as he took the hand she held out to him.

"Leona, this is my friend, Martin Hammond," Aaron introduced him, "My dear friend, Leona Miller.

We're running away from home together, Leona," he chuckled, *"The old folks home!"*

CHAPTER TWO

Alton Willoughby stood in an alcove at the public phone in his hotel, looking mean enough to bite himself. The click of the answering device coming on affected him that way.

I hate that thing! Alton told the impertinent beep. "Blanche, I'm not having much luck catching you and dad at home. I've been running around like a one eyed cat in a field full of mice looking for public phones on my way to meetings to tell you I'll be leaving here in two days and hopefully, will have this trip's business wrapped up in about eight days instead of two long weeks. I hope that's good news to you, though right now it doesn't seem to make much difference to you where I am. And I'd have to borrow some bloodhounds to find you! When I get home, we need to talk. We need to iron out some things between us. We're long overdue for some serious communication. And tell dad I've found him a new fishing hat, if he likes it. It's got room for a lot more lures on it. You can call me here at night, at the number I gave you. I miss you, Blanche, I miss being home."

Alton hung up the phone and gazed at it sadly as if it had just died. *That's one darn poor excuse for communication. No human voice available. It's like talking to myself when I leave a message on that thing. Bitching to myself is what it amounts to. I'm about ten minutes away from losing the arguments! If we had two or three children, maybe I could catch somebody at*

Jackie Griffey

home. If we wait much longer to have any kids, they'll be more like grandkids.

He stalked toward the hotel dining room, his feet punishing the indifferent floor on his way to another solitary dinner.

***

The attractive young receptonist at Coolidge and Quin Law Firm stared at the big bubble of gum she was blowing, fascinated. As it grew, her eyes almost crossed. It collapsed when the phone rang. She poked the remains into her mouth and surveyed her manicure before she reached for the phone.

"Coolidge and Quin Law Offices?"

"Are you asking me or telling me?" The female voice was sarcastic.

The receptonist giggled, "Telling you, I guess."

"I want to talk to Theo Jones."

"Who is calling, please," the bright young voice played secretary.

"This is Blanche Willoughby, and I'm in a hurry."

Blanche drummed her fingers on her writing desk, mentally cursing the quality of office help available these days.

"Mrs. Willoughby," Theo Jones's voice came on oozing friendly efficiency. "I'm sorry to have missed your call this morning, I've just come in—"

"Call me Blanche," she cut him off. "We did go to school together, if you recall, even if it was a hundred years ago."

The smile on Theo Jones's face was audible, "Not quite, it just seems like it sometimes. I'm ah—not sure how I can help you, or what it is you have in mind, from the short note I have here."

"That's the point, what to do. I don't know what I can do, or how to go about it. That's why I called you. What I'm concerned about is my father-in-law. He's got some property and investments, plus other interests, but we, my husband Alton and I, have no idea what or where they are. He could be financing little green men from Mars for all we know. He's got a little office and one employee who works for him there, and that's as far as we know. That's *it.*"

"What is it that worries you?"

"If something happened to him, we wouldn't know which way to turn. He must have quite a bit, the way he spends money, and I don't want to lose it—to see him lose it, I mean," Blanche amended quickly.

Theo Jones didn't comment, waiting for more information.

"I need to be able to get some information so I will know how to handle things, to know what to expect of these investments and properties, or whatever is involved."

"Hum," Theo Jones mused thoughtfully. "Have you asked if you might be able to help him in his office?"

Blanche gasped in annoyance. "I'm not looking for employment! I simply want to know what is going on and what his interests are. Exactly what he has coming in and how much is being reinvested or spent, and where. "I want to know what his investments are and what accounts he has."

"You say he has one employee who keeps his office and he and the employee are the only ones who know what his interests are. If that's the case, that the two of them are now managing on their own, you probably have no cause to worry."

"No cause to worry!" Blanche exploded at his lack of concern. "We don't know that at all. I need to have access to his office, so I'll know what he's doing—what he is spending and where!"

"Now, Mrs. Willoughby—Blanche," Theo tried to soothe her, "I didn't mean to sound uncaring. Are you afraid he's in danger of dying intestate? Is that it?"

"Humpf! Not him! He has a will. He uses it more like a weapon than a legal instrument. He hangs it over my head when he wants to be aggravating, and he wants to be aggravating *often.* I need to know what he's got in the way of property, accounts, all his assets, and what he's doing. Or better still, be able to handle things myself."

"Well," Theo Jones thought that over. "Nobody but his guardian angel can do that, without his power of attorney. Unless, of course—is he perhaps, becoming incompetent?"

"Exactly! He's arrogant, won't let me know anything about any of his business, and he's told his secretary not to give me any information—tells her to say I'll have to talk to him. Last time my husband was home, the two of them went to Canada. To *Canada!*

Just to *fish!* They stayed eight days, that must have cost a fortune!

Theo Jones chuckled, "Then he must be doing something right. I have to juggle time and money just to get out to the lake for a weekend."

"This is serious!" Blanche's voice rose as her anger and frustration became obvious, even to the complacent Mr. Jones. "I know he's got close to unlimited funds—*somewhere!* And he goes around in an old car coat and fishing hat, looking like he hasn't got two dimes to rub together!" She remembered how he had acted when they got to Pleasant Hill, "Or even good sense!"

"Don't shout at me," Theo Jones said mildly but definitely. "Let me spell it out for you. If he doesn't have good sense, that will have to be proved before you can step in and take over his affairs."

Blanche fumed in silence and Theo Jones added with emphasis, "That is not an easy thing to do. Have you considered that?"

"I certainly have. And I've taken the first step. I've put him in a nursing home." She didn't wait for an answer or an opinion, "I'll call you when I need further advice." She slammed the phone down, shaking with anger, frowning at the instrument which had given her so little help.

Incompetent? Maybe. But arrogant and impossible, certainly! The miserable old goat! The way he keeps hinting about grandchildren and that look when the cost of my wardrobe somehow gets into the conversation. The only hobby he has in his old age, is that dumb fishing rod of his, practicing his casting he calls it, and seeing how much he can aggravate me. I'd never have married Alton if I hadn't thought he would have money for us to throw away like his father does.

She narrowed her eyes, a speculative gleam shining in them. *I wonder how much Theo makes in a year?* Blanche shook her head at the image in the mirror. *Too late to think about that now, I wouldn't have had him on a bet anyhow, the scrawny little thing.*

She stood up slowly, her eyes moving critically over her reflection in the gold framed mirror above the desk. *He always looked like the little lab rat that didn't get any vitamins in the drugstore commercials to me.*

Deliberately putting on a pleasant if phony expression, she smiled at the mirror. *We'll see who wins this battle of wits. I'm already way ahead in the looks department.* She smoothed out a wrinkle in the skirt of her designer suit and pushed the record button on the answerphone before walking resolutely toward the stairs.

I'll go down and look more carefully in the pool house to see if he left any papers I can use. He said he closed his account at our bank not long ago, but I heard him tell Alton he paid for their fishing trip with a CD.

*** *** ***

Alton stood up, handing the waitress the little tray with a nice tip added to the money on it. He looked around the room. *Don't see very many people dining alone.*

His self pity was cut short when he realized he was staring at an attractive woman his age or a bit younger.

28

She's alone, and she's—she's smiling at me! Alton's answering smile covered his face with joy, his eyes full of honest admiration, but it didn't last. The smile fell flat as quickly as a retreaded tire. *There must be someone behind me,* he thought as he left.

As soon as he got out of the woman's line of vision, he chanced a look back. *There wasn't anyone behind me, she was smiling at me!* He felt like he'd just gone down the first hill on a roller coaster. He walked on, feeling more alone than when he had gone in. *Whoever she is, she looks like the kind of person I thought Blanche was when I married her.* He pictured the woman's pretty face and smiled, *Better looking, too.*

Alton stole an appraising look in the mirrored wall as he walked, *Guess I'm not over the hill yet, in spite of being married almost ten years.* He frowned. *Or is it Sixteen Beers with the Wrong Woman, like the song says? If I wasn't spoken for, I'd have offered to buy that pretty lady in the dining room a drink. Or had one sent over.* The mirror showed him his face collapsing into hopelessness again. *I've forgot how to be anything but married.*

He stopped at the desk and asked if there were any calls or messages for him. *I'll have to change my drawers if there is.* He had no hope, still in a blue funk.

"No, sir," the young clerk shook his head, then remembering there hadn't been any for this guest the other times he'd asked, he added, "I'm sorry."

Jackie Griffey

CHAPTER THREE

Leona extended her hand with a smile that held nothing but happiness at seeing Aaron again, and welcome for Martin, his friend.

Martin took it and raised it to his lips, returning her smile.

Leona tilted her head, a little laugh of pleasure slipping out at the gallant gesture. "Oh, I like this one, Aaron," she told him with amused delight. "Can we keep him?"

"Like him, do you? I'll chop off his head and have it mounted for you."

"My *dream* way to *go*," Martin chortled, "Done in by a jealous lover!"

"Come on in, you two," Leona stopped to lock the door again, still laughing at them. "And try and behave yourselves while I fix you a little snack." She led the way to the kitchen.

"Just for you," Aaron said.

Martin admired the clean coziness of her kitchen as Leona poured them cappuccino. "Actually," he confided, "Being good is a small price to pay. I'm grateful just to be here. A couple of hours ago, I was sitting in that care facility wondering if I could get out and not a friend in sight to listen to my troubles." He shot a teasing smirk at Aaron, "Now I've got two, some good cappuccino, and all I have to do is remember Aaron saw you first." The chuckle escaped in spite of him.

"Hum," Aaron growled, accepting the olive branch, "If you've got that straight, we've got no problems."

Leona set a plate of sandwiches before them, picking up Aaron's car coat with her other hand. "I'll put your coat in your room, Aaron." She added as she turned, "And when I get back, I want to hear more about this 'running away' business."

Martin and Aaron's eyes met. "We'll have to tell her, it's only right," Aaron reasoned. "You know not to share any of this, don't you?" Aaron reminded him in a low voice as he glanced at the door.

"You told me that as soon as we got to the streetlight, and the position we're in would be hard to forget anyway," Martin spoke softly too. "Besides, who would I tell? I'm about as lone as the famous Ranger."

"Yeah," Aaron nodded emphatically, "Lone is good. I mean to stay that way, keep as low a profile as possible." His eyes softened as he looked up, "Here's Leona."

"Now," Leona went to get a carafe of cappuccino and set it on the table as she rejoined them. "What is this about you two running away from somewhere? And where have you been all these years, Aaron? Your son was graduating from high school the last time I saw you."

"That's right. He's out of school and finished college now, and my wife is gone. My son is married and has a good job with a big company. For the past year or more, I've been living in the pool house at my son's place."

"Grandkids?" Leona asked, sipping her coffee.

"*No!* The woman my son married is a witch on a broom! But I'm getting ahead of myself." Leona sat listening as Martin sipped more cappuccino. "I figured there was something wrong with the marriage," Aaron said ruefully. "And now that I've lived there close to them, I know what it is. Blanche, that's her name, married my son because she wanted money, not him." His eyes showed his sadness, Martin thought as he listened with Leona and watched his face thinking how much body language could tell you. He observed Aaron as he did his patients as he continued.

"I gave them a cruise for their honeymoon. I hoped she'd come home pregnant with my first grandchild. What a joke that was! All she cares about is her looks and having plenty of money to spend."

"Oh," Leona's voice was sympathetic. "But you said your son has a good job—"

"He has. He makes good money. But it's not enough for her, she wants mine too. That's why she waited till he left on one of his business trips, and put me in that place I left tonight."

"Put you in there? But, how could she do that? I don't understand."

"I'll tell you from the beginning. She thinks she's smart, but I've always got more than an arm up my sleeve myself, I was ready for her."

Leona listened, setting her cup down, her attention and sympathy with Aaron as he told them his problems.

"I was practicing my fly casting, thinking about when Alton, my son, comes home, we might go fishing.

Blanche, my daughter-in-law, isn't ever around enough to know he's gone. He could just throw her some cash, like you would a hush puppy to a dog, and she wouldn't care if he stopped the world and got off."

"Aaron," Leona frowned, "Surely you don't mean that."

"You don't know her. I do. I'd been expecting something like what happened, and when I opened the door and saw those two attendants there to cart me off—"

"Attendants? Come to cart you off! Oh, Aaron," Leona looked tragic.

"Well, I knew I'd been right. My mind panicked but my feet stayed put. At least until l demanded my fishing hat and car coat and stalled for a little time to think. When we got there, to the place she had picked out to put me, I made Blanche pay for the few minutes of panic to the tune of twenty-five hundred bucks!" His face relaxed into a satisfied grin, "She was the one in pain when she drove off and left me there."

Martin snickered, admiring Aaron's handling of the situation and they shared a grin like successful conspirators.

"Then they took you to this place, this old folks home you and Martin ran away from?"

Aaron nodded, "Now you know. That's how I wound up on the downhill toboggan, courtesy of Blanche the Greedy."

"At least you were smart enough to make her pay for it," Martin admired his success. "I'm out a month's rent on that cell of mine, I guess." Martin raised his cup of coffee, "Here's to you and your raid on Blanche's wallet."

"I'm so sorry," Leona patted Aaron's hand. "You think she's going to try to—to have you declared incompetent, or something like that?"

"Don't worry about it. It wasn't a complete surprise. knew she was up to something, always trying to get information out of my secretary, she's not hard to read. I made all the arrangements I needed to before Alton left on his business trip. It was the logical time for her to make her move, that's all."

"It's a difficult thing to have someone declared incompetent," Martin assured him. "I'd say impossible in your case. I don't think you have anything to worry about."

"I'm not afraid of her being able to pull it off. She hasn't got the smarts or the friends in high places to accomplish a thing like that," Aaron had a more than confident gleam in his eye. "What I'm hoping she'll do, is show Alton what a mistake he made in marrying her," he smirked mischievously. "Now that we're safely out of there, I'm going to make like I'm invisible and watch the fun and fireworks while she hunts for my ass and my assets!"

Martin laughed wholeheartedly, "Aaron, you've got a mean streak in you, sounds like a fun game!"

Only Leona seemed to take the situation seriously. "What about your son?" She frowned, "Won't he be worried about you?"

"No," Aaron's response came promptly, without doubt. "He knows Blanche well enough to figure out what happened, there's no way she can hide it now that she's done it, and he's got faith in his old man. I'm going to sit this out and watch her hang herself."

He turned to Martin, "It's your turn. What about you, what's your story?"

"No story to it," Martin shrugged, "I've been thrown away."

"Thrown away, is that right," Aaron challenged. "A doctor, a famous surgeon." He stuck his tongue in cheek, not buying a word of it. "Thrown away?"

Leona smiled encouragement at him, "Somehow, I can't see that either," she coaxed gently.

"Well, if you insist," Martin gave in. "But, it's going to make me look like a near terminal case of the dumbs, the way I was set up."

"Can't see that. Must have taken you by surprise," Aaron grunted, "What happened?"

"You're right about the surprise. Though I should have seen the signs, now that I look back on it." He spoke more slowly, remembering past events.

"There were hints about retirement, and there were rumors too. But there are always those. The rule any place that's big as St. Josephs seems to be 'if you haven't heard a panic rumor by ten o'clock, start one.' I'd have been more alert with my head in the sand, the way it looks from here. The most consistent rumor was that a conglomerate big enough to be taken seriously, was trying to buy controlling interest in the hospital. I didn't pay any attention to any of that until the administrator called me in to talk to me about retiring. *Retiring!* I didn't think he was serious at first, then he told me they had already been talking to another surgeon about 'filling my shoes.' Can you beat that?"

Aaron watched, sympathizing with how he felt as he saw the blood suffuse Martin's neck with a tell-tale temper flush.

"Fill my shoes! My number elevens! I was still in them, and I reached across his mahogany desk and grabbed the little weasel by his cheap lapels—"

Aaron slapped the table, rooting for Martin, "I knew you were a fighter when you pulled that little rubber hammer out of your pocket!"

"I told him in no uncertain terms, I was *not* retiring!" He stopped with a sigh. "It didn't do me any good though. At that point it was already too late. The deal with the conglomerate was already in progress. It went through, and they sent a big dog to see to the transition, since the administrator was too chicken to handle me, or didn't have the clout necessary. I don't know which, and was too mad to care by then. Their big dog was not only a world class jerk, but an experienced jerk with the necessary skullduggery tools. He required immediate updates of all our health records, me included, of course. They said I had a touch of Parkinson's. I managed, never mind how, to read what they had on the results of my exam and there were no tests to back them up, just someone's summary of creative fiction. It sounded like I shouldn't start reading any continued stories. They were going to use that as an excuse to replace me as chief of surgery. I could stay on, the weasel said, if they could find a place for me. I swore I'd fight them tooth and toenails, but I sounded a lot braver and smarter than I was. All I had actually, was I knew I don't have Parkinson's. I went home and crawled into a bottle. I don't know how long I stayed drunk, but it was long enough for them to get in another strike against me. It gripes my soul how much I helped them with that. I dimly remember the weasel, which is what I always called the administrator, since that's what he looks like."

Aaron pictured the ferret he'd seen at Pleasant Hill.

"Anyway, I dimly remember the weasel and someone else taking me somewhere, which turned out to be Pleasant Hill. I was too weak to be dangerous by then. I sobered up there in the nursing home with a month's stay paid in advance, on my own credit card, of course, and termination papers in my room. The conglomerate won that round, no contest."

"Their methods sound familiar," Aaron leaned forward, interested, "Do you still have those termination papers?"

"No, I threw them in a trash can as soon as I realized what they were."

"Do you remember the name of the conglomerate?" Aaron's eyes held his, "Or the name of the big dog they sent in?"

"Um," Martin tried to remember, seeing Aaron's interest, then shook his head. "I didn't pay much attention until it was too late, I guess my hindsight got a little pickled," he looked sheepish. "I'm sure the name was on the papers, it would have been, wouldn't it? But I don't remember what it was except that it was a long title. Long enough to sound like all the other legalese you see on things like that or in the newspaper's business section." He stopped, looking grim. "But the big dog, I do remember. He was Denghen Po, they told us, as if that would impress us. I only saw him once, but the strange name stuck in my mind. That was his name, Denghen Po. That much, I'm sure of."

"Denghen Po," Aaron mused thoughtfully, leaning back in his chair.

Leona touched his hand. "Your coffee's cold, would you like a warm up?"

"No, I guess we've kept you up long enough with our up close and personal soap operas," Aaron shook his head. He glanced at Martin, who agreed, looking tired.

"Come on then, I'll show you your room."

The room Leona showed them to was big and comfortable, with ample closets and two double beds. It reminded them both they hadn't any clothes to put in the closets, and it had been a long night.

Right now we're about an eyelash above homeless, Martin realized. The bed looked inviting to him as he turned his attention to what Leona was saying.

"Your own bath is right through here," she finished the tour. "I used to rent it to girls going to the business school near here," Leona added uncertainly.

"Thank you. This is great, just right to be comfortable," Aaron approved.

"It sure is," Martin spoke from the bathroom door. "Unless you want to go first, I'm going to hit the shower and the sack, in that order."

"Sure, go on. Leona and I have some talking to do." He left with Leona, holding her hand.

Martin had no trouble getting to sleep, now that they'd made their escape. He dreamed of chasing a weasel with the administrator's face down a long hospital corridor as Aaron and Leona spoke quietly in the living room.

"I didn't think I'd ever see you again, Aaron." She asked no questions, waiting for him to speak.

Aaron smiled, "I kept up with where you were. My wife is gone now, she didn't suffer and lived to see our son married. Pneumonia, it was. She went quietly in her sleep, I was there. Didn't realize she was gone till I reached over and touched her hand..."

"I'm sorry, Aaron."

"Thank you, we had a good life together." He raised his eyes, "My boy is raised now. And doing well on his own. Or will be as soon as Blanche realizes she's not going to get any of my money." He smiled grimly. "But that's not a thing to dwell on, it will work out. I've got some other things to finish up and take care of, but I'm here now, and things will work out for us this time, if you want them to?" He laid the hand he had been holding against his cheek, his eyes tender with affection.

"I think you know the answer to that," Leona smiled and kissed him, moving closer to snuggle in his arms. "But this Blanche," Her soft brown eyes were worried, "Are you sure she can't do anything to hurt? People like that are dangerous, Aaron."

"She's nothing to worry about. I've moved my office, so she can't bedevil my secretary. That's the next thing she would try. I'm not hiding because I'm afraid of her. I'm hiding because I don't want to be bothered with her while she shows her true colors. I want Alton to wake up and smell the coffee, as Ann Landers says, and this should do it. All I have to do is sit back and wait." The things he had in mind to help her fall on her face, he kept to himself.

***

Alton looked out the plane window at the fleecy clouds without seeing them. *Soon as I get home, I'm going to talk to Blanche,* he promised himself again. *No matter what kind of penny-ante errands she has to run, or if the garden club's got a bumper crop of blooming idiots or anything else, we're going to talk. She hasn't returned one of my calls since I left. We'll talk when I get home or our lawyers will talk for us.* His hand clenched into a fist on the arm rest.

***

Blanche stood in the bedroom window looking down at the pool house as if it had answers to her questions written on its roof in some indecipherable language.

All they'd tell me at the bank is Aaron's closed his accounts there. That's no help, I knew that. He's always free with useless information, but I can't find out anything else without account numbers, even if they were in the same bank. He didn't know he was going to Pleasant Hill. I can't believe there was nothing at all with any useful information in it among his things. He's not that smart, he only thinks he is. The way he spends money, he's got to have an almost unlimited supply. Probably got interest and other things direct deposited into different accounts, if I only knew where they are! There's got to be a way to find out what his investments are, what stocks he has, and where at least some of his property and holdings are located.

Her pencil thin brows drew together in a bitter frown, "*I've got to get him in as good a humor as possible too, with Alton coming home. Alton's not going to like this. I hope Aaron's done something by now that's so totally off the wall outrageous, and he's certainly capable of it, that it will show the world and Alton he's exactly where he should be! I don't know why I didn't think of this before.* She gave herself a mental pat on the back, feeling better, congratulating herself. *With his temper and the regimentation there's got to be in a place like that, it's not going to be long before there's a clash between him and whoever they've got in authority there.* She frowned. *I hope it's not so bad they won't keep him, just enough to show Alton he's definitely in need of their care.*

She looked at the phone, *I know, I'll kill two birds with one stone. I'll call Aaron right now and offer to call his secretary for him. Maybe I can get some information that way, and it will sound good.*

Pleased with herself and her own good taste as she admired the room, she looked up Pleasant Hill's number and dialed, deciding with part of her mind she would buy better looking bedroom furniture as soon as she could locate some of Aaron's money.

Someone at Pleasant Hill picked up the phone as she was picturing some English antiques she had been looking at that would be just right in the bedroom.

"I want to speak with Aaron Willoughby," she cast the antiques aside temporarily. She listened a moment, the pleasant expression freezing on her face. The smile broke and reformed into wide-eyed panic as she sprang to her feet, clutching the phone tighter. Her eyes snapped, her mouth got dry, disbelief and denial took over.

"Gone!" Her voice was an unpleasant screech, *"What the hell do you mean, he's gone?"*

Jackie Griffey

CHAPTER FOUR

Blanche gaped in disbelief at the phone in her hand. speechless after her initial outburst.

"Just a moment, please," a timid voice ventured after several seconds of silence. "I'll let you speak with our director."

Blanche's legs folded, lowering her back into her chair. Uncertainty, which up to now had been a complete stranger to Blanche, ran large as life pictures of the dire consequences of losing Aaron through her imagination.

"Mrs. Willoughby," an older voice breathing authority came on.

"I'm the director here at Pleasant Hill," the woman explained briskly. "We have been trying to reach you."

Blanche found her voice, "Whoever answered the phone told me my father-in-law is not there. I *took* him there myself, how can he not be there?"

"That's why we have been trying to reach you. To tell you he left, and see if he went home."

"Oh. No. No, he didn't." Blanche paused, uncertainty fled as she regained her composure and sought helpful information. "Did he watch for someone coming in and get out that way? It seemed to me when we were getting him registered, the door was kept locked."

"The door is kept locked at all times. He did not leave through the front door. He got a window open, though it too was locked, and got out that way. He left sometime after the last check, which is about an hour after dinner."

"I, ah—I know he was a little upset," Blanche pictured Aaron running down the middle of the street, his robe flying out behind him, "How long has he been gone?"

"He left the first night."

"The first night! And you've heard nothing from him? Did anyone see him go?"

"Not that we've been able to locate. He evidently took the contents of a small case with him. We found it empty on his bed."

Blanche's voice hardened as she faced the reality that Aaron was gone and the woman could be of no further help to her. "I see. Then please leave it at the front desk and I will pick it up when I come for my refund check."

"Pleasant Hill does not give refunds," came the chilly reply. She made the pronouncement sound chiseled in stone.

"And I do not pay for services I do not get. Must I bring my attorney with me?"

After a moment's hesitation, the director recognized an attitude as implacable as her own. "No. That will not be necessary."

"I will be there within the hour."

Blanche wasted no time at Pleasant Hill. She took care of her business there and left the building, darting furtive glances in all directions as if Aaron might be lurking in the shrubbery or somewhere else nearby.

She hurried to her BMW, the shaving kit with her check in it clasped tightly to her breast.

I'll go by and put this check in the bank on the way home. At least I managed to get their check so I'd have my money back. But where can he be? Aaron would do anything to make me look bad, but it won't work. Blanche's foot transferred her temper to the accelerator. *His brain really has turned to jello if he thinks it will!*

Blanche pulled into the bank's parking lot to make out a deposit slip, her mind still racing. *This disappearing act of his is something I never expected, but maybe I can use it. Maybe I won't have to tell Alton about the nursing home, at least not yet, there must be some way this can be used to work for me, if I can just find him. I've got to get hold of that secretary of his. I'll bet she knows exactly where he is! Then I'll decide what to tell Alton.* Blanche got out and slammed the door, resolved to pry some information out of that close-mouthed secretary.

***

"Good morning," Martin greeted Leona as he entered the kitchen.

"Good morning to you, too. Aaron's got his mouth full, we've got eggs, bacon, white or wheat toast, or some not so fancy and fruity cereal if you would like some."

Aaron swallowed, "I highly recommend the eggs and bacon," he beamed at Leona. "How's that for an unsolicited testimonial?"

47

"This is great," Martin sat down looking pleased with the world in general and breakfast in particular. "I'm not used to this. Let me have two eggs over light with bacon and whole wheat toast, before some sadist ends all this by waking me up!"

"Wakes you up, huh? Now don't tell me you're a breakfast skipper," Leona accused him, breaking eggs in the skillet.

"I didn't plan it that way, it was just habit. My routine was to get to the hospital early and get coffee there. Tasted like tree bark and bile, but it was hot. Then I'd have a couple of creams and some sugar to round out my meal," he added as if trying to make points.

Leona scooped eggs out of the skillet and set his plate before him with a scornful glare. *"Eat,"* she commanded.

Martin ate. "This is delicious, Leona," he managed between bites. He reached for another piece of toast. "I'd get down on one bony knee right now and propose, but Aaron wouldn't let me live long enough to finish this."

"You got that right. No wonder you're such a wiry specimen, your tapeworm probably died of shock right after the first three bites of Leona's good breakfast hit bottom, not that I believe a word of that sad, tear-jerker of a story."

"You're questioning my word?" Martin's conversation didn't slow at all his wolfing down his food, but he took time to smile up at Leona as she poured him more coffee.

"Not exactly," Aaron corrected him. "You don't so much tell lies, as you just tell the truth to suit yourself. But forget about your bad habits, we've got to make some plans. I'm going to take Leona with us and rent two cars, in her name. She will drive me, and you can use the other one."

"No need, I'll manage. I'm going to a clinic where a former student of mine is in charge, to see if I can work there."

Aaron was dubious, "What about our low profile, won't they broadcast their good fortune in getting you?"

"No," Martin shook his head. "Rob knows the politics at St. Josephs. He was there off and on when this replacement business started. Also, the clinic is too far away for me to run into any of their staff. I'm sure the clinic needs me, and it will do me good to be needed, after being thrown away. I'm still a doctor, and a surgeon."

"Of course," Aaron's brows drew together in anger at any doubt of that. "The conglomerate and baloney poultice couldn't change that, and don't you forget it! I can understand your feelings though, since I've been thrown away too. It's not that I don't think you can manage, it's easier to get the two cars. That way, you can come and go when you want to and we won't have to bother with any transportation hassle for either one of us, and I still might need you to get something or pick up something for me. I've seen a lot of expense accounts with less justification," he argued. "Mostly, it's just the easiest way."

"It would be less trouble all right." Martin's eyes twinkled, "Since you've got this game with Blanche going, I'd like to be posted from time to time?"

"I'll do that."

"And while you're nodding your head, keep track of all this so I can reimburse you when things get straightened out."

Aaron lost his cool. *"Hell no!* I told you, money's not my problem. Quit worrying about it like a three legged dog! I've got more money coming in than I could spend if I made a nine to five job of it. The only bad thing about it is it attracts maggots like Blanche, but I've got plenty to compensate for that too, if I have to."

"All right, all right. Point taken. Aside from the money angle." Martin put his hands up to ward off blows, "You and Leona need me like that dog needs three legs!"

Aaron laughed. "You can put your hands down. I appreciate your offering to pay me back. It's simply a matter of it's not being necessary. As for hanging around, I need you to sharpen my wits on even if nothing more important comes up and you can't ever tell when you'll need a doctor." He got serious, "And there might be something I need done where I would need someone I trust and can count on. I can do most of what I need by phone and keeping in contact, but I might need you."

"Hadn't thought about that…"

"Well, think about it. And if it will make you feel better, when I get far enough along in this game I won't need you anymore, I'll give you the ax." Aaron winked at Leona, "How's that?"

"Okay." Martin buttered the last piece of toast on the plate and grinned at Leona who had stood quietly listening. "You're a glutton for punishment, Aaron Willoughby."

"For what my opinion's worth," Aaron told him, "The hospital's going downhill fast. They took their first step in the wrong direction when they let the conglomerate get hold of them, and another giant one when they cheaped out and replaced you." His eyes met Martin's, "I've heard of some of the things you did."

"Thanks for the kind words. At least I don't have anything to feel guilty about." Martin stirred his coffee and looked up at Aaron mischievously, "Let me know when the ax is going to fall. And just tell me flat out. I've already proved the hard way, I can't take a hint!"

***

A man in slacks, sports coat, and tie entered Pleasant Hill and stopped at the reception desk. There was no one there. He stood looking around for help.

"Hey, you there in the hall? You're in white, are you a nurse here?"

"Yes, sir," the nurse glanced around. No other help was in sight. "I'm an LPN," she explained, "Are you looking for someone?"

"Yes. That is, I need information about someone who was here—"

"Oh," she assumed a sympathetic expression, thinking a loved one had passed on. "What do you want to know? And who—"

"Aaron Willoughby. Do you remember him?"

"Big black man, didn't talk?"

"Didn't talk?" The man was puzzled.

"Not that I know of. The woman who came in with him answered all the registration questions. I didn't see him again except in the dining hall."

"And he left that night? The same night he came in?" He pounced on it. "Has that happened before, people leaving like that?"

"You'll have to talk to the director about that," the nurse told him, sensing trouble. "Are you—a relative?"

"No. I'm not a relative, I was hired to find him." He held out a business card, "I'm a private detective. My name is L.D. Holmes."

The nurse read the card, stifling a smile, "Holmes, as in Sherlock?"

"Yes, I know I've got a name to live up to." He smiled and got on with his questions. "Do you know of anyone Willoughby did talk to, or come in contact with? Or perhaps sat with at dinner? You said you saw him in the dining room."

The LPN shook her head. "He sat by himself. Wouldn't even take off the old coat he wore when he came in here. The only thing he had in common with anyone else here, is like I told you, another man left that same night."

Holmes pricked up his ears. "This other man, if you don't know if he talked to anyone else, do you know who that other man who left was?"

"I'm sorry, I don't remember his name."

"But there's bound to be some kind of record," he pressed. "You can look it up for me, can't you?" His smile oozed nice as he reached for his wallet to add temptation.

The nurse hesitated.

"I'll give you a twenty for your trouble." Holmes glanced down the empty hall when she did. "It's not against any kind of rule, is it?"

"I don't think so," the nurse made up her mind, "And I can use the twenty."

She went behind the desk and searched among the ledgers and papers. "Looks like the whole thing's ready for the recycling bin, doesn't it?"

She opened a folder, running her finger down a list of names.

"Here it is. His name's Martin Hammond. See, right there at the bottom." She held the paper where he could see it. "I'm sorry, I can't tell you if that address is current or not."

"That's okay, it's a start. Thanks, here's your twenty."

***

Aaron, Leona, and Martin exited the rental agency like eager children on an Easter egg hunt.

"Here are our two," Aaron pointed to the numbers painted on the concrete. "Which do you want, Leona, the champagne or the blue?"

"Blue," Leona's eyes sparkled, "I like blue. And it's such a pretty car!"

Aaron handed her the keys, giving the other set to Martin. "You're going to trust me in champagne?" Martin asked with a grin.

"I like to live dangerously," Aaron kicked one of the tires. He pulled out some bills and wrote something on one of them. "I'm writing Leona's phone number on this small bill. You shouldn't have to use it with these others. If you won't be in by dinner, call and let us know what's going on, so we won't think those Neanderthals in the white suits got you."

"Right." Martin pocketed the bills and gave Aaron a sloppy salute. "I'll do it." He added plaintively, "Wish me luck on the job."

"If they don't thank the Lord and grab you, they're too dumb to work for," Aaron assured him as he got into the blue car beside Leona.

***

Nurse Jennie Graves stuck her head into the clinic's doctor's lounge, straining to see in the dim light.

"Only one lamp?" She addressed a lump on the couch whose length seemed familiar.

"Who's that?" The muffled voice came from the depths of the comfortable couch as her hand found the light switch.

"Rob? I thought I'd find you here. Why the dim lights?"

"I'm being kind to my eyes." His nose twitched like a rabbit sniffing clover. "Is that coffee?"

"Not just coffee. I went out and got you some cappuccino and a couple of Danishes. Have you had anything to eat?"

"Don't remember. But that smells so good, I guess not." He moved slowly as a still sleepy bear wakened too early from hibernation.

"What am I going to do with you," Jennie scolded.

Dr. Rob Payne leaned toward her with a leer, "You want suggestions? Speak up, while I can still crawl bravely on!"

"Oh, Rob, your eyes look awful! How long has it been since you got some sleep—and why don't you take better care of the man I love?"

"No time, lady."

He got vertical enough for the coffee to run down and reached for the danish, looking ravenous. He took a huge bite, paying no attention to the white icing he sprinkled over his scrubs. "Unless I luck up on a faith healer who can cram eight hours rest into two," he added. Jennie watched as he licked a piece of apple off his lower lip before continuing, "Can you direct me to the nearest tabernacle?"

"I can do better than that," she patted his chin with a paper napkin. "You finish that Danish and lie back down. I'll watch this asylum while you take a nap. But Rob, darling, superdoc, stubborn cuss, you've got to have some help!"

"You'll get no argument there. As soon as I find a combination thoracic surgeon and philanthropist, I'll *grab* him. No one seems to want to work twenty-six hours a day for the numbers we've got in our budget."

Jennie moved a pillow. "I know. I know. Sleep now, worry later."

"Don't let me sleep more than an hour, if we can go that long without an emergency…"

***

Martin pulled up to the automated gate of the clinic parking lot and took a card, staring back at the tiny red eye in the mechanism as the gate opened to admit him.

I hate dealing with things you can't argue with! And I don't remember ever feeling this alone in my entire life, Martin stewed as he parked the rental car and made a note of the location. *At least it's not a bad drive from the apartment.* He looked for something good in the situation to lift his spirits.

The sprawling building across the parking lot was impressive. *I didn't realize the clinic was so big. I must be needed here, the parking lot's full. Can't help but wonder if the 'sour grapes' vine reached this far, and how much damage it might have done me.* He took a deep breath and squared his shoulders, *I'll soon know if I've got any friends left.*

Martin moved toward the building at a slow walk. *I'm nervous as a government agent in a booby trapped marijuana patch, wondering what's been spread around about me. But heck, they're bound to need help, and unless I miss my guess, don't have much of a budget to get it.* He shoved his hands in his pockets. In spite of his pep talk to himself, it was a long way from where he parked to the clinic, and his feet got colder with every step. *Common sense tells me they've got to need help. All I have to do is convince them it's my help they need.*

Jackie Griffey

CHAPTER FIVE

Martin stood inside the clinic, watching the flow of traffic. Most of the hurrying people were young, all of them intent on their own errands, much too busy to notice him or anything else, unless it blocked their determined progress.

Okay, I've done it. I'm in here. He moved a little farther in, feeling downright invisible for all the attention he got. *Maybe I should have called first.* He wanted to grab someone and ask for directions, but his hand was reluctant to do his bidding as his feet had been in the parking lot. He simply stood there, studying faces that passed by. No one looked familiar, no one approached him.

"Dr. Hammond! Dr. *Martin Hammond!*" The joyful sound rang out behind him. He whirled around at the feminine voice that seemed so glad to see him.

"It *is* you!"

Martin's grin would have made the entire 'possum population jealous. He reached out and took the hands she extended to him.

"Nurse Jennie Graves! You're a welcome sight! This crowd looks like a prep school. I was looking at all these bright but strange faces, feeling like Rip Van Winkle! Now I've found one I know that's beautiful too!" He gave her a heartfelt hug, keeping her hand. He held the hand up, looking at it critically before letting her have it back.

"Hasn't Rob staked a claim on you yet? I thought he was smarter than that."

"We're working on that in our spare time," Jennie sighed. "But there hasn't been much spare time lately."

"Where is that rascal and what's he been doing that's more important than courting?"

"Stand right there a minute and I'll tell you where he is and all the other gory particulars." Jennie turned quickly and disappeared down a nearby corridor before Martin could object.

***

Blanche always looked better than she acted, which was not hard to do. She drove her BMW like a tank going to war and heavy traffic was her chosen battlefield. She was completely ruthless when it came to grabbing a parking place.

"Gotcha!" She hissed it loudly between her teeth. Her grin was pure, evil triumph as she deftly cut off a larger, older model car, and parked near the building that housed Aaron's office.

"Same to you," she spat at the other driver as he flipped her the bird and sped off. She eased her BMW into the parking place feeling like the Duchess of Go or maybe the Queen of Quick. The glee died as her heels hit the sidewalk and she hunted for coins for the meter. She fed them to the greedy slot, begrudging the legal extortion.

Get these down your little metal gullet, you ugly bandit. You're a hold up in more ways than one.

She checked to make sure the doors were locked, then with a determined frown, started toward the building's entrance.

This time, I'll not be put off. If that secretary won't tell me where Aaron is, or give me any information, I'll refuse to leave until she does. Her mouth was a grim line as she vowed to get results. Stepping off the elevator, she saw a man standing in front of Aaron's open office door.

Feeling vaguely uneasy, she wondered who he was and what he was doing there. *He seems to be doing something to the door. I would have called, but I've never been able to do any good by phone, no matter what I threaten. That man is doing something to the door, but it doesn't look like he's working on the lock, I'll see about this!* She hurried her steps.

The man looked up as Blanche stopped beside him but made no comment.

"What are you doing here," Blanche demanded in a voice of authority.

The workman gestured at the door. "What I get paid to do, that's what."

"Acme Freight and Storage," Blanche peered at the unfinished lettering on the door. "That's wrong. This is—" At his insolent smirk, she looked past the workman into the open door.

"The secretary's desk is gone. The place is *empty!*"

"No kidding," the painter exclaimed sarcastically. "All I know is I was sent here to put this lettering on the door."

"Hum, well," Blanche wasted no time arguing with accomplished facts. "As long as I'm here I might as well go in and at least have a look around." She started easing past him, "If you have no objection." She added, already in the door.

"Suit yourself, but make it snappy. I've got more than this one job to do today."

Blanche walked through the small suite, feeling cheated somehow. Things were not going as planned. Aaron was gone from Pleasant Hill, now this! The feeling of cold air circulating around her spine came back as she listened to her footsteps echoing in the empty rooms.

Everything's been cleared out. It's clean as a whistle, and he never said a word about it. Must have been recently, the only thing left is that trash can in there where his office used to be. Must not have cleaned the place yet. She walked over and looked down at the waste can. It had a plastic liner and was about three quarters full of papers. She bent to get a closer look at the ones on top.

Maybe there's a few addresses and some account numbers in this correspondence, some of it looks official. I see one with a business logo right here on top. She took care to check the bottom of the plastic liner before picking it up. *I'll take this with me, maybe I got lucky...*

As she hurried out, the painter looked up again, but she passed him by without a glance, carrying the liner by its top. He watched her walk away, enjoying the view. His brush was arrested in mid air. He thought it was a shame to waste a shape like that on such an anti-social attitude. The elevator doors began closing behind Blanche.

"You're welcome," he sang out, hoping she heard him.

***

Nurse Graves reappeared quickly. "Sorry I had to leave you," she apologized to Martin. "Let's get out of the traffic."

She led him to some chairs at the end of the hall. "I sure am glad to see you," she breathed as she sat down. "Especially if you're here to help." Her pretty face took on a pained expression, "Rob's about out of gas."

"I am hunting work, but what's this about Rob running out of gas?"

Jennie's eyes told him as much as her words, "Small budget, big job, killing himself, to put it in a nutshell." Jennie watched the activity from where they sat as if it was a tide about to suck them under. "You know how conscientious he is. He tries to fill in the gap whenever there's more help needed whether he's had any rest or not. He's good, but he's not superman, and he needs more rest or he's going to kill himself."

"That would do it all right," Martin sympathized. "Is it really that bad?"

"We'll probably get a little more money next year and things will ease up a little, but right now, yes. It's bad. But, if you've come to help, I'll let him tell you about it himself." She stopped where she had stood up and studied his face, "You are serious about working here, aren't you?"

Martin smiled at the pretty, anxious face, "For the second time, yes. Are you trying to talk me out of it?"

"Heaven forbid! That's the best news we could get. Rob's in the lounge." She started walking and Martin fell into step beside her.

"He told me not to let him sleep more than an hour and it's been two," she smiled, the young student nurse Jennie peeking out at him, "But I don't think he's got the strength left it would take to fire me."

In the lounge, Martin looked down at the young doctor asleep on the couch. Rob's mouth was open and one arm dangled, the hand resting on the carpet.

"Worst case of pooped I ever saw." He looked affectionately at his former student. Jennie touched Rob's shoulder and he sat up, rubbing his eyes.

"Someone's here to see you." Martin noted the gentleness in her voice as she woke him, "Dr. Hammond's here, Rob."

Rob's eyes focused on Martin in the lamp light. "Good to see you, sir." He grinned sheepishly, "You caught me sleeping on the job."

"Not the way I heard it," Martin nodded at Jennie.

"Would you like some coffee, sir?"

"I'll get you some," Jennie offered, "How do you like it?"

"No, don't bother," Martin shook his head. "I know you need to get back—orientation?"

"How did you guess?"

"I know the symptoms for that too. You don't have to be taught about the joys and pains of breaking in new help."

"I guess it's obvious, at that. Let me know if you change your mind about the coffee, okay?"

"Sure. Thanks anyway." He joined Rob on the couch.

"I'm here looking for employment," Martin got right to the point as Rob reached for his shoes. "If there's an opening and you'll have me?"

"Have you?" Rob paused, startled. "Oh. You're referring to that baloney factory that pushed you out of their private rat race at St. Josephs."

"Yeah, they're sharper politicians than I am."

"I knew there had to be some sort of calculated evil going on—probably involving money?"

"How did you figure it out so fast about the money?"

"I met the surgeon they brought in. He may some day be half the surgeon you are, but it won't be during my lifetime," Bob grimaced. "He looks a little like Opie on the Mayberry series. I'd hate for his to be the last face I saw before my anesthetic kicked in."

Martin laughed. "I haven't met him. But I wish him luck. To be stuck in somewhere with that much responsibility must be nightmarish for him."

"He should have known better. If he didn't have a clue, he will soon. But tell me, what happened? We got the official word you were off on sick leave, then nothing."

"The conglomerate and the administrator got together and picked them out a younger and cheaper surgeon. You're right about that. But they hit a snag. Me. I wouldn't resign. They were to find another place for me, they said. Then the order came down from Mt. Olympus, Hong Kong, or wherever, for us to update our health records. My exam or the written report they let me see—I didn't get to see any lab work, made me look senile with Parkinson's gaining on me. I could see another position was not going to materialize. I went home and tied on a good one. I drank everything I had and some that must have followed me home. I woke up in a care facility with termination papers in my hand."

Rob ran his fingers through his tousled hair, "Good Lord!"

"I've still got my license, and I want to practice medicine. So, here I am, hunting employment."

"Dr. Hammond—"

"Make that Martin, please. I'm not over the hill yet by a long shot."

Rob smiled. "I know that. But you're my teacher. I learned so much from you. You're my role model, it feels strange to call you by your first name."

Martin's affection showed in his smile. "Work on it, then. You're not softening me up to turn me down, are you?"

"Not a *chance!* If after you hear about it, you still want a job here, it's yours. This took me by surprise. You can go anywhere you want to." Rob's awed expression was reassuring to Martin's bruised feelings.

"You could go back to St. Josephs if you want to, you could sue them—"

"I don't want to sue them. I don't want to go back. All I want to do is practice medicine. Now, tell me about this place."

Rob briefed him on Lincoln Street Clinic's facilities; approximate volume; and limited budget. Some things he didn't put into words, Martin filled in from Jennie's worried expression and his long experience with hospital procedure. He no longer had any doubt about being needed.

"Anything I didn't cover that you want to ask?"

"One thing did cross my mind. I want to operate on or treat anyone I want to, whether they have insurance or can pay or not." He saw Rob's uncertainty and added, "On the non-pay cases, I will pay for the operating room, medicines, and supplies I use."

"Then there's no problem. You said you want to practice medicine and that's what we do here, even if it's hard to recognize sometimes. We need you, Dr. Hammond."

"Martin."

"Martin," Rob laughed, high on happiness at the prospect of working with him.

Jennie stuck her head in the door. "I heard laughter in here as I went by," she eyed Rob and Martin. "Does that mean we've lucked up and snared good help, or did you do something foolish like show him the budget?"

"Insubordination! See what I have to put up with?"

"I'm working hard on feeling sorry for you," Martin laughed with Jennie at Rob as he got up and the hardened icing fell off his scrubs in a cascade of white crumbs.

***

"Pull over there and park just outside that parking lot, Leona. I want to use that public phone."

Leona obediently pulled over and parked, waiting in the car. *I guess all this calling from public phones has something to do with the things he said he had to finish up, and that Blanche he told me about.* She watched him as he stood in the phone booth, glad he was being careful and no one who wanted to hurt him could find him.

Aaron stood with his back to her, looking pleased with himself. "Took the bait, did she?" Aaron's eyes held a sly, satisfied gleam as he listened to the report.

"Yes, sir, she did. I checked with the painter before he left, as you told me to, and showed him the picture you sent me. He identified her. Said she took the sack of correspondence in the trash can and didn't even say thanks to him for letting her in to look around."

"That's Blanche, all right," Aaron chuckled, picturing her clutching the useless information. "His description of the way she looks and the way she acted is a better ID than a picture." He listened, "No. You won't need to find me, and I ditched my cell phone. Just leave word with my secretary if there's something you think I need to know before you hear from me again. I'll be in touch."

***

Martin felt ten years younger as he exited the clinic and crossed the parking lot.

I'm a doctor again! I'm alive again, he breathed, looking forward to getting back to work. *I'm able to function and feel useful again. I'm—I'm darn near naked, is one of the things I am! No one will see me, I'll stop by the condo and park on the street, watching out for anyone who might ask questions. I won't blow Aaron's cover or have to answer any questions I don't want to.* He grinned to himself, noting how much faster he'd got back to the car than he'd traveled on the way in with the burden of uncertainty he was carrying.

At the condo his luck held. He saw no one who even looked familiar either outside or in the elevator. He compared the elevator's quiet elegance to the one in Leona's apartment building on the way up, glad to have a place no one would think to look for them. Entering the condo, he looked around, feeling strangely out of place amid such order. Orderly but not human, not friendly. He realized with a start how much he missed Aaron and Leona. They seemed more real to him than the place he called home.

This place feels devoid of life, but I see the cleaning service has been here. What a mess the bar must have been, I'll put a bonus in their next check. He left his guilty feelings behind and went to the master bedroom. He stood in front of his closet, tossing on the bed what he wanted to take with him, his mind already back at the clinic. Something inside, urgent and unexplained made him hurry, as if he was anxious to get back to another life from this silent place. As he left the condo, the only movement was the small light on the answering machine. It blinked red and silently. Martin didn't notice it.

CHAPTER SIX

Martin rapped on the door of apartment three-oh-three and waited for the panel to open. Instead, Leona opened the door, Aaron standing directly behind her like a large, black guardian angel.

He's taking no chances, Martin guessed. *Being overprotective because of the neighborhood as much as anything else.* As Leona locked the door, he said, "I went by my place to get a few things, but I parked on the street and didn't see anyone who might get curious and," he paused dramatically, his eyes giving away the secret, "I got the job!"

"Had no doubts about that," Aaron patted him on the back. He gestured toward their room, "Come on, I'll show you my new threads."

Martin picked up the small suitcase and the suit bag he'd brought with him and followed. "Been shopping, have you? I was expecting to see a new bike from that sappy grin on your face."

"Better than that, you'll see."

Aaron went to the closet and Martin dumped the contents of his suitcase on the bed and unzipped the suit bag. "Now, the place looks lived in. My apartment didn't."

Aaron eyed the old robe on the bed and reached into the closet. "I got you this, it won't hurt to have two robes." He handed Martin a handsome paisley garment. "Since you're going back to work you deserve to get comfortable when you get home."

71

"Thanks," Martin admired the robe. "I'll have to take up smoking a pipe to do it justice," he grinned. "You have good taste, it's nice and my old one is about shot. I guess you noticed I left one of the holly bushes the one they issued me at Pleasant Hill?"

"Yeah, they must have a one-size-fits-all deal somewhere." He reached into his closet again. "Here's my suit."

Martin whistled, "Good looking! You did mean threads with a capital T, must have set you back at least a couple of hundred."

"Three. Got a couple of shirts and ties to go with it." Martin couldn't exactly place the kind of expression that crossed Aaron's face, but it was kin to some kind of worry. Aaron turned away to put the suit back in the closet as he continued. "Leona mentioned when I feel like it's safe, she wants me to go to church with her."

Martin smiled, thinking of lovely, good hearted Leona and her volunteer work, and she was watching out for Aaron's immortal soul as well it seemed. His eyes fell on Aaron's slippers and his head jerked up in surprise.

"You didn't get shoes?"

Aaron shook his head, the strange expression back in place, "Can't get them on. Been a month or two. One toe sticks up too far, and it hurts. Must be arthritis."

"Must be?" Martin's eyes demanded the truth. "That means you're too stubborn to go to a doctor. Your diagnosis is probably right, but you should have gone." He sat down on the bed, "Take off your sock and stick your foot up here."

Aaron moved slower than the antique elevator, his face taking on the uncomfortable expression popular in laxative commercials. "I don't want it broken," he growled. "Or anything else that hurts and won't do any good."

"Looking at it won't hurt. Stick it up here. Come on." Martin patted the bed.

Aaron reluctantly complied, watching closely as Martin examined his foot and the maverick toe. He was braced to jerk it back at the first sign of danger.

"Looks shot, all right." Martin looked at it critically, "You can forget about breaking it. Wouldn't help. We can cut it off, but being next to the big one you'll walk more naturally if we get you some medication for the rest of you, cut it off, and suture you another one on. Nothing to it. Won't have any feeling in it but you'll walk more naturally."

Aaron maintained a stubborn silence. "It won't make much difference," Martin told him, but it's such a small thing we may as well." He smiled, "Now, aren't you glad you took in a stray surgeon? It won't cost you anything and it will be over in no time."

Aaron began putting his sock back on, not commenting.

"So, how come you're just sitting there? What's the problem? Talk to me," Martin demanded.

"You're living in a dream world," Aaron snorted, out of patience. "Just get me another toe! Just like that!" He snapped his fingers in disgust. "Get real!

Whoever heard of anybody donating toes? Hearts and lungs and kidneys maybe," he conceded, "If you live long enough to get them. But *toes*? Give me a break," he snorted in derision.

Martin paid no attention, deep in his own thoughts. "You're right about nobody donating toes, and we don't want to call attention to this, as you've no need to point out to me again, but…" Martin tapped a finger against his chin, eyes distant, focused on possibilities. "I've got an idea."

"You've got an idea?" Aaron rolled his eyes, "Now I *am* scared!"

"You don't know me that well," Martin grinned like an imp who would try anything.

"The heck I don't! I'm already getting nervous and you haven't even hinted what your brain child is yet."

"You want to wear shoes with that suit, don't you? You want to take Leona to church, don't you? Are you going to sit in a front row, amen pew with her, wearing those slippers?" He glanced at the door.

They could hear Leona rattling pans in the kitchen. Martin leaned forward and lowered his voice, "Suppose some of the enterprising gang members around here decide you should give your Sunday donation to them instead of putting it in the offering plate, or some other reason to fight or run comes along?"

There was a three second silence from Aaron. "What, ah, what do you have in mind?" Aaron mumbled uncomfortably, but was showing signs of weakening. "I'm ah, not all that hell-bent on sitting there with the Reverend looking down at my slippers," he admitted ruefully. "And you're right about my not wanting to disappoint Leona."

Martin smiled sympathetically, "Wait until after dinner, when it's good and dark, then we'll see what we can come up with."

Aaron's resolve wavered, "Good and dark? I don't like the sound of that, I don't know about this—".

"I don't either," Martin gave his arm a pat, "Just go along with me. We'll leave after dinner."

After dinner, Aaron sat on the couch with Leona, watching television. He didn't hear anything the actors said, braced for Martin's suggestion they leave. During the evening news Aaron relaxed a little, believing Martin must have thought better of their toe hunting safari into the night. But as the evening news went off, Martin quietly entered the living room. Aaron jumped at the sound of his voice. Every nerve in his body twanged back to its original reluctance about the whole idea.

"Aaron, I've got to go pick up a few things I forgot to get." Martin winked at Leona, "Why don't you come with me for protection. I'm afraid of the dark."

Aaron scowled, "I'm surprised the dark isn't afraid of *you!*" He resented the emotions he felt, as if he'd been out bluffed in a game of Chicken.

"Shame on you, Aaron," Leona turned to smile at Martin, "But it is awfully late."

Aaron reluctantly got up. "It's all right, Leona. You go on to sleep and don't worry. We'll be together and we'll park in a well lighted area." He turned to Martin.

"Let's go, before I change my mind."

Martin opened the door and held it politely, trying not to smirk. Aaron had the feeling he was going to step through that door to unknown horrors which Martin would think were real rib ticklers, with his warped sense of humor.

The ride down in the elevator was silent until it was over.

"We'll go in my car, I know you don't like to drive," Martin volunteered.

"Okay." Aaron sat in Martin's rental car as he started it, his anxiety mixed with vague feelings of unexplained guilt he didn't quite understand yet and wasn't sure he wanted to. He hadn't fastened his seat belt and he looked back, wondering if he should jump out while he still could. He missed his chance. Martin pulled away from the curb while he was still deliberating. About fifty percent of him was glad to get started, maybe fifty-five. He pictured himself in his new suit, looking happy and handsome and prosperous, sitting beside Leona in church.

Leona's loving smile disappeared as Martin's voice broke into his thoughts.

"I've got to stop by the clinic and pick up some things we'll need."

"I don't want to know what!" Aaron winced, suddenly acutely conscious of his toe.

"Good. Wouldn't do any good to explain it to you."

"I don't know which is the worst, knowing where I'm headed or not knowing anything—"

Martin sighed, "That's how I felt on our first ride together. We can have a class on what we're doing or just go on and do it, there's not going to be enough dark to do both. We've got to locate someone—"

"All right, all right. I don't want to know."

At the clinic, he left Aaron in the car. "Be back soon, don't get into any trouble."

"No more than I'm in already," Aaron mumbled just loud enough to be heard. He turned to watch curiously when Martin returned with a large box and placed it on the back seat. Neither spoke as Martin got in and drove the next few blocks.

"Neighborhood's looking seedier all the time," Aaron noted nervously as Martin slowed down, "What are you stopping for?"

"How do you know this isn't where we're going?"

"I don't. Is it?" Aaron looked around as Martin stopped near a liquor store with iron bars on its windows and the door. He studied the proprietor's precautions. "They must be expecting us!"

"They're expecting the worst," Martin chuckled, "But that's not us. We're only after supplies."

Again, Aaron waited in the car. Martin returned with a sack and handed it to him. "Here, take care of these."

Aaron peered into the sack. There were two bottles of cheap wine and a magnum of equally cheap champagne. He frowned, turning to study Martin's face, "You're not planning on drinking any of this stuff are you?"

"Nope," Martin kept his eyes on the street ahead of him. "Where we're going, that's money."

Aaron's taut backbone wilted as he hugged the bottles, "Ohhhh, my Gooood," he moaned.

The next few blocks took them into the darkness of an old industrial section with run down warehouses and deserted sidewalks. There was no one in sight except a man curled up in a doorway. Martin continued driving slowly, his eyes on the street, sidewalks, and shadows ahead.

"What are we watching for?"

"Vital signs."

"Humpf! Ask a foolish question," Aaron grumbled.

Martin slowed down, pulling closer to the curb.

"Why don't we just go on home and forget it," Aaron blurted out as the front tire brushed the curb.

Martin paid no attention, peering into the dimly lit street ahead as he turned off the key, ignoring Aaron's panic. "We'll leave the car and walk from here."

"I don't know about this. What's that down there that looks like something burning?"

"It is something burning. It's the remains of a fire some street person left to die out," Martin explained quietly, pocketing the keys.

"Our vital sign?"

"You got it. Come on, I won't bother locking the doors."

"Sure. We're living dangerously anyway. Makes as much sense as anything else we're doing," Aaron kept up his grumbling monologue.

Martin picked up the sack and handed it to Aaron. He carried the box, talking back to Aaron as they walked. "Think about it, Aaron. You can't lock anyone out but yourself. A thief would have no qualms about breaking out your windows—"

"The thing that worries me the most, Martin," Aaron kept pace beside him, his slippers slapping the sidewalk, "Is when what you say begins to sound logical to me. Now, *that's* scary!" His eyes moved over their surroundings, examining the shadows between the buildings they were passing, "Almost as scary as where we are," he added.

Martin walked on, his eyes straight ahead.

Aaron squinted, "Are we going down there where that fire was?"

"Close to it. Since it's going out, someone must have lit it to keep warm or maybe to warm up something to eat. We're trolling for candidates, and there's bound to be some around, you can bet on it."

"Um-hum," Aaron walked more slowly and warily, his eyes busy.

"Yeah, there are probably some homeless people around where you can't see them. Only group I know that tries to keep a lower profile than we do," he grinned. "But don't worry, the dark's afraid of me, remember?"

"You want me to carry that box," Aaron changed the subject.

"No, just hang onto those bottles, they're heavier than this box, even with my bag in it." He stopped.

Aaron froze too, moving nothing by his eyes, "What is it?"

"I saw something move. The other side of the building with the trash can fire in front of it. Let's sit down in the edge of the shadow there."

Martin walked over and looked into the glowing trash can before he moved to the side of the building and sat down beside Aaron. "Still enough embers to bake potatoes," he whispered.

"Oh, you graduated from Hobo School too?"

"No, Scout Camp. Put the box on your side, I've got the bag. We'll put the bait between us."

They got settled and Aaron strained his ears, his eyes on the shadow between them and the glowing can.

"Okay, now what?"

Martin's eyes scanned the area, seeing they were mostly in shadow, their feet sticking out in the light given off by the distant street light and the glowing trash can.

"We wait."

CHAPTER SEVEN

After a few minutes, Martin reached into the sack between them and touched the magnum against one of the wine bottles. The clink of glass against glass was unmistakable in the silence.

Less than two seconds later, Aaron felt air moving against his cheek and found himself looking at two legs in a pair of pants which must definitely have seen better days.

"Welcome, strangers." A reedy voice accompanied a wave by an arm encased in a sleeve of the jacket to the salvaged pants.

A Salvation Army ensemble if I ever saw one, Aaron decided, tearing his eyes away from it to see what Martin's reaction to the welcome was.

"What do you mean, welcome," Martin bristled, his face full of meanness and distrust, "Do you own this corner?"

"No, no. Just stay here most times." The smile accompanying the explanation was snaggle toothed, but friendly, "I'd offer you a drink, but—"

"But you drank it all," Aaron finished for him, wrinkling his nose at the scent wafting his way from the stranger. "So much for the Welcome Wagon," Aaron's grumble was hardly audible.

"Mind if I set?"

"No, I won't charge you rent," Martin's voice was grudging as he casually laid his arm protectively across the sack of booze.

Aaron studied the stranger. He looked to be between fifty and sixty. *Must have been a tough fifty or sixty or maybe it's the life he's fallen into now. He's got some sort of shirt under that thrift shop ensemble, and about the filthiest tennis shoes I've ever seen in my life—one of them's missing a string.* His eyes traveled upward. *Probably ate it,* he decided. He kept his thoughts to himself as he looked away, wanting to hold his breath.

"Don't guess you'd have anything to drink," it came from the wino's lips in a plaintiff whine, his eyes were fixed hungrily on the sack.

"I might," Martin's voice was cautious. "In fact, right now, I've got plenty to drink." He eyed the wino, "That's not my problem."

The wino licked his dry lips, "What's yer problem, then?"

Martin gestured at Aaron, "It's my friend here. He needs a toe."

The wino slapped his knee and cackled, "That's a good 'un—needs a toe!" He would have laughed at a pork and beans label to get at what was in Martin's sack.

"It's true. He needs a toe. Show him your toe, Aaron," Martin commanded.

Not expecting anything like that, Aaron shot him a look that would have frozen a lesser man to silence. Martin returned his look, waiting.

Aaron stifled a retort and took off his slipper and sock then stuck his foot farther out into the light.

"Well, I'll be horn-swoggled," the wino observed with wonder, "Thing sticks up, don't it? What be the matter with it?"

"Arthritis," Aaron ground out the word between his teeth. *I'll get you for this, Martin, extenuating circumstances or not, I'll get you,* he vowed.

"You know many people around here," Martin asked the wino in a friendlier tone of voice.

"Some. Why?" The wino was suspicious, a little deflated, "You lookin' for somebody fer some reason?"

"No." Martin didn't look at Aaron, concentrating on the wino, "I was thinking if you knew people around here, you might help us find someone who might sell my friend here a toe."

"Sell? A toe?" The wino scratched his head, "I never heard tell of such a thing. What do you mean, 'zactly, by sell him a toe?" A gleam of interest lit his eyes, "And what would you be offering?" His eyes slid back to the sack.

"Why don't we have a drink and we'll talk about it."

Martin pulled some disposable glasses and one of the bottles out of the sack and poured with all the ceremony of high tea. He handed the wino a plastic tumbler of wine.

"I've got toes," the wino blurted out the words as he took the wine. "Ten of the little suckers last time I checked," he giggled, eyes on the fascinating, irresistible bottle. He gulped the wine.

"You do, do you. How do I know?"

"I'll show you—wait!" The tennis shoe without a string came off quickly, revealing a bare and not too dirty a foot, considering the rest of what it was attached to.

Some of the crud must have worn off, Aaron kept his thoughts to himself, fighting the urge to move a little farther away.

"What's all this?" A deep voice boomed above them. "Show and Tell, or a dirty foot contest?"

Two large black men stood on the other side of the trash can, their eyes missing nothing, certainly not the plastic tumblers of wine.

"We're in the market for a toe," Martin explained seriously, watching Aaron out of the corner of his eye. He was putting his sock and slipper back on. "Have a seat," he invited the newcomers, "And we'll talk about it."

Martin moved over a bit, making room and getting closer to Aaron. He reached into the sack again. "Competition is good for trade, we were about to have another drink and open negotiations."

The two black men exchanged a grin and a shrug and got comfortable sitting across from the wino.

"I'm Pete and my friend here is Homer," the one who spoke first told Martin.

Homer nodded, "How do—what are you drinking?"

"I've got a choice of white or red wine. What's your pleasure, gents?"

"Man, it's a pleasure to have a choice," Pete's teeth showed in a broad smile. I'll have red."

"Me, too," Homer stretched his neck to get a better look at the sack.

"I'll have the same," the wino chimed in and accepted a refill, not bothering to replace his sneaker and take a chance on getting behind in the drinking.

Martin handed around the plastic tumblers of red wine. No one noticed Aaron had none or that Martin wasn't drinking.

With his candidates happily sipping, Martin cleared his throat, "Now then, about the toe—" He looked at Pete, "I guess you heard me, I need to buy one for my friend, here."

Pete and Homer nodded.

Pete downed the last of his wine, "But, I never heard of anybody buying a toe."

The wino had finished the last of his wine first and now held out his empty tumbler hopefully, his eyes on the bottle as Martin picked it up and poured. He drank hungrily. His tongue licked an arrant drop beneath the rim as Martin continued.

"My friend has arthritis in his toe and can't wear shoes," Martin explained to Pete and Homer as he refilled their tumblers. "I'm going to cut his toe off and sew him another one on, so he can wear shoes and take his lady friend to church. You have to wear shoes to go to church," he patiently pointed out the problem to them.

Homer nodded, "Ain't fittin' to go to church without shoes. You got to have respect for the Lord's house. My mama always told me that." He sipped, thinking about home and his mama.

"I'm glad you agree," Martin filled the wino's tumbler again and topped off Pete and Homer's drinks. "Now, I only need one," he studied each face. "Which one of you would—"

"I guess I would," Pete glanced at Homer, "If the price was right, or—if you've got something I want?"

"I've got a magnum of champagne, that's what I'm offering."

Pete and Homer's necks swiveled like a Greek chorus to look at the foil wrapped top of the bottle sticking up out of the liquor store sack.

"I want to see the toe, of course," Martin put in hastily.

"Oh, yeah," Pete laughed. "Can't go buyin' no piggee in a poke!" He chuckled as he took off his shoe and a sock which could have been put on from either end.

"There," he grinned proudly at Martin, "What do you think?" He wiggled his toes and moved his foot a little, regarding it critically, as if trying to see it as Martin did.

"Yeah, it looks good to me." Martin peered at the toe. "I'll give you a local before I take the toe and bandage it for you—"

"Wait," Pete's grin disappeared, "You said, 'take it.' You mean, cut it off, I got that, but not later in a hospital. You mean right here, right now, don't you?'

"Yes, of course. It will be quick, and not all that bad," Martin's voice was professional and informative, "The shot will hurt worse than taking the toe."

A tense silence fell between them. Homer hastily finished his wine, watching them, eyes on his friend. The wino had gone to sleep, his head leaning against the brick wall behind him. Aaron now had his socks and slippers on and was holding his breath again.

Pete looked down at his foot, then at Martin, who was pulling on latex gloves. Pete's eyes grew big and his lips parted as Martin tested the needle, liquid sparking as it shot out.

"Hey, this guy's for real!"

Pete was faster than a speeding bullet, once his mind and his feet joined forces, and Homer was already scrambling to his feet. The two of them took off as if the law was right behind them, Pete running down the middle of the street beside Homer, his shoe in his hand.

Aaron expelled the held breath, "We blew it!"

Jackie Griffey

CHAPTER EIGHT

Martin knelt, arrested in that position, holding the needle. His eyes met Aaron's, "I had to tell them the truth."

"I know. You should have. It's all right."

"We've still got this other candidate—" Martin pointed with the needle at the wino.

"Yeah, he's out like a light," Aaron contemplated the wino's open mouth. He slept as peacefully as if he were in a bed on a good mattress.

"Maybe he's dreaming about selling his other toes and getting some dental work done when he sobers up," Aaron chuckled.

"Could be. He's full enough of that red wine he likes so well to dream about anything. Remember, when he went to sleep the toe contest was still on." Martin moved toward him still in a squatting position, like a toad balancing on a lily pad as he held the needle carefully aloft.

"Hey, you said that shot will hurt. Won't he wake up?"

"Of course! I'm not in the habit of stealing toes," Martin said indignantly. He smothered a laugh, testing the needle again. "When he gets his eyes open, we'll give him the good news he won the contest."

Speechless for once, Aaron watched nervously as Martin used the needle on the wino's bare foot.

"Eeeeeich!" The wino's eyes flew open and focused on them, a surprised expression on his face.

"You won the contest—congratulations!" Martin beamed and Aaron reached over to shake the wino's hand.

"Yeah, the magnum's yours," Aaron affirmed.

The wino's lips turned up in a slightly confused smile that froze when he saw the scalpel flash in Martin's gloved hand. He let out a horrendous, blood-curdling cry before he collapsed, his head drooping back against the brick wall behind him.

"You've killed him!" Aaron screeched as the wino's mouth fell open and his eyes rolled back.

"Calm down, he's just passed out," Martin scowled at him, "That's *good.* Now, push that bag closer."

Martin worked quickly and efficiently. Aaron mumbled something, Martin didn't catch anything but something about Jesus. He kept mumbling and his eyes were shut tight until Martin touched his shoulder.

"Let's go. I've got the box and he's all finished up. You get the bag, and hurry!"

They saved their breath for traveling fast until they were almost back to the car. Aaron panted, glancing at Martin, "That was a nice touch, wrapping his arms around that magnum—"

"Yeah, I thought so," Martin grinned at him, "It'll be like Christmas morning waking up with that magnum and the other bottle we had left." He shifted the box. "There's the car, now aren't you glad we didn't lock the doors?"

The dark street was still deserted as Martin pulled away from the curb and made a U-turn as wide as it was illegal. "Next stop—the clinic!" He darted a quick look at Aaron, "What were you talking to Jesus about back there?"

Aaron shuddered, "I was afraid the wino was dead. I promised Him if He'd get us away from there without going to jail, I'd never listen to you again!"

Martin exploded with unbridled mirth and picked up speed, *"Such rank ingratitude!"*

At the clinic, Martin parked close to the emergency entrance and motioned Aaron to follow him. He clasped the box to him, and Aaron followed closely with his bag.

"The lab's closer to this entrance. Just keep putting one foot in front of the other. If you've got to think about something, think about buying new shoes."

"Don't worry about me, I'm right behind you. It's too late to back out now."

They didn't see many people and Aaron carefully didn't make eye contact with anyone, hoping no one would remember him.

"So far, so good." Martin glanced back down the hall behind them as he braced the box against the wall, opening the lab door with his key.

"I feel like a burglar," Aaron muttered, looking behind him as he followed Martin in.

"Well, you're not." Martin dismissed it. "Sit on that examining table and take off your slipper and sock while I run some tests."

"Tests?"

"Remember the blood sample I took from our donor after he passed out?"

"Must have had my eyes closed. I didn't know what you were doing."

"That gets you an A in blind faith," Martin nodded approval, "But you don't want AIDS, do you?"

Aaron didn't answer. When Martin motioned, he stopped hugging himself to stop shaking and stuck his bare foot out in front of him on the table. He couldn't bear the sight of the needle and shut his eyes again.

"I know this local is going to hurt," Martin apologized, "But you'll be grateful later. I'll give you something else too, for pain. I did the same for the wino, it if will make you feel any better."

"I can still see him sitting against the wall with his arms around that magnum," Aaron admitted, trying not to notice what Martin was doing. "And I'll be hearing that blood curdling scream of his the rest of my natural days!"

"I knew you were a softy," Martin smiled, "That's why you and Leona get along so well. I also left him enough pain killers to get him through the worst of it, but not enough to kill him if he's foolish enough to take them all at once."

Aaron's head jerked up, trying to stay alert.

"Are you getting groggy?"

Aaron tried to say yes, but settled for a nod. The last thing he heard was Martin promising it wouldn't be long.

Martin gently shook his shoulder, waking him.

"Is—is it done?"

"Yes, it's all done. Does it hurt?"

"No, not a bit," Aaron answered wonderingly. "But, shouldn't it?"

Martin chuckled, "You're a hard man to please. The locals took care of the pain for now. I'll give you something for later." He rummaged in a drawer for samples.

"You can look at it now," he tossed over his shoulder, "Before I cover up my work of art with gauze."

Aaron lifted the piece of gauze covering the foot and looked at it. "There it is, all right. And it doesn't stick up, you did it!"

Martin found the medicine samples he wanted and stuck several envelopes in his pocket. "Okay, and we'll take one of those canes there. Soon as I get it bandaged we'll be ready—"

Aaron still sat contemplating his foot. "The only thing is, Martin? This toe is *white!*"

Jackie Griffey

CHAPTER NINE

Aaron and Martin entered apartment three-oh-three quietly.

"Shh, Leona must be asleep," Aaron whispered.

"I'm glad she left the lamp on," Martin waited while Aaron locked the door. "How are you doing?" He watched as Aaron took a few steps.

"Fine, just fine." Aaron looked down at his foot in wonder. "I couldn't believe it didn't hurt."

"It will. I'm not that big a miracle worker. You probably won't need the pain killers until in the morning and the medicine will take care of it. Just walk the way I showed you." He looked at the cane, "You won't be going dancing any time soon anyway, you'll make it."

"Yeah, it's all right. This cane you gave me at the clinic helps. Thanks—for the cane too."

"You're welcome." Martin let him pass and go ahead of him. He kept an eye on him as he walked a few steps ahead like a walrus on the beach, carefully minding the new toe.

Safely in the bedroom, Aaron sat on his bed and cast a wondering gaze at his bandaged foot. "I can't believe I let you sew a white toe on my foot. When you let me see it was the first time I'd thought about it. It looked stranger on my foot than it did in that ice bucket!"

"It's not an ice bucket, it's an organ—oh, what the hell, ice bucket is as good a description as any." The tiredness and the hour hit Martin all at once. He sighed, pulling off his shirt, feeling like it must be fourteen o'clock or at least thirteen as the stress caught up with him.

"Wonder what Leona will say about this white toe," Aaron worried aloud, still staring critically at the bandage.

Martin's reply was an unsympathetic snicker. "If she'll run you off for having a white toe, it's better to find it out now than later." He asked curiously, "What's so bad about having a white toe anyway? You've got a Jewish name. Aaron was a brother to Moses if I remember right."

"The Jewish name is a bow to tradition, there is a reason for it."

"You mean there's a little of the Yiddish in your family tree," Martin listened as he got comfortable, adjusting his pillow.

"Looks that way. I have a great auntee who devoted most of her spare time to tracing our family back to Solomon."

"Solomon?" Martin turned to look at him, "You mean the King Solomon in the bible?" He raised his eyebrows, "Is that why you've got money in Swiss banks and property all over the world?" He squinted at Aaron, "Are you serious, or are you 'funnin' me as the wino calls it?"

Aaron propped his foot on one of his pillows, getting his covers arranged. "That's the one. It's true. You know how it is, with things like that. Nobody paid much attention at first. But, according to what she turned up in her research, it's been accepted as true, by the family anyway. Most of the family records were oral, handed down and told by one generation to the next."

"If it wasn't true, the rumor probably wouldn't have survived this long," Martin murmured, recognizing the logic in the family's acceptance of his auntee's findings and the handed down history.

"She did find records to verify some of the times and happenings that were described, enough to feel most of the oral records were true. We're descended from the children Solomon and the Queen of Sheba had, and of course, their people with them. No one ever traveled alone, what amounted to their courts and families went with them, and sometimes their animals, too. But that's the conclusion, or at least the consensus, that we're descended from their children."

"I see," Martin nodded, his face serious as he thought about it. "You know, I'll bet the oral records are right, at that. Even without much in the way of actual records to verify some of them. The bible does record the meeting of Solomon and the Queen of Sheba, and the attraction between them. It's just been overlooked because everybody and his dog was looking for Solomon's mines and treasure, not his offspring."

"Human nature hasn't changed much, has it?"

Martin smiled, "Not a bit. Most progress has only improved the financial opportunities available. There wasn't much attention paid to birth control in those days either. They just took the careless ones out and stoned them."

Aaron shrugged, "You'd think that would be pretty effective. What convinced me the records were true, is some of our branches and distant cousins still remember their people having come from those regions over there. They had records of some of the same events that took place, and it's been accepted as true, even though there are only a few actual confirmations of the family records."

He pulled the cover up, irritated with himself. "I don't know why I'm telling you things I've never discussed with anybody else outside the family."

Martin's teeth showed in a grin as he reached up to turn off the lamp between them. "Because no one ever got you a toe before." His head settled on his pillow, he said into the darkness, "Thank you and Goodnight, Jesus."

"Are you asking for trouble," Aaron's deep voice rumbled.

"Nope, just playing it safe."

The next morning Martin got up and dressed quietly. He looked down affectionately at Aaron who slept soundly, his mouth slightly open, and tiptoed from the room.

Leaving the building, Martin chuckled to himself, *He'll have to tell Leona whatever tale suits him when he wakes up. He'll be taking my name in vain for sure.* Martin shook with silent laughter, *He's descended from Solomon, he'll figure out something."* He laughed out loud, then stopped short, squinting at his car. *What's that?*

His laughter was cut short by the sight of a paper stuck beneath his windshield wiper. *Somebody selling something, no doubt.* He recalled the accumulation of junk mail at the condo as he reached for the paper.

The note was written on a small sheet torn from what must have been a child's composition book. The words were printed, some of the letters backwards. Martin's mouth compressed into a thin line of distaste as he read.

"We seen what you done last night by the alley."

Oh, boy! Martin took a quick look around. There was no one in sight. He looked again at the note. It was signed 'witnes' with only one s.

***

Aaron yawned and opened his eyes. He was facing Martin's bed. It was neatly made. He looked around the room, no Martin. He tilted his head, listening. No sounds from the bathroom. There were sounds from the kitchen. He smiled, Leona was fixing breakfast. The smile faded as he realized there were no voices accompanying the rattling noises. He contemplated Martin's neatly made bed and glared at it, facing the truth.

He ran out on me, the rat! Left me to explain my condition the best dratted way I can, that's what he did. Well, thank you, noble friend!

Getting from his bed to the closet convinced him to use the cane on his way to the kitchen. He put the medicine Martin had given him in the pocket of his robe, taking back a few of the things he'd been thinking about him.

I'm beginning to need these. He said take one before I eat. I'll tell Leona the truth, but not the whole truth. He scowled, balancing on one foot while he pulled the spread up over his pillow. *Nobody in his right mind would believe the whole truth anyway. Well, here goes.* He was glad he had the cane as he took the first few steps.

Entering the kitchen, Aaron managed a cheery, "Good morning," for Leona.

"Good—*oh*!" Leona's surprise and concern showed in her face. "You're hurt!"

"No. No, I'm not hurt. I'm going to have to use this cane for a while is all." He ignored the awakening feelings in his foot and forced a smile, "Beats hopping like a stork, but not by much."

"What happened to your leg?"

"It's not my leg, it's my foot. Martin found a donor and replaced the toe I was having trouble with." He looked down at the table, not meeting her eyes.

"So that's where you really went last night! But, why didn't you tell me?"

"Because we weren't sure of—ah—the donor." Aaron studied her face as he continued, "It's a white toe."

"Oh," Leona put her arms around his neck, "Thank goodness for Martin! You were lucky to be able to get one."

"Yeah, there was a lot of luck involved, all right." Aaron felt that was a safe statement with enough truth in it to let him hold his head up.

"And I'm sure Martin did all the tests and necessary things," Leona added confidently.

"He did, yes. I hadn't thought about tests, but he made sure about AIDS and of course, being compatible and other things too, he said."

He smiled up at Leona, *Martin was right, she doesn't care if I have a white toe. And I've told her the basic truth,* he defended himself from the twinge of conscience he felt.

"I should have known Martin would help you," Leona talked while she worked.

"Soon as it heals, I can wear a shoe on that foot again."

"I know. You can get you some new shoes to go with that new suit. That's wonderful! Did it hurt a lot?"

He was tempted to say *yeah, a lot!* And just bask in her love and concern but he was ashamed of himself so he just felt in his pocket for the samples Martin had given him.

Aaron took out the sample envelope and shook it. He laid a tiny pill on the table. "Not a bit. But he gave me these for when the shots he gave me wear off. I'm going to take one before I eat."

Leona handed him a glass of water and examined the little pill. "Such a tiny thing, must be potent medicine." She watched as he took the pill. "I'm glad Martin operated on your foot so you can wear shoes again, but I'll bet he had to talk you into it, didn't he?" She smiled knowingly. "You hadn't said a word about it, and I remember trying to get you to go to a doctor once before, a long time ago," she teased him. "You're almost—anti medicine," she giggled.

"All I'm admitting is it was his idea when he saw I hadn't bought shoes to go with that suit you like." Aaron put on his martyr's face, "I did it for you."

Leona put her arms around his neck again and kissed his lips and then his cheek, lingering a moment with her arms around his shoulders, "And I love you for it. It was a sweet, wonderful thing to do. It was good of Martin, too." She turned back to the stove "He's a good friend and a good doctor."

"I know it. I just don't think it's a good idea to tell him too often and mess up a good thing."

Leona laughed with him as she set his plate before him. "Maybe, but he told me he will do hip replacements for two of the patients where I work as a volunteer. They both need them, but they don't have the money or any insurance to cover the operations."

"Even if he donates his services, the hips and other things will have to be paid for," Aaron mused out loud.

"Oh," Leona stopped, her dish cloth in her hand as she turned back to him, crestfallen. "I hadn't thought about that. He said not to worry, so I thought the hospital had some kind of fund or something—"

"He's right, don't worry," Aaron quickly assured her. "The artificial hips aren't much. One of my affiliates handles them and other prostheses. Between the two of us, there won't be any great expense involved. He was probably going to pay for those and the supplies himself."

Tears glistened in Leona's eyes. "He is so good and good hearted with it, Aaron, like a doctor should be. I could see us helping people who have no money, who don't have any hope. All I thought about was the people I've seen in pain and needing help. How wonderful it would be if we could help them…"

"We can, Leona, don't cry. We can help them. Martin wants to help, and I've got the money for anything he needs. We can help them. All you need to worry about is breakfast," he patted her hand then stretched his neck, trying to see into the skillet from where he sat.

"I'm so hungry, I think both my legs are hollow, right down to my new toe."

Leona smiled, wiping her eyes. "That's something I can handle. There's not going to be any hunger in my kitchen!"

She heaped his plate and kept his cup full until Aaron laid his fork in his plate and said, "Uncle! I may not be able to get up!"

He did manage to get up in spite what he called his balancing act, and put his arms around her, his cheek resting against the top of her head as he held her.

Jackie Griffey

CHAPTER TEN

Blanche worked harder than she ever had in her life, trying to uncover some of Aaron's extensive operations and holdings. She sat at the writing desk in her bedroom, the phone in her hand.

"Thank you," she said sadly. She was so discouraged, she had lapsed into politeness. She replaced the phone with a weary sigh, her eyes on the papers in front of her.

In spite of all the inquiries I've made on my own, I've met nothing but dead ends. I was hoping there would be something helpful in all these papers I found in his office. That big pile of papers, all that correspondence, and there's nothing! I've come up with nothing at all. He's closed his accounts at the bank, which isn't news. They evidently only told me that much to get me off their backs. And they won't give out any information at all about CD's without account numbers and all kinds of identification and written consent, whatever that might be, so I don't know if the CD that financed the fishing trip to Canada was the last one he had or not. It's sure beginning to look that way.

Blanche sat staring at the window, depressed, weighed down by her failure to find anything that showed Aaron had any assets at all.

His office is gone, at least it's empty. I saw that for myself. She looked at the pile of papers with a soulful longing. *There was nothing but bad news there. Those papers, even the ones with official letterhead and logos I was hoping would help me locate some of his holdings were no help. Everywhere I called to check, every business is either bankrupt, sold, phones disconnected, or there's been some kind of merger and they won't give out any information about it.*

She gave the papers an angry push, grinding her teeth. *They didn't even have any reaction when I mentioned his name at some of those places. It's as if he's made being anonymous an art form! Damn!* She kicked the metal trash can and leaned on the desk, unwilling to accept the failure of her project.

Desperate, Blanche picked up some of the papers that had fallen and put them back on the desk. Methodically, she checked each one to make sure there was nothing she could have missed, a business she hadn't tried to contact. There was none. She pushed the armload of papers down, making them fit in the can that was more ornamental than functional and regarded them, her shoulders sagging, the picture of despair. A frustrated tear appeared at the corner of one eye.

"He's broke! Broke," she moaned aloud to the empty room.

Bitter as it was, hating having wasted her time in the futile hunt, she gave in to the obvious conclusion. *He has no office, those businesses I've found any information on are closed or sold out, no wonder they were in the trash can. He's got nothing. He's run out of money. That must be the real reason he moved into the pool house here. Aaron's broke!*

She straightened, narrowing her eyes. *He's old enough this year for social security, though.* Her lips drew back in a mirthless grin, *As if anyone could be 'socially secure' on what the government doles out. If Pleasant Hill won't keep him for what he can get when we find him, we'll find a cheaper place that will. I'll tell Alton when he gets home.*

The manicured hand on the antique desk clenched into a determined fist as she got up, her decision made.

***

Leona hurried to the ringing phone. "Leona Miller," she answered expectantly.

"Hello yourself, pretty lady. This is Martin. Let me speak to our not so pretty roommate."

Leona giggled, "Yes, he is pretty, I mean, good looking, and he's got other good points, too. Just a minute."

Aaron was standing nearby, listening. He took the phone. "What jail are you in," he growled winking at Leona as she turned to go back to the kitchen.

"I'm still running around loose, but I'm going by the condo for a couple of things. Thought I'd let you know."

"Oh, good. Glad you did. We need to talk about some of the things you're planning on doing when you get back here."

"What things? And what did Leona think about your new toe?"

"There's no problem, no thanks to you—running out on me like that!"

"I'm just a surgeon, not a social worker," Martin chuckled before asking again, "What things do you mean?"

"The two hip replacements."

"Oh. I've got that in the unfinished business wrinkle of my brain right now. But since you brought it up, I need your help with something."

"As long as it doesn't involve cheap booze and a dark alley—"

"Get over it, Aaron. What I want you to do, is look around for some space we can get that's close, cheap, and not too obvious or accessible to the outside world."

"Why not too accessible to the outside world?"

"Such distrust—such suspicion—"

"Call it caution. Why not too accessible to the outside world?"

"Because I don't want to be bothered with the outside world. The main thing is, it needs to be close. Has that apartment house we're in got any basement space?"

"Don't know. Should have. I'll find out. Are you going to give me a clue what you want it for?"

"I want to fix up a couple of rooms for our patients and bring a nurse from the clinic to care for them until they're able to go back to their usual routine, whatever and wherever that is. I want them to be close to keep an eye on them, and I don't want to be bothered by any curious outsiders. Do you approve?"

Aaron's smile deepened enough to be audible, "Not that you care a rat's ass, but yes, I approve."

Martin smiled into the phone, he could hear the relief mingled with Aaron's approval. "And you'll find us some room?"

"I'll look into it today."

"Fine. See you tonight."

Turning away from the phone, Martin's hand touched the note n his pocket. *I'll show this to him tonight when I get home,* he promised himself.

Martin stopped to check his mail before going up to his condo. His box was full and he glanced around as he pulled the mail out. *I feel safer parking on the street, people who don't bother with the amenities upstairs, get talkative in the parking level for some reason. I didn't realize being a workaholic would pay off so well when it comes to privacy.*

He entered the elevator looking through the accumulated mail. The whole top was advertisements, it seemed all the planet's population was selling something. He pulled out a receipt from the cleaning service.

He smiled to himself, *Someone remembers Captain Kangaroo's magic words, Please and Thank You. They wrote 'thank you' across it.* He chuckled, feeling better about the world in general and the mess he'd left in the bar.

In the condo, he gathered up things he forgot on his last trip. Sticking fingernail and toenail clippers in his pocket, the blinking red light on the answerphone caught his eye. There was only one message. He pushed the play button.

"This is Dick Chelsea. I'd like to talk to you when you get in. Please give me a call or drop by as soon as you have a minute."

Dick Chelsea, wonder what he wants. He didn't say if what he wants to see me about is personal or something to do with his job as building manager.

Martin gave the immaculate living area a last look, his eyes lingering on the glass doors to the terrace with its breathtaking view.

The terrace always reminds me of Mildred. She bought the view, I think, when we moved here. All this other stuff was just thrown in as dull old necessary. He pictured her standing there by the glass doors and swallowed a lump in his throat. *I'm glad we had some happy times together.*

He set down the sack of things he had gathered up and locked the door on the way out.

Wonder what Dick wants? I know it's late, but I'll stop by and see him whether it's business or not. There's no telling when he left that message. He pushed the button for the ground floor with his elbow.

Outside Dick's apartment, he shifted the sack and rang the bell. Dick himself opened the door.

"Dr. Hammond! Good to see you. I was wondering if you got my message."

"Dr. Hammond?" Martin gave him a shocked gasp, "How long have I been gone?"

"Martin," Dick laughed, "Come in, come in. Set that sack down somewhere. Want a sandwich? I'm batching tonight—"

"No, thank you," Martin looked Dick over, pretending to look for scars or bandages, "I've just got your message, sorry if it's been a while. Good thing you weren't bleeding to death!"

Dick laughed, "Heck, no problem. I'd have made a lot more noise if I'd been in pain, you can depend on it! Probably wasn't important anyway."

"What wasn't? What did you want to tell me?"

"About a week or so ago, maybe a little more, a man came here asking questions about you."

"About me?" Martin's surprise showed before it turned to curiosity. "What kind of questions? May have been selling something. I had a box full of junk mail, even more than usual, waiting for me."

"No, he wasn't selling anything," Dick's face got serious, "Come sit down. Do you want a drink?"

"No, thanks. Who was the man?"

"He said he was a private detective. Showed me an ID card with his picture on it. His name is L.D. Holmes"

"L.D. Holmes," Martin repeated the name, "Doesn't ring any bells…"

Dick scratched his chin, recalling the man. "He wanted to know for starters, if you still own the condo, where you work, then worked up to if you work at St. Josephs. I didn't think anything else was any of his business, so I told him you own the condo, you work at

St. Josephs, and he would have to ask you if he wanted any more information."

"You did exactly right. Interesting that he wanted to know where I was." Martin shifted his sack before setting it down by his foot. "I'm not at St. Josephs now. They must think I'm going to take them to court or something, to send a detective around trying to locate me."

"You're not at St. Josephs?" Dick's pleasant expression rearranged itself into worry wrinkles. "You've left St. Josephs?"

"Didn't have much choice. A conglomerate bought controlling interest in it recently. Don't discuss that with anyone else, there are still some good people there. You were right to refer any further questions to me. I won't bore you with the details, but the change naturally caused a lot of upsets. Things had got to the point where the only desirable thing about my being there at St. Josephs was it was close enough for me to walk to work."

Dick digested that, then asked hesitantly, "You wouldn't by any chance, be thinking of selling the condo, would you?" He looked sheepish, "Not that I could afford it if you were."

"Hadn't given it any thought, but as little as I've been up there the last ten years, I suppose I might as well. You know more about condos and real estate than I do, what do think it's worth?"

"My guess would be about two hundred and fifty thousand—which would put me out of the running."

Martin laughed at his frustration, "That's what you get for being honest." He moved the sack a little, looking at a nearby clock. "If you were to make me a non-haggle, best I can do offer on it, what would it be?"

Cautious hope returned to Dick's pleasant features, "Are you serious?"

"Are you? I asked, didn't I? Talk to me."

Dick rubbed his chin, thinking. "I don't think I'd have any trouble raising a hundred and ten or twenty thousand on this place. And I've got a lodge up near Lake Tahoe that was worth a hundred thousand ten years ago, that's what I paid for it. It's not a cabin, it's a lodge. Big place with five bedrooms, four and a half baths, and forty-five or fifty acres around it. We don't get a chance to go up there much any more, and it needs some work, but I'll see what I can get. That condo of yours has always been my favorite, and I doubt I could get my wife in from that terrace long enough for a game of bridge—"

"I get the picture," Martin chuckled, "I'd like to know someone was enjoying it as much as Mildred and I used to."

"If you're serious about selling, I'll go to the bank and make sure I can raise the hundred and ten thousand on this place." He shook his head, uncertainty returning. "But, I'm not too sure about the lodge or how much it might have depreciated by now. There isn't a caretaker, and we haven't had time to go up there in about three years." Martin could tell he was picturing it as a stopover for migrating geese.

"Don't worry about it. I'll take it as is, valued at the hundred thousand you paid for it. That and the hundred and ten thousand you can get on this place will do it, if you want the condo. If that's agreeable with you?"

"More than agreeable," Dick nodded emphatically. "It's downright generous! I'll go in the morning and get the bank started on the paperwork."

"There's something else."

"What?"

"I want our business to be two separate transactions. The lawyer who handles the condo's business for you can handle them, with no witnesses except himself and his secretary. The condo will be sold to you for the hundred or hundred and ten thousand you get from the bank. You will transfer the lodge deed to me for a token amount, no connection with the condo. Don't give anyone any information except that I no longer own the condo, and that I left no forwarding address. Also, the things and furniture I take with me from the condo will be sent to friends and delivered where I tell you. The move will be done in your name with your name on the moving contract, but I will pay you for it."

His eyes met Dick's, "No information is to be given to anyone about me or my belongings." This speech had a sobering effect on Dick, he touched Martin's arm, his brows drawing together in concern.

"If there's something wrong, some problem. I'll help you Martin, any way I can."

"No," Martin smiled to reassure him, "There's nothing wrong. I just don't want to be bothered. I've been wrapped up in my work so long, I've come to

114

appreciate privacy. Might want to go up to that lodge and live like a hermit when the mood hits me. Do we have a deal?"

"We do." Dick reached out and they shook hands on it. "And don't worry," he squeezed Martin's hand, "I can handle the privacy."

CHAPTER ELEVEN

The sound of the ringing phone was all Alton heard, the hated answerphone was not on. He gave up and replaced the receiver, looking around the airport. As he picked up his bag, he spotted a van driver with a hotel's logo on his lapel.

"Hey! *You!* Van driver! Wait a minute!"

"Yes, sir," the driver came toward him. "Imperial?"

"No, but can I slip you a five to take me with you? I can get a cab home from there without second mortgaging my house," Alton eyed him hopefully.

"Sure can," The driver took the five from Alton's hand. "Where do you live?" He bent to look closer at the tag on Alton's bag. "For another five bucks, I'll take you on home. It's not that far, but I'll have to drop my people first."

"Enterprise," Alton beamed, "It's what makes America great! Best offer I've had this trip!" He picked up his bag and followed his benefactor.

When he got out of the van at home, a let down feeling settled over him. His bag felt like it had gained ten pounds as he walked up the driveway. *No sign of Blanche's car, sometimes I wonder where she spends all her time, it's sure not here...*He grumbled all the way up to the house.

He let himself in with his key. The heavy door opened on a silence that was almost tangible. He took a quick look into the kitchen, then took his bag upstairs.

His soft footfalls on the carpeted stairs were the only sounds he heard.

She could have left a note in case I got here before she got back from wherever she is.

He looked around the neat, expensively furnished bedroom and set his suitcase down. It was the only thing out of place in all that well planned order. *This place looks like it's ready to be rented or sold. It looks like nobody lives here, and that's just about right!* He felt his anger rising.

He walked to the window and looked down toward the pool house. *Don't see dad anywhere either. Maybe Blanche took him somewhere.* His heart thawed a bit, but the thaw turned into an ache. *No, I've been living in a dream world long enough, I know better than that. But dad must be around somewhere.*

He looked happier as he started downstairs, *I'll surprise him!*

He glanced back at the pool before sticking his head in the pool house door, a slight frown settling around his lips. *Not practicing his fly casting? He usually does about this time of the day.* He raised his voice, "Dad, I'm home!"

There was no answer, no sound of anything moving came from the silent house.

He may not even know I was coming home early. There's not been any sign Blanche even got any of my messages, much less shared them.

As he went in he called again, to no avail. He stopped. *Something's different here.* Alton felt vaguely out of place and uncomfortable. *The place seems a lot neater, none of his lures or anything lying around. Maybe he's*—He looked into the little room where Aaron had his television set. *No robe or slippers or a cast off shirt? This place is so neat it's beginning to get scary!* The seeds of fear sprouted, they grew into full grown panic as he reached the bedroom door.

The pool house hasn't been this neat since dad moved in! He felt unaccountably weak standing in the door. The bed was neatly made. *That designer spread makes the place look like no one's slept here—ever. The pool house looks as ready to rent out as the rest of the place!*

His eyes fell on the magazines on the bedside table. *Harpers Bazaar? Ebony? Elle? What happened to Field and Stream and Country Living?*

His mouth was dry, he had to make his legs function well enough to get to the double closet. He flung wide the folding doors. He crumpled, leaning against the facing, letting out the breath he had held without realizing it. Relief flooded him at the sight of the crowded closet.

He hasn't left us, his clothes are here. He laughed out loud at himself. *And I was halfway to the orphans' picnic!* His eyes took in the clothes and the shelves beside and above them, the feeling of something wrong wouldn't leave him.

These are certainly his clothes, but where's his old coat he likes so well? And his fishing hat! It's not here on the shelf where he always keeps it. He looked wildly around the room as if the furniture could talk to him, tell him where his father was. The sound of a car sent him to check the driveway.

About time! Blanche is home.

***

Martin arrived at apartment three-oh-three a little after eight o'clock, the burden of what was churning in his mind showing on his face.

"You missed a good dinner," Aaron greeted him, "Roast beef."

"All Leona's dinners are good. Have any luck finding us some space?"

"Found some right here in the basement. It's got possibilities. It's available to rent and you can fix it up any way you want it, as long as you pay promptly. That's what the agent told me. Like all other businesses, it's got no heart and no stomach, just pockets."

"I'd already discovered that, Aaron," Martin's pained expression underlined his sentiments.

"Oh yeah, sorry, I forgot."

"That's okay, I'm trying to forget it, too." he shrugged it off.

"I've got a crew from one of my subsidiaries on stand-by to do the work, if it's what you want."

Martin's good humor resurfaced. "It's where I want it. Aaron, if I was paying you, I'd give you a raise. Let's go down and look at it."

"Wouldn't you like something to eat first," Leona called from the kitchen door.

"A roast beef sandwich would hit the spot."

"I'll make you one, but you have to eat some vegetables to get it," Leona good humoredly held the sandwich for ransom. "Squash or peas or both?"

"Make it squash—and thanks."

Aaron opened the door, calling back to Leona, "We'll be a little while."

In the elevator, Martin tilted his head, listening. "Something seems to be missing here. Some noises and some side to side motion where there's only the correct going up and down now."

"I wondered if you'd notice," Aaron was pleased. "I took care of the side to side thing when I was alerting the stand by crew. I couldn't put in a new elevator without attracting a lot of attention, so I had the works inside done. Everything's new except this same old cab."

"That was a stroke of genius, we'll be using it a lot." The elevator came to a stop. "And we've arrived! It's faster, too." He raised an eyebrow, "What are you going to do if someone asks about that?"

"Look dumb and keep quiet, what else?"

"Sounds good to me," Martin laughed as Aaron stepped off the elevator and hit a light switch. "There's an outside door as well as this one and the stair. As devious as you are, I figured that would come in handy."

"You can't hurt my feelings amid all this splendor! This is great, more room than I was hoping for." Martin looked almost afraid to ask, "Is it—all of it—"

"It's all available and can be partitioned off any way you want it. The only restriction is the space around the furnace. The building manager has to have unlimited access to it for the janitor to fuel and service it."

"That's reasonable. I'll put doors where I want privacy."

"I figured you could handle that, the way your mind works. You're usually about two blocks ahead of me and I thought I was the King of Be Prepared."

Martin grinned, "It just scared you I was so pleased, that's all that's wrong with you. But I'm glad to get all this space." He paused in his exploring, "Are we needing money yet?" He quickly added, "I've got some coming in, is why I'm asking."

"If you're getting a fair amount, you should put it somewhere to give you an income. You could run into circumstances where you'll need it. You're just devious, not immortal," Aaron reminded him. "What's about this money? Did St. Josephs give you a nuisance fee not to cause them any trouble? If that's where they hurt, let them sweat."

"No," Martin shook his head. "The conglomerate's got too tight a grip on the purse strings to make an offer like that, and I've got better things to do than cause them trouble. Not that it wouldn't be highly entertaining if some irresistible opportunity should arise," his eyes held an impish gleam.

"Hum, figured you'd leave the door open about that."

Martin pointed at two decrepit lawn chairs near the furnace, "This must be the custodian's summer place. Pull up a chair, I want to talk to you. I'm selling my condo."

Aaron joined him in the other chair before answering, "Sudden decision, wasn't it?"

"When I got home, I had a message on my phone to call Dick Chelsea. He's the building manager as well as a friend, so I stopped by to see what he wanted. He told me a private detective was there asking questions about me." He leveled a speculative look at Aaron, "It wasn't the hospital that sent him. They never operated that way. And from what I've seen of their operation, the conglomerate's too cheap not to use their own people if they want information."

Aaron's teeth ground together in the ensuing silence.

"Blanche! It's the next thing she'd try, hiring a detective."

"We did go out that window at the same time."

Aaron shook his head. "Blanche isn't smart enough to ask about that, but a private detective would be. He'd start at the nursing home. But, you don't have to sell your condo. We can manage without making contact there, you have so far. It won't be long until Blanche hangs herself, and it will be safe for you to go back."

"It was slick, planting that can of correspondence at your office," Martin grinned.

"Yeah, I enjoyed picturing her frustration. She's grabbing at straws, that's for sure. That's why I figure it won't be long. So there's no to need to sell your condo unless you want to."

"It's all right. It wasn't much more than a laundry drop since Mildred, my wife, died. Dick Chelsea and his wife want my condo, so I'm selling it to him." Martin pictured Dick's face when he realized they had a deal. "He's as happy as a kid with circus tickets and the school closed. Also, the sale will be done in private, handled by his lawyer, and the furniture will be moved in Dick's name."

Aaron nodded his approval. "Good arrangement. I may be able to teach you to worry about the right things yet." Aaron shifted, leaning back in the chair. "Then you can take calculated risks instead of being plain old not scared of anything, with a warped sense of humor," he stifled a chuckle.

"Never mind doing me any favors," Martin leaned back too, getting comfortable as he could. "I'm happy the way I am."

"This sale seems too sudden not to involve some sacrifice, how much of a loss are you taking?"

"Not much. Dick's getting half the money from the bank on the condo he's got now. In a separate deal, he's giving me the deed to a lodge up near Lake Tahoe for a token amount. It's valued at a hundred thousand —or was ten years ago. It needs work, he said, but it's big. Has five bedrooms, four and a half baths, and has forty-five or fifty acres around it."

"Forty-five or fifty acres around Lake Tahoe? That's a *lot!* And in that location, in any condition— you did say, Lake Tahoe?"

"That's right. And no one will think to look up the records on property that far away if they're hunting somebody around here. Now, if we have to or want to get lost for some reason, we've got a place to go. You said I was devious," Martin grinned.

"Maybe I should be taking lessons from *you.* You've got a much better deal than you think on that property. You must be at least half Irish, the way good luck follows you."

"After what I've been through, it will take more than a good property deal to even the scales, I think."

"What are you going to do with your furniture?"

"I don't know yet. Got any ideas?"

"How's this? You can get the apartment across from Leona's to put your furniture in until you decide where you want to move. Leona told me today she had talked to the people there, and they will be gone by next week. The manager asked them if they knew of anyone who wanted it, they said, so it's available."

"That is luck, I don't want to store it. I told you I feel like a third leg there with you and Leona. I probably would have had to settle for putting my things in storage, like it or not. The apartment and the basement were both strokes of good luck." He looked around them appreciatively, "And you're right about the outside door being a good thing. I'll draw up a rough draft tonight of what I want done here. Rooms first. I'll need two rooms for my hip replacements, and a larger place for some equipment I'll need to run tests and other things."

"Fix it however you want it and get whatever you need. Leona's excited about being able to help people, and there's no point in your ever asking about money again. There's no pattern the earth's plates can shift into that would sink all my boats."

Martin eyed him curiously, "Doesn't that take all the fun out of it?"

"Nah," Aaron gave a short bark of laughter, his eyes alight with the challenge of life and competition, "It's like a great big game of monopoly!" He got up, "Are you ready to go?"

Martin got up, laughing with him, but the laughter stopped abruptly when he remembered the note in his pocket.

Aaron stopped dead still, a sinking feeling in the pit of his stomach, "What is it? I know that look, you told me the good stuff first, didn't you?"

"The good stuff is always the most important," Martin insisted, "Hold that thought." He fished in his pocket and held out the note.

Aaron took it carefully, as if it might suddenly bite him.

"I found this under my windshield wiper this morning," Martin explained.

Aaron read the note and looked up, "Not from a rocket scientist, but we'll have to deal with it." Did you see any likely suspects hanging around when you got home?"

"No. Nobody. figure he'll be around and watch the car and contact us again that way."

Aaron started toward the outside door, "Yeah, I'd bet *big* on that. Let's go see if the windshield has grown anything else in the fertile city dark."

Martin and Aaron stood outside the basement door and looked around. There was no one on the sidewalk and no traffic, all the places along the curb were taken.

"Don't see anyone yet, where did you park?"

Martin pointed, "Nearly at the end of the block. Let's go stand by the car a few minutes."

Reaching the car, they stood facing each other, watching in both directions.

"That was quick," Aaron said quietly in a few minutes. "They must have been watching for us. Two white men coming this way. Must have been in one of the basement stair wells. One of them's about five foot eleven, the other I'd guess, about five foot eight, both poorly dressed. Um-hum, they're coming right to us."

Martin slowly turned to stand facing the men with Aaron. He noticed as they got closer, the shorter one had the naive countenance of a child.

"The smaller one is walking half a pace behind the other one. That one in front must be the chairman of this trouble committee," Martin observed, his lips barely moving as he spoke softly.

"You must be right, that one in front looks as mean as a hunter taking prey out of a trap," Aaron kept his eyes on them assessing the strangers as they got closer.

The two men stopped in front of Martin and Aaron. None of them spoke immediately.

Martin kept his face blank as he stared silently back at the men. *Darned if I'm going to help them out any,* he thought grimly, knowing Aaron was standing beside him as solidly unmoved and unmovable as a cigar store wooden Indian.

The taller man's eyes wavered. He seemed daunted by the obvious absence of fear in his intended victims.

"I left a note on your car this morning," he ventured tentatively. His head swiveled from Martin to Aaron, "I put it under the windshield wiper."

"I got it," Martin said flatly. "It's my car."

"Me and my friend here, we was in the alley when you talked to those two men that run off and to Rummy. We seen what you did."

"Rummy?" Aaron inquired coldly.

"That's his name. The man what you—"

Suddenly, Aaron's cane was aloft. Martin hadn't seen him raise it. It sang in the air as it descended. The blow fell on the tall one's head with a crack against the skull that jarred Martin's ears.

Shaking, the shorter man clutched his partner's arm, his innocent eyes wide, watching Aaron, but glued to his partner in his fear.

The blow did not knock the taller one down. He stood as if frozen upright, a trickle of blood starting down between his terrified eyes which were locked on Aaron.

Aaron spoke in a low, solemn voice. "Now that I've got your attention—"

"Yes, sir. Yes, sir." The would be blackmailer mopped at his head with a dirty handkerchief. One eye had a nervous tic as Aaron continued.

"Do you think you can find this man again, this Rummy?"

"Yes, sir. I know I can." Hope creeped into the fear and respect the cane's resounding whack had loosed from the hard cranium.

"If I hand you a hundred dollar bill and tell you to find this man and *kill* him," Aaron's eyes nailed him, "Will you do it?"

The smaller partner continued to cling to his friend's arm, mute and terrified. The blood had dried between the leader's eyes, which now took on a glaze of greed.

"Lemme see the hundred."

Aaron took a hundred dollar bill from his wallet, but held it just beyond the man's reach as he talked.

"I don't want you to find him. Or kill him. *Forget him.* This hundred is a retainer fee. You're both working for me now." He handed over the bill.

"Yes, sir. My name's Tom Burke, and this here's Harry Jones." The bill quickly disappeared into Burke's worn billfold.

"All right. Meet me here at eight o'clock tomorrow night. I'll give you a beeper. Keep it with you."

Regally, in spite of the cane, Aaron turned and walked away without a backward glance. Martin followed, feeling like a bit actor following the star off stage.

Jackie Griffey

CHAPTER TWELVE

Alton went into the house, his temper not improved by the fact that Blanche hadn't noticed him looking out the pool house door. She turned when he opened the door to go in.

"Oh, you're home."

"Yeah, I can see it's cause for wild celebration," Alton spat sarcastically. "Where's dad?"

"He's—he's gone," Blanche fished unsuccessfully for better words.

"Gone? I can see that, where is he? Tell me where he is." He took her arm and shook her, feeling frustrated.

"Alton," Blanche gasped, "You're wrinkling my jacket!"

Alton stopped abruptly, upset with himself on top of all his other problems. He dropped her arm, looking contrite. "I'm sorry. I'm upset, that's all. I looked for dad, then I went in the pool house and it looks like he was never there. I guess it sort of threw me. You say he's gone, gone where?"

"I'm afraid I don't know—right now," Blanche faltered.

"Right now? What do you mean by that? Did he say he was going somewhere? Where did he go?"

"Come on out to the den," Blanche stalled, "I'll fix you a drink, or do you want a coke?"

"A coke will be fine. If you don't know here he is, when was the last time you saw him, he can't have just disappeared?"

"I was afraid he'd wander off, sometime when I was gone. I, I—I ah—"

"You what? What did you do, Blanche? *Answer me!*"

Blanche cringed at the unaccustomed anger in his voice. "I—I put him in Pleasant Hill," she blurted it out.

"Pleasant Hill?" Some of the wrinkles in his forehead straightened out. "Oh, that nursing home near here." He stared at her, frowning, "You put dad in a nursing home?"

"It's a nice place," Blanche pointed out defensively, "Where he will have people his own age to talk to. And he won't be able to wander off, or—or anything."

Disbelief replaced Alton's frown, "And he went?" He shook his head, "That doesn't sound like him." His eyes narrowed, coming back to hers.

"He—ah—they—sent two attendants for him. To see that he got there safely," she quickly explained.

Anger blazed from Alton's eyes, *"You mean you had him shanghied!"* He shouted at her. "That's what you did," he stood, hands on hips, accusing her. "Blanche, this is the last straw! I'm going to get him." He stopped, "Pleasant Hill, you said?"

Blanche wrung her hands, "He's not *there,* Alton!"

"What do you mean he's not there? We seem to be going in circles here. You just said you took him there or the attendants did, is he there or isn't he? I'm not going to play games with you, Blanche. Where is dad? *Where is he?* You tell me, and you tell me *now!"*

"I don't know, I don't *know!"* She stared at Alton's grim face, his clenched fists, he was barely hanging onto his anger. "He left there. He left Pleasant Hill. I talked to them, they don't know where he is either."

"He might not have gone far, did you put out a missing person's report on him?"

"No!" Blanche gasped, "Think of the scandal!"

"Scandal, my ass!"

Alton looked ready to kill. Blanche's words tumbled out through dry lips, talking fast. "I have a private detective looking for him."

"Call him then, whoever he is. Call him—now!"

Blanche went to the wall phone and dialed the number L.D. Holmes had given her. To her relief, he answered immediately.

"This is Blanche Willoughby, Mr. Holmes. My husband, Alton, wants to speak with you." Her hand shook as she handed Alton the phone.

"Have you located my father," Alton asked without preamble. He listened a moment. "I see. That's it, then. I'll take over, now that I'm home. Send your bill to Blanche, she's the one who hired you." He hung up the phone and turned to Blanche, who looked like she wished she'd had the nerve to sneak out of the room while he talked.

"I'll go and report him missing. But first, we have to talk."

"Talk? You're blowing this all out of proportion, Alton. He'll come back."

"This has nothing to do with dad. I'm talking about you and me. About our marriage."

Blanche nodded, relaxing a little. "Our tenth anniversary will be in three months."

"We're not going to make it, Blanche."

"Not going to make it? What do you mean?"

"We have no life together, nothing in common, and no family. You knew I wanted children when we got married, I thought you did, too."

Blanche avoided his eyes. "But, Alton, I don't think now is the time—"

"Not time," Alton snapped back in disgust. "You're pushing forty! Do you think it will ever be time?"

"No! No, I don't!" Blanche's temper erupted like a long dormant volcano. Alton stood with his hands on his hips again, listening to her as if she were a stranger.

"I don't want to lose my breakfast or my figure either! And I wouldn't be out in the cold without you," she added disdainfully. "There are lots of men who would appreciate being married to a woman like me!"

"Find yourself one, then! Our marriage was a mistake. Either you get a lawyer or I will, or we both will, whatever it takes." He pointed a finger at her, "And don't plan on any alimony or keeping the house, either. You've got enough education to find a job. We'll sell the house and split what we've got right down the middle, fifty-fifty. That's fair, and it's all you're going to get. Call whatever lawyer you want, and get out!"

Blanche was stunned. "Get *out?* Me? You're the one who should get out."

"No, I'm staying here in case dad comes back, and to show the house. You call a lawyer, whoever you want, and I'll call a real estate agent. As soon as you leave, I'll go down and take care of the missing person report. You can put your things in that BMW you're so crazy about. You're welcome to that, no contest!"

***

As soon as Martin and Aaron got inside and the basement door closed behind them, Martin doubled over with the laughter he'd been holding back since the confrontation with the would-be blackmailers at the car.

"Your hiring practices must save bushels of paperwork," he gasped out between spasms of glee.

"Keep it simple," Aaron responded complacently, "That's my motto." He grinned at Martin's mirth. "It's like making the punishment fit the crime. You do whatever the current situation calls for."

"I'll have to hand it to you. The threat is gone and you've got local help. That poor fellow will do anything you want him to, you've established that, sure as God made little apples!"

"With the far out ideas you get, that's bound to come in handy," Aaron pointed out trying to take some of the pressure off himself.

Martin subsided and sat down, still grinning. "Can you beat having Burke and Harry working for us?"

"You know those two?" Aaron raised his eyebrows.

"No," Martin laughed again, his sides were beginning to hurt. "Never saw them before."

"Then what's so blamed funny?"

"Burke and Haire were the body snatchers who supplied Dr. Frankenstein with spare parts! Now we've got our own Burke and Harry."

"Oh," Aaron groaned, "I hope this isn't some kind of sign. The wrong side of the law is a dangerous place to be."

Martin sobered, his laughter having run its course. "You're right about that. I've always obeyed the law and played by the rules, even when I didn't agree with them, or they hampered my work." He came to a sudden decision. *"No more!"*

Aaron jumped, startled.

"My only rules now are going to be my oath and the ten commandments."

"The ten commandments?" Aaron squinted at him, "Is that a promise? It would be a load off my mind. Sometimes you scare me, Martin."

"I scare *you?*" Martin scoffed. "Did I hear right? How do you think I felt when your cane landed on Burke's head? You could have cracked his skull! Tell me the truth, would that have bothered you?"

Aaron fidgeted uncomfortably, "Somewhat. Yes."

"Um-hum, somewhat," Martin seized on that, "But not a great deal. You play by your own rules too. Admit it," he demanded.

Aaron turned without commenting and headed for the elevator. "Let's just agree to do the best we can. Your squash is getting cold."

CHAPTER THIRTEEN

Entering the clinic to go to work, the first face Martin saw was beaming, beautiful, and belonged to Nurse Jennie Graves, who was holding Dr. Rob Payne's hand. They stopped and Jennie flashed Rob a confident grin before speaking to Martin.

"You told me to find you a nurse, and have I got a nurse for you," she beamed at the accomplishment.

"Good morning," Martin's smile included both of them, "And that's great. She must be classified Guardian Angel to rate that much enthusiasm," Martin couldn't resist teasing her.

"Anyone trying to hire nursing help would certainly think so," Rob put in, agreeing with Jennie.

"Maybe not Guardian Angel, but pretty close. She's a nurse practitioner," Jennie explained. "So she's not hard up for work or probably money either. She's an excellent nurse, and she says she'll work any time she's not on schedule to work here."

"That's why we can still be friends," Rob wore a pleased grin.

"Well, that's good, I won't be stealing your good help then. I've got a couple of LPNs and some sitters to fill in. When can I talk to this paragon, or do I have to call Mount Olympus to get an appointment?"

"Since you know how lucky you are, I'll page her for you now. Her name's Hilde. Hilde Haschold."

"I'll get on then, and let you do your own contracting, Rob said. "But before I go, I want to tell you how much I admire what you're doing for all these people you've been treating who need your help so badly."

"Sure," Martin dismissed it, "You can help me polish my halo in your spare time."

"Spare time's spoken for," Jennie waved him away and led Martin to the desk to page Hilde.

***

Alton answered the doorbell and found a stranger on his porch. The stranger sported a rumpled jacket, no tie, and a face that was devoid of any recognizable emotion.

"Alton Willoughby?"

Alton nodded, noticing he didn't seem to be carrying a vacuum cleaner or anything else to sell.

The stranger shoved a large envelope full of papers at him, turned, and left without another word.

She didn't lose any time. Alton recognized his divorce papers. He scanned through them. *No alimony, good. We will split everything down the middle, just like I told her. I see the grounds are irreconcilable differences. He's got that right, whoever Theo Smith is.*

The doorbell rang again. Alton glanced at his watch as he hurriedly hid the papers in a drawer in the low coffee table in front of him. *Must be the real estate agent. She said they'd be here at ten and it's five till. Hope she's that prompt in selling the house.*

Alton took a deep breath and braced himself to be pleasant in what was to him, an already unpleasant situation. He opened the door wide and the phony smile froze on his face.

In that fleeting second, his teeth got dry, his tongue refused to work, and his heart skipped a beat.

The attractive woman he was staring at seemed to be similarly afflicted. *"Oh,"* was her only comment.

The real estate agent looked from one to the other, wondering why her client had fallen apart like a car out of warranty. She could see no cause in the customer she had brought.

"Mr. Willoughby," the agent spoke cautiously, "This is Honor Dean. I've brought her to see the house, as I told you I would. Have you two met?"

"Yes!"

"No!" Honor Dean spoke at the same time.

The real estate agent smiled at the obvious attraction between them, "Can we discuss which it is inside?"

Alton moved aside quickly, "Yes! Please, come in. I was on a business trip," he felt compelled to explain, "We stayed at the same hotel."

"We happened to be at the same hotel, but we didn't meet," Honor clarified. "We only saw each other in the hotel's dining room. I guess we noticed each other because we were both dining alone..." Honor finished lamely.

"Yes. Yes, that's how it was," Alton agreed, beginning to perspire. "I—I was surprised to see you again," he spoke to Honor, then quickly told the agent, "I've got coffee made." He knew he was talking too fast, but couldn't seem to stop. "For after you show Miss—Mrs.—" He gazed at Honor Dean.

"Miss. It's Miss," Honor Dean explained. "And please, call me Honor."

"Thank you for fixing coffee," the real estate agent smiled at Alton, trying to put him more at ease. "That was thoughtful of you."

She turned to Honor, "Shall we get started?"

Alton went to wait in the kitchen, acutely aware of exactly where they were during their tour of the house. Then when they had seen everything but the kitchen, they moved on to the surrounding grounds.

The grounds were as well kept as the house, the agent pointed out. She told her the dimensions of the pool and pointed out the landscaping, in spite of the fact her client's eyes kept returning to the kitchen door.

"I'll let you look around the kitchen for yourself, the appliances are all in working order, some of them new."

She finished the sentence talking to herself, Honor had already started toward the house and that magnetic kitchen door.

Alton appeared in the door before they reached it, to open it for them. He tried to be both hospitable and nonchalant, poses which mixed like oil and water with his nervous state and only made him more uncomfortable. They sat down at the table where Alton had set the coffee pot, cups and cup cakes in an attractive array.

"Shall I pour?" The real estate agent didn't trust Alton with hot coffee, and gently took over. "How nice, you have cup cakes too."

Alton managed to nod, looking anxiously at Honor. "Wanted to make a good impression for a family minded person," he spoke to the agent but stared intently at Honor Dean. "Are you—ah—"

"I'm helping my sister look for a house," Honor explained. "She's expecting her third child, and they need more room. "I'm not married and have no family yet."

"The nice large pool will be good for keeping children entertained at home," the agent pointed out.

"The house is very nice, too," Honor spoke to Alton. "My grandmother passed away, and her will gave me and my sister a choice between a sum of money and a family property back in Tennessee. A farm. I chose the farm, and my sister is using her money to get them a larger house. Her husband doesn't want to leave his job here."

"His job," Alton parroted, his brain on hold while his feelings were in charge.

"I have a job, too," Honor said, "I'm a teacher here, but I plan to move to the farm in the near future."

The real estate agent set down her cup and consulted her watch. "I have two other places to show you, Miss Dean, whenever you wish to see them. It's getting a bit late—"

"Yes," Honor agreed quickly. "Some other time. I'm going to make some notes about this house to show my sister. I'll take a cab home."

"All right," the agent hesitated, but agreed. "Let me know when you wish to see the other properties. The card I gave you with the office number on it has my home number on it as well, so call me any time you wish."

They had been moving toward the door and the agent smiled at Alton, "Thank you, Mr. Willoughby."

Alton nodded, too busy opening the door for her to waste time commenting. He watched in silence as she got into her car and started down the driveway. When she got to the iron gate, he shut the door quickly and turned to Honor.

"I thought she'd never get the hell out!"

"Me either," Honor laughed.

Alton folded her in his arms, holding her close before he kissed her long and passionately. Honor's arms stayed around him as he murmured against her forehead, "I've wanted to do that ever since I saw you in that hotel dining room."

"I felt the same way," Honor looked up at him as she drew away, her eyes sad. "But it's too late. You're married, aren't you?"

"No! No, I'm not. My marriage was a terrible mistake, and the divorce is almost final. That's why I'm selling the house." His usually pleasant features registered pain, "And don't draw away from me, please?"

Honor's full breasts touched his chest as she moved back, "Um—my heart wasn't in it. Drawing away, I mean," she smiled up at him.

Alton began unbuttoning her blouse, kissing the cleavage as he went, then taking her in his arms again, like something precious. He savored the warmth of her against him as he kissed her again. She returned his warmth and his kisses, it was like coming home, somehow, filling a hunger and a need for them both. He led her upstairs, holding her hand as if he was afraid she would run away, that he might lose her as suddenly as he found her.

They made love, exploring each other in delight, breaking only for nourishment when Alton made more coffee and Honor made omelets, giggling as she hitched up his oversized robe to keep from tripping on it.

They skinny-dipped in the pool at midnight, and enjoyed the paradise they found in each other until exhaustion overtook them and they slept, their bodies curled around each other.

***

At the clinic, Martin stood up when he saw Jennie coming, accompanied by another nurse.

"Dr. Hammond, this is Nurse Hilde Haschold. Dr. Martin Hammond. I'm going to leave you to get acquainted," Jennie's smile pronounced them two of her favorite people as she turned away.

"Let's sit down and be comfortable," Martin suggested, and waited while Hilde got settled.

"I'm grateful for whatever help you can give me. The operations I'm going to do are hip replacements. Routine, no complications, and they will both be done tomorrow, one before and one after the heart surgery I have scheduled. The two patients will be here the first night, then go to my place until they can return to their care facilities. There will be two LPNs to handle the medicines, and you can come whenever your schedule here allows. You can sleep the whole shift after you check the patients, if you need to. The others will be there and hopefully, there won't be any emergencies."

Hilde nodded, "That's easy to arrange then. I may as well be there as that place I pay rent on. I had a cat, but it got old and died, and I've never been very good with house plants," Hilde told him candidly.

Martin smiled, "No responsibilities to feed and water? Your life style sounds like mine. I'm either at work or asleep."

"That's it, all right. I never lucked up on anyone who appreciates plain and homely. I gave up looking. Are you divorced?"

"No," an instant of hurt flashed over Martin's features but was gone as soon as it appeared, "My wife died ten years ago. Ovarian cancer."

"I'm sorry," Hilde voiced her sympathy, wishing she hadn't asked. *Dr. Hammond must be a good and caring person for Jenny and Dr. Payne to think so highly of him.* She concentrated on what he was saying.

"You're not plain and homely, what gave you that idea?"

Hilde shrugged, "Mirrors and other people's reactions." She paused as if weighing that, "Or maybe it was lack of reaction." She straightened her shoulders, dismissing that as unimportant. "But I'm a good nurse, and I think what you're doing for these two women is wonderful. If you're sure it will be all right to sleep some, I'll go with you from the clinic when you take the patients out."

"Thanks. You can help me get them settled. I'll manage to get your clothes washed for you and your pay will be portal to portal, asleep or awake."

Hilde's strong, perfect teeth showed, "That's a fantastic deal!" Her pleasure showed in her handshake, "I'll stick my things in the trunk of my car. I'm ready to go to work. I need the money."

As they got up, Martin asked curiously, "No cat, no plants, if you don't have any responsibilities, why do you need the money?"

Hilde's eyes held an impish gleam, "I'm ah..." A little embarrassed, she laughed at herself, "I'm thinking of buying a tadpole." She left before he could ask any more questions.

Martin scratched his head, admiring her legs as she walked away from him. *A tadpole?*

Jackie Griffey

CHAPTER FOURTEEN

As good as her word, Hilde went with Martin and the two patients when he moved them to the apartment building.

"I've pulled some strings and I'm taking them in one of the ambulances. I'm taking my car, if you want to leave yours here?"

Hilde hesitated.

"I'll bring you back and forth when you have to come, if that's what's worrying you, and it may be a good idea to leave it here—"

"I couldn't place the apartment building or the street you told me it's on is why I hesitated. I had a battery stolen out of my car not long ago."

"It could happen there. Come with me. I'm in a rental car and the insurance is paid up."

Hilde laughed, "Why don't I feel better? Is this place as dangerous as it sounds?"

"No, not really. But there are lots of people, all different kinds and philosophies and unless I miss my guess, some gang activity."

"I'll take you up on your offer then, and go with you."

At the apartment house, Martin watched a moment as Hilde stood checking the chart he had attached to the second patient's bed. He turned as Aaron came through the door near the elevator.

"Got them all settled in, I see." Aaron glanced through the door nearest him at Hilde and the elderly patient. "How's it going? And is there anything I can do to help?"

"Everything is going well. They both have strong constitutions from growing up on hard work. That helps," Martin told him. "There's nothing I need you to do for them, but I'm glad you're here. I want to talk to you." He beckoned to Hilde as she came out and left the patient's door open a few inches.

Martin sat down at the card table and laid a paper on it as they joined him. Aaron explained to Hilde this was the Leona Miller Memorial Card Table, since she had insisted they would need it. And he had decided immediately he liked Hilde as the good and helpful person Martin had told him she was. They shared a smile as Martin spread out the paper.

"This is Hilde Haschold," Martin gestured at Aaron, introducing them formally, "My good friend and sparring partner, Aaron Willoughby." Hilde smiled again, making a note of the sparring partner title as they turned their attention to the project Martin put before them.

Aaron studied the paper but was puzzled. "I don't understand anything on here but the word skin and a dollar sign." His eyes held humor as they met Martin's. "If you're going to skin somebody, Martin, we do need to talk." He winked at Hilde.

"Classic example of a little knowledge being a dangerous thing," Martin snorted derisively. He pushed the paper closer to Hilde.

"It's things for a burn patient," Hilde explained to Aaron as she studied the paper.

"Right."

She looked up at Martin, "Is this the little girl who was brought to the clinic, then sent to the burn center the other day?"

Martin nodded. "Skin means just that, Aaron. Skin grafts. The child is eight years old, a poor kid burned in a tenement fire. She's responding well. If we can get all this and she has the strength, she'll make it. Being a healthy eight year old, she's got a good chance."

Hilde's reaction was immediate, "If they can't pay for help, I'll do what I can."

"No." Martin shook his head. "The burn center is handling it. I saw the doctor in charge and asked for this estimate of what will be needed. I told him we will get what he needs," his eyes met Aaron's.

"Money and supplies are no problem for us," Aaron confirmed, his brows drawing together, "And I assume the medicines are available, but skin?"

"That's what I wanted to talk to you about. I've got a plan."

"I'm listening."

"I'm going to offer to cover the extent of the skin donated with thousand dollar bills folded twice and take care of the donors free of charge of course, until they're healed. Burke and Harry should be able to round up some very willing donors with that kind of an incentive, and we've got to have those donors *now*."

Aaron wrinkled his nose at the thought. "I've got a better idea. I will go to the Salvation Army Soup Kitchen around the corner and tell them our problem, what we're trying to do. The chance to give a child back her life, plus the money incentive, will give us a better quality donor to work with."

"You're right. Absolutely right. That's a much better idea. You approve, then?"

"Yes. You deserve a pat on the back for thinking of it." He got up, "I'll go down there now."

"Fine, I've got to get back to the clinic."

***

Preoccupied, Martin hurried down one of the clinic's busy corridors and realized someone was calling his name.

"Dr. Hammond! Dr. Hammond!"

"Jennie! I didn't see you," Martin stopped.

"I was trying to catch up with you to tell you I've just checked on the little burn patient and she's doing so well, you can hear 'good prognosis' in the doctor's voice."

She smiled at Rob as he joined them. "Filling him in on the burn patent?" Jennie nodded.

"That was some idea you had for getting skin donors in a hurry, they had to turn people away," he laughed. "How are your hip replacements doing?"

"Doing well. Since we've got the rooms, we can afford to be a little over protective, but Hilde and I are going to let them go in a couple of days."

"Great! Hang in there," Rob hurried away.

"You and Hilde are working well together then," Jennie smiled. "I told you she's good."

"Yeah, she's some nurse, and got her head on straight, except for a couple of things."

"What do you mean," Jennie got defensive, "What couple of things are you talking about?"

"One, she's got the idea she's plain. She's not, she's just somehow decided that all on her own. And two, she mentioned she might use the extra money she's making to," He rolled his eyes at the ceiling. "To—are you ready? Buy a *tadpole!*"

Jennie burst out laughing. Unable to speak, she patted Martin's arm and turned to get on with her work.

"Hey! Wait a minute! What's so funny about a tadpole?"

Jenny stopped. She took a breath as she stepped closer and lowered her voice. "Dr. Martin Hammond, what, when you put them under a microscope, looks like a lot of little wiggling tadpoles?" She turned away again leaving Martin staring after her.

Tadpoles—oh! Tadpoles! His mouth flew open when he realized what Jennie was trying to tell him. *Hilde's thinking of going to a sperm bank!*

***

The afternoon sun was bright as Aaron entered the apartment house foyer, his paper folded under his arm. Leona stood looking out a front window. "Two Blocks to the newsstand is plenty of exercise for a fugitive from the old folks' home. What are you doing?"

"I'm watching." Leona answered without taking her eyes from the window. "It's my turn."

"Your turn?" Aaron walked over and stood beside her, looking out the window. He saw nothing but children passing by, on their way home from school.

"What is it you're watching?"

"That man down there. See that black car with the door open down there?"

"Yes, I see it now. Is he there to pick up a child?"

"Not if we can help it. He does awful things to little children, he's been in jail for it several times."

"What? He molests, *children?"* Aaron was shocked. "Why don't you call the police?"

"Several of the parents have. But, they won't do anything, Aaron. They say they can't, unless he does something against the law. As long as he's just sitting there, there's nothing they can do. So we watch him. This building and the one across the street. I watch when I'm not doing my volunteer work somewhere. I'll only be here until the children have passed by, then I'll go up and make us some coffee."

"Here," Aaron handed her the paper. "You can go on up, I'll watch until that last group gets by, they seem to be the last of them."

"Oh. All right. I'll put us some cookies in the oven, I had some batter left."

He watched until the elevator door closed behind her and the indicator stopped on three. Then, grasping the door knob as if strangling it, he went back out. He walked across the street and strolled down the block until he got to the car with its door open across the sidewalk.

Aaron stopped at the open door and smiled politely, addressing the man who sat in the car. "Excuse me, did you know your fly is open?"

"What's it to *you*," the man was as hateful and vile as his reputation.

"Not a thing, cowboy, I prefer women, myself." Aaron bent down, lowering his voice, "Not to mention, I'd want a cleaner, better looking partner!"

The short, burley, spoiler heaved his oversized belly out of the car, looking like a lynch mob all by himself, and threw a punch at Aaron. It was a big mistake. Aaron grabbed his arm with one hand, his other hand landing a hard blow to the pervert's ample belly. It knocked the wind out of him. As he doubled over, Aaron delivered a well placed rabbit punch, then landed two quick blows to his head in the eye and nose areas as he flopped back onto the car's bench seat.

Winded, the angry predator sopped his bloody face with the tail of his shirt. "You musta broke my nose," he whined.

Aaron remarked pleasantly, "You asked for it, I aim to please. But," he frowned in mock concern, "I see your fly is still open."

Reaching into the car, Aaron took hold of both sides of the open fly and ripped the pants beyond any hope of repair. He straightened up and smiled benignly down upon the sprawling villian's pitiful condition. "Been *most* entertaining talking to you," his phony pleasantry was back in place as he spoke. "I'm sure if you're here about this time tomorrow, we'll meet again."

The pervert stared up at Aaron in disbelief, as if he just might be dealing with an over the hill mental case. Aaron reacted by slamming the heavy door of the old model car on the still extended leg, and turned to stroll back toward the apartment house. As he ambled happily away, he heard the old car's tires screech as the pervert burned rubber getting away.

Martin heard Aaron come in the basement door. He was sitting at the card table writing. "You're in early," Aaron observed. "What is that you're doing?"

"Spending your money. The earth's plates haven't shifted, have they?" Martin looked up, "Good Lord! What's all that blood on your shirt? What happened to you?"

He asked questions as he pushed aside his work and pulled out a chair. Aaron sank gratefully into the chair, more winded than he was ever going to admit.

"Out with it, and did you get in a few licks?"

"That's not my blood you're looking at, but I *am* a little tired." He mumbled almost inaudibly, "Not able to leap tall buildings, you might say…"

Martin reached for the box of kleenex and started wiping Aaron's face. "Tell me what happened. And why didn't you call me instead of hogging all the fun?"

"Wasn't time." Aaron made a face as Martin wiped the sweat from his nose and forehead. He half expected him to say 'now—blow!' "I had a difference of opinion with this nasty thing on the street," Aaron explained. "He thinks it's his right to entice children into his car and do anything he wants to with them as long as he doesn't get caught."

"A pervert? You tangled with some kind of pervert? I'm glad you got some licks in," Martin said with feeling. His face was grim. "All this blood is proof of that. Take off that shirt, I've got an idea."

"Oh, Jesus, have mercy!" Aaron closed his eyes as if in pain as he handed Martin the shirt, "No—No! Not one of your ideas, not on top of everything else!"

Martin ignored his grumbling, disappearing into the lab with the shirt.

Aaron went to the door and looked out, checking to see if the pervert was really gone or might have returned. He walked out to the sidewalk and looked both ways before going back in, satisfied.

Martin was back in a few minutes, looking thoughtful, and handed Aaron his shirt. "Here, I rinsed it and dried it under the hand drier while I was doing the tests."

Aaron looked down at the sleeve he had put on, "It's still a little damp."

"I don't guarantee satisfaction like Sears and Wal-Mart." Martin refused to worry. "It will keep Leona from fainting when she sees you."

"Humpf!" Aaron finished putting on his damp shirt."

"That jerk's blood is too good for him. He hasn't got anything dangerous, and he's a type 'O' donor." Martin's eyes narrowed, "We could put him down here, lock the door, and have a handy emergency supply. I thought about doing something like that when I gave blood at the burn center."

"What about the ten commandments," Aaron squirmed nervously, trying to get the last button through the damp shirt material.

"I'm not suggesting we drain and kill him, only keep him out of trouble for a little while."

"I don't know, let's think about it some more. I'll beep Burke and Harry and see if they can locate the slime ball. What were you working on when I came in?"

"A list of equipment I need so I can do organ transplants here, you need equipment to harvest organs."

"Here? Harvest organs here?" Aaron's eyes widened in surprise, "You've got the clinic, why here?"

Martin sighed, "Because," he explained patiently, "Not all of our donors will be cheerful givers like the Lord loveth, Aaron."

"Aaaaaaaaaach!" Aaron threw his hands up over his eyes in horror, picturing Martin harvesting spare parts. Less than a second later, he raised two fingers and peered between them at Martin.

"You're thinking of the pervert," he said, having figured it out. "We could give someone an organ they need from the pervert." He put his hands down. "Humpf! It would probably be the only good thing he's ever done in his miserable life!" Aaron's brows drew together, "But, what—how could we—"

"You keep trying to make a business man out of me, and I'm catching on—"

"But, what if someone complains, or goes to the police, or what if—what if—someone *dies?"*

"We'll see that no one stays around long enough to go to the police, and hopefully, nobody is going to die. But, if we need to ship a witness too far away to testify, or due to no fault of our own, someone does die—"

"You would get in that little bit of legalese, wouldn't you? All right, what would we do?"

"We'll do what any successful business executive would do, we'll delegate, Aaron. We'll delegate."

"Delegate," Aaron echoed blankly.

"Right. We'll delegate that responsibility to Burke and Harry. They can put the pervert, for instance, on a slow freight train when we're through with him. There are lots of ways. The slow freight, drive them across the state line, and there are cargo ships that leave here every day."

"I guess I'm a goner, I'm beginning to see all kinds of possibilities here." He fingered his sleeve, "My shirt's dry now. Go on and order your equipment and I'll get you a check from one of my places to cover it." He grinned at Martin. "You have to keep current in the business world, and recycling is the 'in' thing now. We'll be recycling humanity!"

"Exactly," Martin laughed with him. "Recycling humanity!"

Jackie Griffey

CHAPTER FIFTEEN

Two days later when Martin came home from work, Aaron greeted him at the door looking suspiciously pleased with himself and followed him into their room.

Martin hung his coat in the closet and put on his slippers before asking, "What have you been up to today, you look full of news as a gossip column."

"I am. I got a call today you'll be interested in. Your equipment will be here and installed tomorrow."

"So soon?" Martin appraised the aura of satisfaction, "Your money must have talked for us."

"Yeah, that, and that cane you gave me is a pretty good devining rod when it comes to finding good help, that's what I'm so impressed about. Burke and Harry are more efficient than the detective Blanche hired. I heard from them this morning."

"That was quick. With no more than they had to go on, I'm surprised they found him that fast."

"They were more than fast, they were as efficient as a dose of salts! They now know the pervert's name, record, address, his usual haunts, and best of all, they know where they can lay hands on him if we want to—ah—*talk* to him."

Martin laid his hand over his heart, "I'll never knock your hiring practices again. What's the slimy joker's name?"

"It's Ollie. Last name Borden, just like Lizzie's."

Martin nodded, "That's good, it will be easy to remember. And didn't Leona tell you his record was why they were watching him? And that part of the record is he's been in jail for molesting children before?"

"Yes, he has. And he doesn't discourage easy, I'm sorry to say. He's back. He stayed away a while after I had my little talk with him, but he's up to his old tricks again. Been down there where he was parked before, for the past two days. I hadn't noticed him, but Leona told me, and I looked, and sure as fog on the coast, there he was." He raised his eyebrows, "Shall we send for him?"

"If it was my child he was trying to get into his car, I know I couldn't see any point in waiting." Martin paused, "Since we know where he's going to be, I could give him a shot and we could get him in here ourselves, but I don't want anyone to see him being brought in here. Burke and Harry can bring him in after dark, so I guess that's the best way to go."

"I'll beep them then, and tell them to bring him in here between nine and ten o'clock tomorrow night."

"That's settled, then. I've got some news to tell you, too. Guess who was brought into the clinic feet first today?"

"I don't quite trust the way you said that—just tell me?"

"Denghen Po."

"Denghen Po!" Aaron was instantly alert, "You mean Denghen Po, the big dog the conglomerate sent to get rid of you? Are you sure? Did you see him? Do they know who he is?"

"No," Martin broke up with glee, "They've *no idea!* That's what makes it so funny! They haven't got a *clue!* There was a four vehicle collision involving a city bus, a cab which must have been Denghen Po's, and two more vehicles. Several people that were in the bus and the other vehicles were examined, some treated for minor cuts and abrasions, the usual phonys who just wanted a piece of the action. All of them were released. But Po and another man were unconscious and they were admitted."

Aaron frowned. "Why don't they know who Po is? Didn't he have identification on him?"

"None at all," Martin chortled. "Some enterprising citizen at the scene relieved him and the other unconscious man of their wallets."

"Why am I not surprised," Aaron grunted. "So he had no ID?"

Martin added with a self satisfied grin, "None. Besides which, I stole his clothes!"

"You *what?"* Aaron broke up too, "You nervy rascal! What have you got in mind? Knowing you I know there's got to be something—"

"I thought it would broaden Po's education to see how the other half lives—without his connections. I threw away his vest, tie, and coat. Then, since the other patient was about the same size, a laborer in his work clothes, I swapped the rest of Sir Denghen's clothes to him for his work pants, sports shirt, and cheap underwear. He wasn't wearing any socks, so I presented the fortunate fellow with Po's silk knee lengths. There he was, unconscious as if the mortuary had laid him out and better dressed than he's probably ever been in his life. Sort of poetic justice in that, don't you think?" Martin paused as if expecting applause, obviously proud of himself.

"That's my boy! You're all heart, Martin," Aaron gave him a thumbs-up salute. "I forgive you for every goose bump you've ever given me with your weird ideas. Do you think you can keep them from finding out who he is for a couple of days, if it really is Po?" Aaron's doubtful expression came back.

"Probably can," Martin nodded. "And it *is* Po." Martin glanced down at his slippers, "Do you want to go and see for yourself? No sense wondering, he's certainly in no position to object."

"Could I do that without anyone knowing?"

"Easy. Piece of cake as they say on the street. We can go now, if you want to."

"I do. I'll tell Leona we're going out for a little while, while you get your shoes back on."

"Okay. Do you have any carbon paper around here?"

"No, why?"

"Never mind. Get a bottle of nail polish remover."

Aaron stopped dead, too puzzled to frame a question.

"Just get it, I'll explain later."

They met at the apartment door. Aaron gave Leona a brief kiss on the cheek while she told him to be careful.

"As if 'be careful' would cover it when I go out with you," Aaron rolled his eyes toward heaven and mumbled as he closed the door behind them.

"Oh, and here," Aaron stepped into the elevator and handed Martin a bottle of nail polish remover. "This was in the medicine cabinet, so I didn't have to ask for it. What do you want it for?"

"Denghen Po was the only one of the accident victims with a manicure." Martin added smugly, "I mean to mess that up."

"Makes sense, he would have a manicure, if it's really Po."

"I only saw him once, at St. Josephs, but it's Po all right." Martin's face turned grim, "I had good reason to remember his face."

Martin parked near the clinic's side door and they made their way directly to Po's room without seeing anyone who asked any questions.

Slipping quietly into the room, Martin and Aaron stood looking down at Denghen Po. He was still unconscious.

"It's Po, all right." Aaron nodded and gazed down with awe, "His connections aren't doing him any good now." He gestured, "What's wrong with him besides the leg?" Aaron gestured at the raised limb.

"Besides the leg in traction, he has internal injuries. There was internal bleeding which hopefully has been stopped, and his spleen was removed. The head injury caused swelling, they cut a section of the bone to ease that. It's the most serious of his injuries. I didn't work on him, I'm going by his chart and what I've overheard."

They watched him a few seconds in silence and Martin tilted his head, viewing Po from a different angle, "He doesn't really look Chinese, does he?"

"I've heard his mother was an Australian missionary. Too bad he didn't take after her. If he's here incognito a couple of days, I can take advantage of his absence at the helm of some places to pull off a couple of financial coups that will make your equipment bills look like petty cash."

There were dollar signs in the eyes he turned to Martin. He demanded the truth as far as Martin could estimate, "How are my chances?"

"Excellent," Martin replied positively. "He's in no position to tell anybody who he is and I doubt his name would mean much to the personnel here, even if he could. You've got your two days easy, probably more. Wait here a minute."

Martin left before Aaron could object.

"What do you mean, leaving me here in a position like this," Aaron demanded, looking ready to explode when Martin stepped back into the room.

"Keep your pants on, I had to get these," he waved a handful of forms.

"What are *those?*" Aaron cast incredulous eyes on the handful of papers, "We can't be supplying any information on him!"

"We don't have to use them for forms just because they *are* forms," Martin's voice was full of disgust, "The bureaucracy has you brainwashed! I got them for the carbon in them." He turned to get on with it. "Watch what I do, then you can help me."

Martin laid the forms and a packet of cotton balls on the night table and started to work. Seeing Martin use the cotton balls and polish remover, Aaron started to work on Denghen Po's other hand. They worked quickly getting the clear polish off his nails.

"That's got it," Martin said when they finished. He used the water in the pitcher beside the bed to get the scent of the remover off Po's hands and dried them on the sheet.

"Now we use the carbon." Martin extracted the carbon from a couple of the forms and handed some to Aaron.

Aaron watched, then chuckled, "Damned if you're not a genius! Devious as hell, but a genius!" He helped himself to more of the carbon and worked with Martin, rubbing it into Po's knuckles and under his fingernails.

The job didn't take long and he leaned back to admire their work.

Martin examined Po's nails critically. "Looks good, doesn't it? I got the idea from the laborer's hands. He got his honestly, from grease and hard work, but these will do."

"You don't know how to fake a couple of calluses, do you?"

"No, you have to work for those. Gather up all that paper and let's get out of here before someone comes to check on him."

***

Burke and Harry were as efficient as Aaron said they were. Promptly at nine fifteen, Burke knocked on the basement door. Martin and Aaron answered the knock together.

"What did I tell you," Aaron bragged, reaching into his pocket.

Ollie Borden stood between Burke and Harry, his hands tied, feet loosely shackled, and his mouth covered with duct tape. His wild eyes were set on maximum mean, and promised a good tussle when the restraints were removed.

"Leave the duct tape on, I don't want to listen to his filthy mouth," Aaron instructed. He handed Burke eight one hundred dollar bills, "This is for both of you."

"Yes, sir," Burke's eyes were greedily counting the bills as if he couldn't believe his good fortune. "Do you want anything else," he asked hopefully.

"Not now," Aaron dismissed them, "But keep that beeper with you, and close the door on your way out."

As soon as the door closed, he joined Martin in the lab. The pervert was sitting on the examining table as if in a stupor.

"He looks groggy," Aaron observed uneasily.

"He is. I gave him a shot. Shut the lab door and let's get him out of these grubby clothes. He'll be asleep before he gets embarrassed."

"Or enjoying it," Aaron's lip curled in disgust.

CHAPTER SIXTEEN

Aaron and Martin sat at the card table after getting the pervert cleaned up and settled.

"It will probably do him good, just getting the crud off," Aaron glanced toward the closed lab door. "It somehow rubs me the wrong way knowing we did something that will benefit him."

"We can even up the score by making him help someone else."

"Shame we can't just stop the world and put him off, with his record. Leona's right, about all they and the parents can do is watch him."

"There's something else I've been mulling over in my mind—"

"Is it dangerous, illegal or fattening? I can handle expensive."

"I don't think so. You remember how many volunteers we had when you contacted the soup kitchen about the skin grafts? What about getting some of them to donate blood? I don't mean donate as in no money, we would pay them the rate other places pay for it. The money would help them, and the clinic could use the blood. What do you think?"

"I don't know. You don't want them coming here, do you? I like being a hermit, but the mail system is tough enough on plain packages, think what damage they could do with blood!"

"Cute, Aaron. What I'll do, if enough of them seem to go for it, is go to them, like the Red Cross does. The equipment won't be much."

"I don't see why not. And since there's a going rate to stick to, it won't call too much attention to us. We were lucky we could run the skin grafts payments anonymously through the hospital, but we don't want to get too obvious."

"When I get off tomorrow, we'll go down to the soup kitchen together. We'll let them know I'm with the clinic," Martin grinned, "So they won't think I'm the neighborhood Dracula."

The next day, Aaron introduced Martin to the man and his wife who were managing the soup kitchen.

"Dr. Hammond," Aaron introduced him, "This is Don and Dee Dee Davis—Dr. Hammond."

Martin shook hands with Don and smiled as he extended his hand to his wife, "Dee Dee?"

"My name's Diane, the DD is short for Diane Davis. I'm glad to meet you. Dr. Hammond. We know how you helped the little girl who was burned."

"Yes, sir," Don agreed, "Is there something we can do for you?"

"I'm not sure. I thought when the little burn victim was being treated, I'd come and see if people here in the neighborhood would be interested in giving blood—to have on hand to use for things like that."

"I don't know," Don was uncertain. "Would they have to go to the clinic?"

"No," Aaron assured him "We thought we would see how many might be interested and if there is a lot of interest, we would bring equipment here," he glanced at Martin, "Say, once a month?"

"I don't see any harm in it," DD told Don. "If they want to do it."

Don smiled, "Well, it's their blood. Do you want me to make an announcement or do you want to do it.?"

"I'll do it. You just get their attention." Martin looked around the large dining room. Don picked up a glass and tapped on it with a fork. Several people looked around, then gradually most of them paused to listen.

"Ladies and gentlemen, my name is Martin Hammond, Dr. Martin Hammond. I want to thank you all for the time you donated and skin grafts and help for the little girl who was burned. If you are interested in giving blood for future use in cases like that and others here, in this area, I will bring equipment here and pay you the going rate."

It was another great idea that never got off the ground. No one showed the slightest interest in giving blood.

"People started turning away when you finished thanking them for the help with the burn victim," Aaron said quietly.

Don moved closer to Martin and raised his voice, "Anybody interested in giving blood, will you hold up your hands?"

There still was no interest, not one hand showed.

"I'm sorry," Diane told Martin. "I'm not sure I would either, when I think of a needle drawing blood. It was good of you to try, though."

"Will you stay and have a bite with us," Don invited as Diane went back to her work.

"We'll take a rain check on it," Aaron said.

"Yes. Thanks for letting us check and see if anyone was interested."

Martin and Aaron looked back as they reached the door. "The first notice they took when Don got their attention was to see if there was something free being offered," Aaron said, "After that, they lost interest faster than bankrupt brokers."

"Looks like I took time off from the clinic for nothing." Martin's disappointment showed as they started walking home from the soup kitchen.

"It's just something about a needle, like DD said. I know how I hated to see that one you used on my toe. And we can't go around offering a lot of money for blood, that wouldn't do."

"No, that would make them suspicious anyway. Guess I was about due to strike out with one of my great ideas."

"Now don't tell me it hasn't happened before, as many of them as you get?" Aaron turned to grin at him but stopped.

"What is it," Martin whispered, not turning his head.

"Let's walk on, slowly. I think we've picked up a shadow."

"A shadow? Does he look dangerous?" Martin's eyes cut sideways. "I don't see anybody."

"It's a kid. A little boy. Looks to be about—eight or so, I'd guess. But he's definitely following us."

"Let's stop and see what he wants," Martin turned around, eyes searching for he child.

"Now you've done it, he's gone!"

"I see him running. Are you sure he was following us?"

"I'm sure. He'd stop once in a while, stand behind a waste bin or something, then he'd come out and come on, keeping us in sight."

"Did you see him in the soup kitchen?"

"No, but that doesn't mean he wasn't there. He could have been there and heard you ask if anybody wanted to give blood."

Martin frowned, "If that's why he was following us, it must mean he needs a doctor for some reason." He kept walking back in the direction the boy was running.

"Martin," Aaron was exasperated, but kept walking, "You must get all your exercise jumping to conclusions. What makes you think he needs a doctor?"

Martin walked faster, "I can't think of any other reason, can you? Come on, move," he walked faster.

"Okay, okay, but just to see you strike out twice in one day."

"There's no sign of him," Martin said after the next two blocks.

"There's a little girl sitting on the steps of that second house, looks like it's been cut up into apartments."

"Let's ask if she's seen him. You ask, she might talk to you, I don't want to frighten her." Martin stood back a few feet as Aaron approached to within talking distance of the little girl, who was dressing her doll.

"Have you seen a boy, light skin like yours, wearing jeans and a black baseball cap?"

"Jist Kendall."

"Kendall?"

The little girl nodded, "He lives here. Him and his momma and—him and his momma."

"There he is," Martin came to the steps, looking up at the child on the stairs inside. "Are you Kendall?"

The boy nodded. "I saw you at the soup kitchen. You a doctor?"

"Yes, I am. Do you need some help?"

The boy looked up the dark stairway, "My momma does, but we don't have no money," the boy looked away.

"You don't need money, I'll see what I can do for her. Martin went in and started up the stairs with him. "Has she been sick long?"

"She's not sick. She's hurt."

They arrived at a worn and warped door and the boy opened it, letting Martin enter first. The door creaked and Aaron went in behind them. He stood beside the door as the boy led Martin to his mother. The woman sat on a box near the one window in the room, holding a wet cloth to her forehead. She looked to be in her late twenties, pretty but shabbily dressed.

"Miss," Martin said gently. "I'm a doctor, let me see if I can help you." The woman lowered the cloth and looked up at him. There were bruises on her face and a laceration where she had been holding the cloth.

Her nose was swollen and the eye under the laceration was on the way to being blacker than the rest of her.

"How did this happen?"

"It was Hamp done it," the boy spoke up. "He hits her all the time."

"I don't have my bag with me, if you can walk, come with me and I'll dress that laceration and medicate the other places." Martin reached to help her up, but she drew back her hand when the downstairs door slammed shut. She gasped in terror, as heavy feet climbed the stairs.

Martin turned toward the door to see a man taller than he, but smaller than Aaron appear in the door with a sack in his arms. He shifted the sack and the sound told Martin there were cans in it. *Beer,* he thought, *Not groceries. It figures!*

The man's eyes slid past Martin and fixed on the woman. He looked capable of murder as he started to step into the room. Out of his range of vision, Aaron's foot shot out and tripped him. He and his sack both fell heavily, the cans rolling across the floor.

Martin took the woman's arm. Dragging her along at first, he quickly followed Aaron who was already hurrying down the stairs with the boy's hand in his. The four of them ran to the accompaniment of loud curses coming from the upstairs apartment.

At the next corner, Aaron grabbed Martin's arm as he caught up, "Quick, back here!"

Aaron, Kendall, Martin, and the woman cowered behind a commercial trash bin, hardly daring to breathe.

Squatting on the sidewalk, Kendall peered through the crack between the bin and the wall of the building.

"He's going the other way," the boy reported.

Martin chanced a peek over the top of the bin. "He's turning down toward the soup kitchen. Quick, let's go!"

They ran the rest of the way to the apartment house, making for the basement doorway.

Aaron reached it first and held it open for the woman and Kendall, looking down the street behind them.

"There's someone we need to see," Aaron pointed.

Martin went around him and stood in the middle of the sidewalk, waiting for the uniformed policeman who was coming toward them.

"Officer, would you come with me a minute?"

"What's the trouble?"

"I'm getting ready to treat some cuts and abrasions, if you'd come in?"

Aaron put his hand on the woman's arm, "It's all right. You just tell the policeman what happened to you."

"I'll tell him," Kendall spoke up, "Hamp beat her up—again," he eyed the policeman.

"Della," the policeman spoke to the woman, "You've got to let me put him in jail. He's going to keep hurting you until you do, and he might do the same to your boy."

"He'd beat his own son," Aaron looked at Kendall.

"He's not *my* daddy," Kendall's young voice was bitter. "He talked my momma into coming up here with him, took the salary she made, and bought booze with it until she got fired because she couldn't work—"

"All right, son." The policeman put his hand on Kendall's shoulder and turned to Martin. "I've been called before, by neighbors, about this man. None of this is news to me. I know who he is, but she's got to stand up for herself."

Aaron bent to talk to the woman, "Della, that's your name?"

She nodded.

"Della, you've got to sign a complaint against this man. He's not going to hurt you any more. You don't have to go back there. You can stay here until he's gone. Where is your home? Kendall said you came here with Hamp. Where did you come from?"

Della began to cry, "I can go home, I can stay with my sister until I get a job. She's been asking me to come, said she would come and get us. But I was afraid of him, of what he'd do."

"I'll go and get him now, and put him in jail," the policeman told her. "And this man says you can stay here until he's put away where he can't hurt you or anyone else. Does Hamp know where your sister lives?"

Della shook her head, "No, I never told him, or about her saying I could go to her." She squared her shoulders and squeezed Kendall's hand. "All right, I will. I'll sign the complaint, and go to court this time, then we can leave after he's—he's gone."

Kendall put his arm protectively around his mother's shoulders.

Della looked up at Aaron, "But please, tomorrow, I want to go and get some of my things I want to keep."

"All right. We'll do that."

The patrolman left to round up Hamp, and Martin began cleaning and dressing Della's face.

"I'll be back in a little while," Aaron gestured upstairs and Martin nodded.

Leona returned with Aaron, her eyes on the little boy. "I brought you a coke," she held it out. "Aaron says you ran all the way here. Come sit down here with me."

"Thank you," Kendall sat down at the card table with Leona to drink his coke.

"Della," Aaron told them, "You and Kendall can stay in the room Martin and I stayed in before he got his apartment. We'll go with you tomorrow after Martin gets home from the clinic, and get your things you want to keep. You will be safe here until your sister comes for you. You can call and talk to her tonight."

"Thank you. I know I should have done something before now, but I—I was so afraid."

"It's all right now, you'll be all right," Leona had come to stand beside Aaron as he stood up. "Aaron said that man doesn't know where your sister lives—"

"No. No, thank goodness. He doesn't know. She knew where I was, because once I called her collect, when I had to go to the emergency room. But he doesn't know where she lives."

Martin was finished. Leona shepherded Della and Kendall upstairs, Aaron and Martin, looking after them.

"Turns your stomach, doesn't it? Good thing your furniture got here when it did." Aaron spoke softly as he helped Martin put medical supplies away.

"What hurts, is there's so many more in the same boat, with no none to help them."

"We'll just have to do the best we can. And," Aaron hesitated, "I'm sorry the idea about the blood bank didn't work out."

"I'll live," Martin smiled as he started toward the elevator, "I'm a tough guy to discourage."

Aaron raised his coke bottle as the elevator door opened, "I'll drink to that!"

***

Martin knocked on Aaron's door the next day. "You must have sneaked off on time, for a change," Aaron remarked when he opened the door.

"I just saw that Hilde left on time, I think she's fonder of work than I am."

"Couldn't be," Aaron shook his head as Della joined them.

"I heard Dr. Hammond come in," she smiled at him. "Kendall's watching television with Leona. I'm ready to go."

"Okay. She knows we'll be back soon. Let's go and get it over with."

"I don't have much, so it won't take long," Della apologized.

"Pay no attention to him, sometimes he forgets to listen to what he's saying."

"I only mean, to break all ties with the past—to make a new start."

"We know, we know," Martin looked superior, aggravating Aaron as much as possible and Della giggled.

At the shabby apartment, Della looked around the small rooms. "I guess I should straighten up some—"

"No, you shouldn't. All the straightening that needs to be done is being done by the police."

"You got that right. Just get what you want, Della."

It took only a few minutes to get the few clothes she wanted and the things she wanted for Kendall together.

Aaron carried a small suitcase as they left, Martin and Della carried paper sacks. As they reached the place where they had hidden behind the trash bin, a figure stepped out into their path.

"Hamp!" Della froze.

They must have let him out, Martin thought, taking in the five o'clock shadow and the mean look he gave Della. Hamp started at them, raising his arm.

Aaron quickly raised the suitcase and blocked the first blow Hamp aimed at him. At the same time, Martin pushed Della out of harm's way, then carefully set the two sacks against the side of the building.

Hamp and Aaron were warily circling each other. Hamp landed Aaron a blow which set him down hard against the trash bin, but Hamp got overbalanced, and fell in the opposite direction.

Martin leaned over Aaron, "Do you need some assistance?"

"I'm just getting warmed up," Aaron growled, *"This* one is *mine!"*

As Martin straightened up, Hamp raised his foot to kick Aaron while he was down. Martin saw the movement out of the corner of his eye and deftly put his hand under Hamp's calf and lifted, sending him sprawling again.

"Just evening things up a little," he told Della as he joined her.

"Oh—up there in the next block," Della's eyes widened with hope, "Here comes Officer Smith!"

Della looked relieved, the policeman had seen her and what was going on. But Martin raised his hand to get his attention and shook his head, pointing to Aaron.

Aaron paid no attention to approaching people or anything else. He had gotten his second wind and was giving Hamp the record beating of his mean, maladjusted life. Every time he thought of other people Hamp might have hit or bullied, and times he had hit Della, Aaron let him have the force of righteous indignation he deserved. Hamp's nose was bloody and one eye was swelling and the look in his eyes had nowhere near the confidence they held when he'd thrown a fist at the suitcase.

Patrolman Smith carefully wiped the smile off his face, covering it with a bland expression as he slowed his pace. He stopped to examine numbers lettered on the curb, petunias in a couple of window boxes, and various other points of interest as Hamp bled on his clothes and the sidewalk from a lot of painful places.

Aaron again slammed Hamp down against the trash bin, and this time he stayed there, feebly raising a hand to signal he'd had enough.

"I guess I'd better run," Aaron growled at him as he spotted Officer Smith, "Before I get arrested for littering," he sneered at Hamp who leaned limply against the trash bin. He briefly considered throwing him into it, head first.

Officer Smith took over, smiling at Aaron as if he could read his mind. "Do you want to press charges," he asked, "I saw this man trying to snatch your suitcase."

"I guess not, but this bird's breath smells like a brewery, isn't that against the law?"

"Public drunkenness is, yes. Drunk and disorderly." The policeman eyed Hamp, "Assault and battery." His smile faded, disappointment taking over. "Too bad you didn't knock him a little farther so I could get him for resisting arrest, or leaving the scene of the accident he looks like he was in."

"There was nothing accidental about any of this," Martin guffawed.

Aaron glared at him. "With friends like you, I'll never need enemies," he scolded. "We'll just settle for the charges we've got," he told Officer Smith.

"What's he doing out on the street, anyway," Martin wanted answers.

Must have let him out until court, but this will fix that mistake. He won't be out again until he's sentenced."

"Need some help getting him back," Aaron asked as Officer Smith handcuffed Hamp.

"No, he'll probably be glad to get back, from the way he's moving," Officer Smith laughed. "But thanks for the help, and entertainment."

Jackie Griffey

CHAPTER SEVENTEEN

Martin paid for his lunch at the end of the clinic cafeteria line and looked around for a place to sit.

Ah, there's Hilde. I'll see if she wants company.

Martin paused beside Hilde's table. She hadn't noticed him, seemingly lost in thought.

"Need some help watching that cup of coffee get cold?" Martin smiled down at her. "You look like you're pondering the impossible, mind if I join you?"

"No, sit down. I was considering all the pros and cons I know about something."

"Pros and cons, hummm. Looks like from your expression, the cons are outnumbering the pros. Do you want input, or is it something private—like solitaire?"

"It's private, but it's complicated enough that I need some input." She regarded Martin with more interest. "It's a thing with a built in time limit and not much in the way of guarantees or safeguards. And since you've asked, I realize you are more than qualified to give me some input."

"I doubt anybody can get 'more qualified' since perfect is perfect and honest is honest, qualified must be qualified, period." He made a funny face at her. "But you look too serious for humor. Must be one of those calculated risks Aaron keeps trying to educate me about."

Martin opened his sandwich to examine the inside, carefully not looking at Hilde. "These pros and cons, are they about the tadpole you're thinking of buying?"

Hilde didn't answer.

"All life is a calculated risk at best. It took me a while to figure out what you meant when you said you were thinking about buying a tadpole." Martin spoke softly, though there was no one close enough to be interested in their conversation.

"I know, but since it's something you have a choice about, it takes serious thought. A sperm bank sounds ideal for someone like me, who wants a child, but it's got its down side too. It's exactly what you called it. A calculated risk."

She gazed intently at Martin, "Remember that louse who got caught supplying his own sperm at the sperm bank he owned?"

Martin nodded, "I remember reading about it in the paper."

"There's a class action suit against him, but the damage is done. Imagine choosing the donor characteristics you want, thinking you have chosen well for your child to be healthy, intelligent, and have a good start in life, and then learning something like that happened. They should have lynched him instead of merely suing!"

"I agree. They should have skinned him with a dull knife. What I'm talking about is commitment, I suppose, not the physical side of it. Hilde, there's never any guarantee what a child will be like, no matter how carefully you choose your mate or your sperm bank."

Martin's mind returned to happier years, forgetting his food in his concern for Hilde. "My wife, Mildred, and I never had children. We would liked to have had, it just wasn't in the cards for us. I remember once, when Mildred thought she was pregnant, she told me, 'our child will be beautiful to us. If it has a wart on its nose, we'll just think that wart is the absolute best wart *ever*,' is how she expressed it." Martin's smile was affectionate, remembering Mildred's excitement.

Hilde giggled, "I know just what she meant. But, it's only human to want the very best you can get for your child."

She leaned on her elbows, her eyes half closed, "I'd want someone...He wouldn't need to be drop-dead gorgeous, but nice looking. And I'd want to see health records, too." She sat conjuring up a mental picture of a desirable donor. "I'd like fair to medium coloring, like mine," she decided. "And if at all possible, someone in the field of medicine like I am—"

She stopped suddenly, staring at Martin. "That's *you!* You can see that, can't you? I hadn't realized it until now, but that's you! You fit the description to a tee! So, what do you think, Dr. Hammond, would you be willing to sell me one of your little tadpoles?"

Martin sloshed coffee in his saucer in his haste to set down his cup. *"Not me,"* came out a little too loud. He looked self-consciously around but no one seemed to have noticed.

"I'm drop-dead gorgeous, so it can't be *me,"* he tried to laugh it off.

"I can overlook that," Hilde dismissed the small discrepancy. "You're shocked, that's all. I was too, when it dawned on me I'm sitting right here looking at all the characteristics I've been hunting." Her features were taut with anxiety, "I'm serious. I wouldn't have to worry about any kind of mix up or any of the other things that can go wrong." Her face glowed with the discovery, "It's the answer to my problems!"

Leaning slightly forward, her eyes implored understanding. "Would you consider it, please," she asked with childlike politeness and hope in her eyes.

Martin glared at his plate and the half eaten tuna fish sandwich. "This is the strangest lunch I've ever had."

"You're not sterile, are you?" Hilde pursued what seemed to be her perfect solution, the end of the problems that plagued her dreams. "You and Mildred did have tests run, didn't you?"

"They said I wasn't," Martin admitted. "She wasn't either. Then we found out about the cancer."

"Oh, the ovarian cancer…"

"Yes." Martin sighed, "Thank goodness she didn't suffer as long or as much as some I've seen…"

"I'm sorry." Hilde spoke from her heart. "I really am. But, she's gone now, and the past is not part of the problem now. I know she wouldn't object to your having the child you both wanted."

"No," a short laugh escaped, "She'd more than likely vote for it! How old are you, Hilde?"

"Never mind that tired excuse." She leaned forward again, elbows on the table, stating her case. "Dr.

Hammond, I'm forty-one years old. And I'll be forty-two when this child is born. Never mind telling me I'm not old, that's ancient for someone to be having a first child. But I've still got time to raise it, and care for it, and love it, even if it does have a wart on its nose. And I make good money—"

"Hilde, I'm honored. I am, I can't think of any higher compliment. But please, think about this. I am closer to ancient than you are, my time's limited, too. So it's important to keep that in mind."

"I realize that, I will think about it. But please, will you think about it too? Will you please, just consider it?"

Martin couldn't find it in his heart to flatly refuse. "I'll think about it."

***

That night Martin had to concentrate to do justice to the good dinner Leona had fixed. As soon as Aaron put down his coffee cup after dessert, he said, "Aaron, if you're finished, come downstairs with me. I want you to help me with something."

Aaron exchanged a serious look with Leona before answering, "All right. I need to talk with you about something anyway."

Entering the basement, Martin went first to the lab to check on the pervert. Aaron followed and looked down at the sleeper. "Darned if I don't see improvement," he examined the chubby face critically.

"Clean living, no doubt. I'm not going to bother with vitals. He's warm, looks all right, and his foul mouth is shut. Go on out, I'll lock the door."

Martin joined Aaron at the card table. "Now, what was it you and Leona were exchanging mysterious glances about?"

"About a woman she saw at the charity hospital where she worked today. The woman goes there for dialysis, and Leona knows her general situation. She always knows all their life stories before she leaves."

Martin smiled, picturing Leona with the patient.

"Anyway, today she found out the woman's not even on a waiting list for a kidney. She's in her late fifties, not sixty yet, and has her daughter and her little granddaughter living with her. They need her disability check just to make ends meet for all of them. There's no money for a transplant. I don't know what the government would pay or even if it would be covered, but they couldn't pay their part of the bill even if they could get a kidney. The woman was working and had insurance when the first kidney was removed, but there's no hope now. Leona wants you to agree to do the transplant. That way, the woman can at least get on a waiting list and have some hope. Leona can't stand not trying to help her, even if it's nothing but giving her hope of a fighting chance."

"That's what makes Leona, Leona," Martin's features softened with affection. "I'll talk to her when we go back up. I'll see the woman, and do what's necessary, I think we may be able to help her."

Aaron made no move to get up. "Are we going to —ah—recycle the pervert?"

"Yes. He'll be our donor unless something shows up in the testing to rule him out. But, I'd bet against that. We won't tell Leona anything until we're sure. I'll do the transplant to the patient at the clinic, taking the kidney in one of the 'ice buckets' you so generously provided. We do need a name to use for the donor when I do the paperwork."

"No problem about a name, or any other information you may need. "I'll give you the name and ID of a dead board member at one of my places. He was a stingy turd, he can do a good deed posthumously."

"Great. I knew I could depend on you," Martin quickly crossed it off his worry list. "And 'posthumously' reminds me, Denghen Po died some time last night. That head injury is what got him."

"Do they still not know who he is?"

Martin shook his head, "Never regained consciousness."

"What will they do? I never thought about a situation like that before."

"He's an unidentified John Doe, same as the laborer I gave his clothes to. They're both at the morgue by now. If no one claims Po's body, and no one will, he's headed for the precinct's pauper's field."

"Tough! But it serves him right, he was more than a little bent. Is that what you wanted to tell me? About Po?"

Jackie Griffey

"No. It wasn't." A strange look came over Martin's face. Aaron saw it and braced himself, lips parted, wondering what was coming.

"I'm—thinking of becoming a father," Martin said quietly.

"A *what?*" Aaron felt he'd endangered his blood pressure for one of Martin's jokes and immediately calmed down. "Becoming a father? Am I hearing right?" He waited for the punch line in spite of Martin's serious face.

"That's right. You heard me. *Me!* A father! At least, I've been invited."

"Invited? To be a father! You don't just get invited to be a father, Martin. You're going to have to clear this up for me." Aaron stared at him, waiting for an explanation or an end to the joke.

"A nurse at the clinic was considering going to a sperm bank, is how it happened. But, to make a long story short, she wants to buy the sperm from me."

Aaron was speechless for once.

Martin added, "The nurse is Hilde."

"Hilde!" Aaron sputtered, "She's a good twenty years younger than you!"

"That won't matter in a case like this."

Aaron took a few seconds to digest the news. "Well, are you going to do it? Sell it to her?"

"Not sell. But yes, I think I'll give her the sperm."

Aaron rolled his eyes heavenward, "You're all heart, Martin. Or maybe it's a phrase I'm looking for. Lucky Son of a Sea Biscuit—yeah, that fits." Aaron got up and started walking toward the door as if his legs were on automatic pilot. "Here I am," He mumbled aloud, "Mourning the fact I'll never have any grandkids, no more little Willoughbys making footprints in the sands of time, and *you!*" He glared at Martin beside him who seemed as stunned by it as he was, "You just *get invited!*"

***

Honor put the finishing touches on the table as the doorbell rang. Alton heard it and joined her as she opened the door.

"Alton," Honor beamed, "This is my sister Janetta, and her husband, Tyson Long—Alton Willoughby." Honor's love showed in her eyes as she introduced Alton, and Janetta smiled at them thinking what a handsome pair they made.

"I'm glad to see you," Alton extended his hand to shake, "I've been looking forward to meeting you."

"Thanks, same here," Tyson smiled back, "My wife likes your house so much, she hasn't looked at another one since Honor showed it to her."

Alton enjoyed getting acquainted with Honor's sister and her husband, feeling even closer to her now. He and Tyson were friends before Honor served dessert.

"I was an only child," Alton told his new friend, "Now I feel like I've got a family, after all these years."

Only Honor noticed the fleeting haunted look before Alton looked down at his coffee cup.

He's thinking about his father. She wished she was close enough to reach out and touch him.

After dinner, Alton and Tyson went into the den to talk about the house, leaving the women to enjoy their visit.

"Now that they're gone," Janetta exclaimed, "Let me see that *ring!*"

"Isn't it beautiful?" Honor held out her hand, admiring it with Janetta. "He gave it to me today."

"It's not only beautiful, I'm sure it's a set. He got the wedding ring too, didn't he." Janetta pressed.

"He didn't say anything about it," Honor said happily, "But I'm hoping."

Alton and Tyson managed to get together on the details involving the house, and Honor held Alton's hand as they waved goodbye to their guests.

"I'm glad you like them, I really enjoyed our visit. And I know Janetta likes the house. It's just right for them." She laughed, "Looking around the living room she picked out where she's going to put her Christmas tree this year."

Alton laughed too and looked around the large room, "You hear that, house? Love's going to live here," he squeezed Honor's hand. "It's a good place for children, I think it's just right for them too. And I don't blame him for not wanting to move away, he's got a good job. It's good to know someone will have the house who will enjoy it. When we were talking, we agreed on the lowest appraisal as a price on the house, with a moving date in six months."

"Six months," Honor murmured.

Alton added, "That should be long enough to finish the repairs you said are in progress on the house on your farm."

"Progress in repairs makes it sound impressive, I didn't have enough money to do much. They're only going to do what's necessary to the roof and a few things that have to be done to make it at least livable."

Alton nodded, "I've applied for a transfer to that area, we can work on it when we get there. I'm hoping dad will come back before then, or at least get in touch with me."

"We'll find him, Alton. Did you talk to the police today?"

"I did. I even went down to look at a couple of dead bodies. John Does, but no luck, I'm glad of that, hope these men are found by their families. But Dad's got to be around somewhere. Probably doesn't even know I'm home now."

Tears of sympathy welled up in Honor's eyes and he took her in his arms. "Somehow, I know he's all right. What worries me, is he hasn't contacted me or tried to find out if I'm home. Surely he knows I wouldn't have sent him to Pleasant Hill, or anywhere else. When I leave for work every day, I drive around some of the places we used to go, he's sure to turn up."

Jackie Griffey

CHAPTER EIGHTEEN

Martin looked for Hilde before he started to work, searching the halls until he saw her hurrying along. He reached out and caught her hand, drawing her out of the human current.

"I'm going to agree about the tadpole," he told her hurriedly. "But we have to talk—dinner?"

Hilde winced in aggravation, "Can't. Don't get off till eleven. I know a nice piano bar with good food, if you can keep from starving until then?"

Martin nodded, "Parking lot door—eleven plus!"

At five past eleven Martin saw Hilde coming toward him, pulling on a gray sweater with pearls embroidered around the neckline.

"This is as close as I can get to out of uniform," she told him, looking embarrassed.

"You look fine." He felt somehow protective as he held the heavy door for her. "We'll go in my car." Hilde nodded, adjusting the neck of her sweater.

"Where is this piano bar," Martin asked as he pulled out of the parking lot.

"Not far, and they do have good food. Did you manage to get anything to eat?"

"Tuna salad. It's become my main diet," Martin grinned.

"Mine too. At least they fix it every day, and it's fresh. Turn left at the next light."

"The parking lot's well lit," Martin observed as they slowed to turn in where the sign indicated.

"It is," Hilde smiled, "Weird hours make you notice things like that."

When they entered, a waiter with an armload of menus met them and guided them to a table.

"No waiting? And I like the place. Their regular patrons must be keeping it a secret like a good fishing hole." He looked around as he held her chair.

"I don't know. The lights in the parking lot and the number of people who come in, I just put all that down to the weird hours I keep," Hilde shrugged.

"The pianist can play things I recognize. That's what music is supposed to sound like," Martin commented as he picked up the menu.

"Um-hum, it's easier on the ears than hard rock—your digestion too. I know I can relax and get a good meal when I come here."

Hilde paused, not meeting his eyes, "You did say yes—about the tadpole, didn't you?"

"Yes, and there's something I want you to do. It's not a requirement, it's only a request. I want you to go, at my expense of course, and get 'the works' at that beauty salon near the clinic. The one with the French name."

"Oh, you mean Henri's. The works, huh? How did you know I was going to ask?"

"Ask?" Martin's mouth fell open in surprise, "Ask what?"

"About the sperm. I was going to ask if you'd have to put a sack over my head to do it normally?"

Martin gasped, shocked to his socks, *"My God, Hilde!"* He glanced around quickly, lowering his voice.

"I want you to get the works because when you see how good you look, you'll know you have a lot of better choices than me for this."

"You're my choice, but I'll go to Henri's for your sake. You didn't answer my question."

"I'd be delighted to do it normally, and no, I'm not going to put a sack over your head." He laughed briefly at this weird conversation. "What a thought! Listen, won't you? What I've been trying to tell you is you can do better."

Hilde was not swayed. "Getting on with our plans, I think it will be best to stay together until I conceive, but I live in an apartment house for women—"

Martin's features immediately drew downward into a comic frown, "I refuse to be loaned out," he announced emphatically.

Hilde laughed, "Not a chance! Though some of those women at the sperm bank would fight over someone with your good points, and a sense of humor too!"

"Slice it a little thicker, I like baloney," Martin grinned happily. "But flattery always sounds good whether you face the fact it's flattery or not. And staying together will be no problem. I have an apartment in that building you worked in with the hip replacements. But we won't stay together until you get the works and see how pretty you really are."

Martin got serious, "There's one other thing. This one is a condition."

"A condition," Hilde repeated, studying his face. "That sounds chiseled in stone serious, is this the last one?"

"Last and most important. If and when you do conceive, we will be married. There won't be any strings attached. You can stay, go home, or whatever you want to do. And you don't have to worry about my making any demands. I'm too old to want custody. But I'm not going to have our little tadpole arrive on this planet without a last name and the sure knowledge that both sides of his gene pool care for him."

"Or her," Hilde corrected, watching his face with interest.

"Or her," Martin agreed with a smile, wondering how in the world Hilde could look in the mirror and think she was plain.

"Deal!" Hilde reached out to shake hands on it. "Now, we can eat." Her eyes scanned the menu. "Everything is good, but order three of whatever you decide to order for us."

"Isn't it a bit optimistic to start eating for two just yet?"

"Not for me, for him," Hilde nodded at someone, "Musicians are always hungry."

Martin looked in the direction she indicated. The pianist was coming to join them.

"This is Donnie Albright," Hilde introduced them, "Dr. Martin Hammond."

"Oh." Donnie's voice fell flat. "A doctor." His pleasant face rearranged itself, stopping just short of a disapproving frown.

"You don't like doctors," Martin raised an eyebrow, studying him. "Had a bad experience? Vaccination didn't heal?"

"Nothing like that. No, nothing like that. They just don't know when to quit." Donnie poured himself some wine from the bottle on the table. "When I found out my liver's shot, I prearranged my funeral and quit worrying about it, any further advice they want to give me is unnecessary and irrelevant aggravation— professional nagging," he pronounced it.

"Can't get a transplant?"

"No. They won't give another liver to an alcoholic who's already pickled his own." His eyes met Martin's briefly, "I did ask about that. No sense worrying about a thing you can't fix, so I just suit myself." He raised his glass in a philosophical salute.

"Some of that liver must be working," Martin observed with a smile that held no censure.

"Quitting now won't help, and I don't intend to die thirsty."

"I'm not going to argue with you, the wine will help you digest that steak."

Donnie was delighted, "You'd better hang onto this one, Hilde," He smiled beatifically at Martin, "I hereby forgive you your Hypocritic Oath!"

Martin and Hilde laughed and Donnie inhaled his steak and most of a baked potato. He left them for his piano, taking a refilled glass with him.

***

The day Martin had scheduled the kidney transplant, Aaron accompanied him to the basement. "Lucky everything matched up as you call it. You're going to take out the pervert's kidney here?" Aaron glanced at the lab door.

"Yes, that's my plan. I'll take it to the clinic and give it to the woman who needs it."

"I didn't know you could do that without help."

"Oh, I've got help," Martin said, obviously not at all worried.

Aaron stood still, watching Martin making preparations until he went to get his scrubs. He followed, feeling on edge for some reason. Martin took two sets of scrubs from a cabinet.

"Who? Who—" Aaron felt perspiration pricking out on his forehead and his back; his mouth felt suddenly dry. He stood mute and motionless like something that had taken root. He glanced through the lab door at the washed and prepped pervert till he was aware of Martin approaching him. Martin advanced wearing a smile that was downright diabolical, holding one set of scrubs out to him.

"No," Aaron shouted. "No!" He backed as far as the door to the lab as Martin advanced to the door with the scrubs. He braced his feet on the sides of the door, hands gripping the door facing on both sides. Spreadeagled in the door, he refused to move, mumbling incoherent negative sounds as Martin drew near.

"Me? No! No way! I didn't agree to this—not anything *like this*! *No! No!*" He held on like a barnacle.

Unperturbed, Martin tickled him with his free hand and pushed him ahead of him into the lab. "Put these on."

"Not me!"

"Of course, you. There's nothing to it. All you have to do is stand there and do what I tell you when I need you."

Aaron continued mumbling angrily under his breath, "I can't do this. You never warned me about anything like this." He looked down at the scrubs, tentatively touching them.

"Another one of those 'fits all' deals," he continued mumbling angrily under his breath. "I can't do this." He shook out the folded scrubs and slowly put them on, Martin paying him no attention.

Standing in the scrubs, still mumbling, about as comfortable as he would have been with them stiffly starched and on sideways, he took the soap Martin handed him.

"I never—*never* agreed to this."

Martin didn't waste time on conversation. Scrubbed and gloved, Aaron still felt pasted together. He stood stiff as a cardboard paper doll. He ground his teeth as Martin made the incision, making a rattling noise deep in his throat.

Martin kept talking to him while he worked, to keep him from bolting out the door.

"See, I told you there's nothing to it. We'll have this kidney in the old ice bucket in no time."

The pervert made a moaning sound.

"Oh, *Lord!*" Aaron moaned right along with him.

"Put your finger right there," Martin ordered, "While I tie this off. And don't you faint on me, or I'll bury you out there by Denghen Po!"

Finally after adding a good ten years to Aaron's age, the operation was done. Martin dismissed him with a nod as he lifted the kidney.

Aaron made it to a chair beside the card table and collapsed. He took several deep breaths and was nearly back to normal when Martin appeared in the lab door, beckoning to him.

"He's gone. I couldn't save him. Could have had an aneurysm or something I didn't know about. I'm sure he didn't either. If he'd been out on the street, he'd have probably been gone before now."

"Are you sure?"

"No, I'm not sure," Martin snapped with unaccustomed impatience, "And I'm not going to waste time I don't have to autopsy him."

"I meant, are you sure he's—he's gone?"

"Oh yes, I'm sure about that."

"What are you going to do?"

"Take his liver. Come and help me."

"Oh, my Gooooooooooood," Aaron walked back into the lab like a zombie under a spell.

The washing up took longer than the second operation and the two organs were, miraculously it seemed to Aaron, ready to go to the clinic.

"I've got to hurry," Martin said, "Mary Cartwright, the kidney patient, is being prepped now, so I'm right on time. Get a grip and listen to what I'm telling you—this is important."

Aaron swallowed, or tried to, his throat was dry. "I'm listening," he managed to croak.

"Beep Burke and Harry and keep the lab door locked until they get here to remove the pervert. Call Hilde, the number's there on the table. Tell her to get Donnie Albright, even if she has to drag him away from the piano. Tell her to get him to the clinic—*now!* I've got a liver for him."

Martin turned, "And dig up another one of those board members for the paperwork on the liver."

Martin worked fast and appeared in the door with the organs as Aaron started talking to Hilde. He reached for the phone and heard Hilde say, "He's at work by now. I'll take an orderly with me. Where did Martin get the liver?"

Martin spoke quickly, "Accident. Organ donor died. We'll do the tests at the clinic. The orderly's a good idea. *Get moving!*"

***

Inside the piano bar, Donnie Albright gazed dreamily at the tip glass on top of the piano. There were only three or four bills in it. But, the evening was young, Donnie thought philosophically, enjoying his work. He smiled as his fingers caressed the keys, coaxing a golden oldie out of them. He raised his head at a stir in the room's atmosphere.

What's everybody looking at? People were turning to look toward the entrance. *What's this all about, it's Hilde.* His fingers missed a couple of notes. He stared as the customers and waiters were.

Hilde's in her uniform and moving like she's on some kind of mission. That guy with her, I don't know him. It's not that doctor, Martin his name was, I liked him. But this one's got on a white uniform like Hilde...

"Hilde," Donnie grinned when she got close enough. "What's your hurry? Did someone go up there and drink Canada Dry, like all the signs say?"

He chortled at his wit, but there was no fun registering on Hilde's face or on that face accompanying her. They were close enough to detect any humor if it had been there. He decided he didn't like the man's looks, not as nice a guy as Martin by a long shot.

"Who's the guy in the uniform," he demanded of Hilde.

"I've come to take you to the clinic," Hilde told him briskly, "We've got a liver for you."

Donnie stared, big eyes with a combination of outrage and disbelief stared as the orderly took his arm.

"A liver? You know I can't get a liver! *Hey! Watch it there!* What's he think he's doing," he glared at Hilde.

Hilde firmly took Donnie's other arm. "You're going. Do you want to walk or be carried?"

She didn't wait for an answer. Scooping up the bills from the tip glass, she stuffed them in his pocket, not missing a step as she and the stalwart orderly briskly propelled Donnie toward the door.

Jackie Griffey

CHAPTER NINETEEN

Aaron paced, waiting for Burke and Harry. *I feel like fleeing the scene, as they say in the movies. But this is the kind of thing you can't get loose from.* He wiped the perspiration from his palms, trying not to think about what he had shut up behind him in the lab.

The knock of the basement door brought him back to stark necessity. *Too late to make tracks now!*

"Who is it?"

"Burke and Harry," came the prompt answer, "You beeped us."

Aaron opened the door cautiously, "Okay, get in here—*quick!*"

He leaned out, hand on the door, and craned his neck, looking up and down the street. He let them scurry in and locked the door behind them as Burke and Harry stood waiting. He gestured at the lab door.

"I've got something in there I want you to get rid of."

Harry grabbed Burke's arm like it was a security blanket, eyeing the closed lab door as if it housed all the Halloween goblins in the world. It was the same expression that witnessed the blow to his partner's head.

"I don't care where you get rid of it, and I don't care how, but I don't want it to turn up anywhere anytime soon, and certainly *not* around *here!*" He walked over to the door and opened it for them, but he didn't look in.

Burke paused only a second before going in. "You can wrap it in that sheet it's on," Aaron told him. "There's no laundry mark or anything on it."

Burke pried his partner's fingers from his arm. "We'll take care of it," he assured Aaron.

***

It was past midnight when Martin got home. He let himself in the basement door with his key, noting the lamp on the card table was on. Out of the shadows, Aaron's voice greeted him, "How'd it go? Mary Cartwright and the one you gave the liver to?"

"Everything went fine. Percentagewise, their chances are excellent." He glanced at the lab door, "We'll have to use these rooms again, neither one of them can afford to go anywhere else."

"I cleaned up in there, after Harry and Burke left, but you'd better check and see if I missed anything. I'd have had to take lessons to jump out the window, the state I was in."

"I know I should have warned you, but you'd have run, wouldn't you?"

"No doubt about it!"

Martin smiled at his honesty. "I knew you could do it and you did just fine. Did Burke and Harry give you any trouble?"

"Not a bit. The little one, Harry, was scared. But Burke took over and handled it like a pro. Harry and I watched him put it in their van."

Martin went into the lab to look around, Aaron followed, his aversion to the place having vanished along with the body of the pervert.

"You did a good job cleaning up, I'm proud of you. The transplants went well and Burke and Harry did their thing, Mary and Donnie will have better and longer lives, the world is rid of the pervert, but…"

Aaron stopped dead on his way out of the lab, "But?" He cringed, "But what?"

Martin grinned, "We've lost our blood donor!"

***

As Martin entered the clinic the next day, someone called to him. "Dr. Hammond," he turned as Hilde came toward him.

"Martin," he smiled down at her.

"Martin—between us, Dr. Hammond on duty," Hilde amended. "I got an appointment at Henri's for three o'clock tomorrow, and Henri himself is going to work on me!"

"He can see how well you will turn out and he wants to hog all the glory for himself."

Hilde gave him a skeptical smirk, "Or I'm such a challenge he couldn't resist. Anyway, I'll get the works like you wanted me to, and from Henri himself."

"Are you off tomorrow? Want to have dinner?"

"No, I'm scheduled to work until eleven, and I hate to rush dinner. I would like to go over and see Donnie a few minutes, though."

"All right. Come in from the salon and I'll take you over there so you won't have to park again."

"That would be fine. Thanks. And you can go home tonight and rest up," she teased him. "Then tomorrow night, after I get 'the works,' and my shift over, we can go to the piano bar after eleven, if you want to?"

"Sure, it would be downright criminal not to show off at a time like that! And they do have good food."

"Right." Hilde resisted the urge to kiss his cheek, "See you after the works tomorrow."

***

Martin got home early, finding a place not quite half a block away from the apartment house to park. As he got out of the car he saw Leona coming from the other direction. She was walking, carrying a sack of groceries.

She doesn't see me, probably thinking of all the good vitamins she's going to feed Aaron, he chuckled to himself as he got out. The chuckle was cut short by the realization that a man was following Leona, and he was catching up fast! Just as she got to the steps, he reached toward Leona's shoulder bag and at the same time, raised his arm to hit her with something he had in his other hand.

Darting at them, Martin tackled the man before he touched Leona, but he and the man rolled against her legs, then down the two steps onto the sidewalk below her.

Turning, Leona gasped as Martin's fist landed on the man's jaw. "I didn't even know he was *there,*" she screeched. Her head jerked around, anxiously watching the fight and clutching her sack of groceries in a reflex motion, not knowing what else to do until one of Martin's rights laid the culprit out. He sprawled on the sidewalk below her.

Martin started pulling on the man, slapping his face a couple of times, trying to get him conscious enough to stand up. "Leona, go get Aaron!" He slapped the man sharply and put his arm around his shoulder as Leona turned in. "Tell him to come to the basement—hurry!"

Leona nodded as she disappeared into the building. Martin half carried the man toward the basement door. He had just managed to get inside and settled the man down when Aaron burst through the inside basement door, pulling up short when he met Martin.

"Leona's scared to death, is that the rat who attacked her?"

Martin nodded, catching his breath as he went to stand in front of the stranger. Aaron breathed easier, studying the man. "Nobody I remember seeing before around here. What's the matter with him? This is the one, isn't he?"

"That's the one, I just got him in here. He tried to hit her with that," Martin gestured toward the card table outside the lab. "It's a sock full of sand, There's nothing the matter with him. I gave him a shot."

"A shot?"

Martin took a deep breath and grinned at Aaron, "Meet our new blood donor."

"Ha!" Aaron grinned back, "Picked the wrong sandbox to play in, didn't he?"

"Wrong for him, right for us. Help me get him comfortable so I can get some blood to test."

Between the two of them they soon had the would be mugger roused a little, sitting on the examining table with his shirt off. He looked groggily around the lab at the equipment and the table he was sitting on, then at Martin advancing on him with a needle and a determined expression.

"Is ah—this ah—a clinic, or something…"

Martin administered the shot and eased him down on the table, talking to Aaron as he worked. "This is mild, but it will serve our purposes for now. And no one saw him come in, Donnie's door was shut."

"That's good."

"Hilde's getting the works at the beauty salon tomorrow," Martin paused to say. "She told me to come home and rest up tonight," he smiled over his shoulder as he put the donor's dangling arm up on the table.

"She's going to that French place you told me about? I'd like to see her after the works."

"You can. She's coming over to see Donnie for a few minutes after she leaves the salon, before she has to go on duty at the clinic. He must be asleep now, since the door was closed. Guess I'd better lock the lab door, now that we've got us a new blood donor."

"If you don't, I will," Aaron said with feeling, "Aren't you paying attention to these worrying lessons I've been giving you? I don't want to have to explain to anybody what we've got this unconscious lug in here for!"

"You're a worrier, Aaron. All we'd have to do is tell them what happened. That he tried to mug Leona and we brought him in here. Heck, it would look like we rescued him off the sidewalk out there. But, you go right on and worry if you want to."

"Somebody's got to, I don't think you're programmed for it."

"Well, good. Now that you've taken over that chore, I won't need to." He gave a satisfied look around. "I'm through, and the new donor is comfortable—"

"And *quiet.*"

"Right, and quiet. Let's go." Martin locked the lab door but didn't test it the way Aaron always did.

"I'd hate to have your nerve in a tooth," Aaron muttered.

***

After leaving Henri's, Hilde walked on air as she entered the clinic. The first person she saw was Jennie Graves.

"Hilde! Is that you?"

Jennie admired the works from all sides, delighted with every possible angle. "Wow! Wait till Dr. Hammond sees!"

"Till Dr. Hammond sees what?" Martin and Rob emerged from a nearby corridor.

Martin stopped, staring at Hilde in open admiration for a few seconds. Rob playfully pushed him out of the way. "I was looking for Jennie to go to lunch with me, but—introduce me to this *beautiful woman!"*

"Just hold on there," Martin pushed back. "I knew the works would open your eyes," he told Hilde, "But I wasn't prepared for *this!"* He let his shoulders droop, his face fell into a comic mask of tragedy as he murmured sadly, "Well, I guess this is goodbye…"

Hilde laughed, "Henri only changed my looks, not my plans. Can we go see Donnie now?" She glanced at her watch, "We have time."

"Sure, let's go." He turned to Jennie and Rob, "I'll bring her back in a little while." He smirked, "Maybe."

"If we don't see you in the next two or three hours, we'll know you eloped," Rob called after them.

***

At the apartment house, Martin knocked on Leona's door, then stood aside, leaving Hilde standing there alone.

"Hilde," Leona cried joyfully, "You're beautiful!"

Aaron joined them, smiling at Hilde. "I'm impressed, you certainly do look nice. But let's not stand here in the door, come in."

"Yes, do. I've got fresh cookies made," Leona added.

"I'd like to, but I've got to go back to work. Martin was nice enough to bring me over to see Donnie a few minutes."

"Okay then, Come back when you can."

Donnie's door was open as they entered the basement. He welcomed Hilde with a smile as she and Martin came in. "There you are. I was waiting to get a chance to say thank you. You took me by surprise, and I've been out like a light most of the time since." He looked at Martin, "The sitter and I both had naps this afternoon. So, thank you, Dr. Hammond."

"Dr. Hammond? I don't remember removing anything that would affect your calling me Martin." He assumed his hurt look, but his humor was lost on Donnie. He was staring at Hilde.

"Hilde, you sure do look *good* in daylight!"

He grinned at Martin, "It's usually the other way around with most of the people I meet at the bar."

"That's only because I've just come back from having 'the works' at Henri's salon. It will be back to Cinder-Nurse tomorrow, without my fairy God-Stylist."

"Don't give him all the credit," Donnie insisted, he had to have something to work with, you know."

"That's what I've been telling her," Martin agreed. "But, I've got to get her back to the clinic. You behave yourself!"

Donnie rolled his eyes at that, "As if I had any choice! You know what you've done, don't you?" His pleasant features managed to register pain, "I've got to quit drinking now, and rejoin the human race!"

"Bummer!" Hilde laughed without mercy.

Jackie Griffey

CHAPTER TWENTY

On the way back to the clinic, Martin's eyes kept returning to the masterpiece Henri had created.

He pulled up carefully and stopped at the clinic door to let Hilde out. "Are we having dinner tonight?"

"Certainly! Are you trying to chicken out on me?"

"No, just afraid you'd had a better offer. We can go somewhere else, if you want to?"

"No, the piano bar's fine. I wonder who they got to replace Donnie while he's out on sick leave?"

"Never can tell. If it's a rapper and some break dancers, we can eat fast, or just look and leave fast."

"Aw, they wouldn't do that to us. And besides, there isn't enough room back there by the piano for break dancers, you know how wild they get." She smiled, putting Martin on cloud nine because it was for him, "See you at eleven!"

At eleven plus Martin got to the door first and saw Hilde coming, "Excuse me, ma'am, have you seen a nurse—oh, it's you!"

"I can see why you'd be confused," Hilde looked down at her cocktail dress. I brought this with me. No sense wasting the works on a uniform."

"You look like the cover of Vogue, or maybe Glamour," Martin admired her. "You sure you don't want to go somewhere else?"

Hilde looked at the clock, "The piano bar's probably the best place anywhere near here at this hour. Besides, it's the first place we had dinner together."

"You're right. Let's go." He held the door and took her arm, his feelings catapulting back to college days because she had chosen him, no matter the motive. He wasn't one to look a gift horse in the mouth. He spared a split second to be glad Aaron had found Leona again.

Entering the piano bar, Martin pointed, "Looks like your faith in the establishment was justified."

"My *goodness,*" Hilde's reaction was incredulous, "Is that a *harp* I see?"

The approaching hostess heard the question and smiled at Hilde, "It's a harp, all right. I had the same reaction. We were lucky to get her." She turned, admiring the professional looking musician. "She's with the symphony, but she is really great at all kinds of music. She's going to play swing for us here, until Donnie Albright comes back."

"A harp," Hilde whispered again with awe. She watched in fascination as the musician smiled around the room and sat down at her instrument.

"I'll put you where you can hear without too much distraction," the hostess promised, and turned to lead the way.

"Thanks," Martin took Hilde's hand and followed her to a table near the harp. They ordered seafood and an expensive wine to celebrate the works, enjoying the food and the music as Martin stole admiring glances at Hilde across the table. He tasted the wine and the wine steward poured it for them and discretely disappeared.

Hilde peered at the label on the bottle. "I'm going to make a note of this wine for future occasions to celebrate," she told him happily.

The seafood was good and the music seemed written just for them as Martin smiled at Hilde in the candle light, wondering how she could ever have found anything wrong with her reflection in the mirror. Her eyes met his and she smiled at him and the wine bottle, "Yes, I'm definitely going to remember this wine, for the good effect it has."

Martin shook his head at the waiter, hovering near. "It's not the wine and you know it," he declared. "I'm just old and out of practice, not *blind!*"

Hilde laughed and it turned into a sigh, it had been a long day.

"It's been quite a day for you," Martin said, "Are you ready to go home?"

"Yes. Briefly."

"Briefly," Martin raised his eyebrows.

"To get some clothes and things and go back with you."

"You—haven't changed your mind?"

"No," Hilde stated positively, "And I'm not going to let you." She got up and laid her hand on his arm.

He got up too, and smiled down at her, *Aaron's right, I'm a lucky son of a sea biscuit!*

There was no one stirring in the building when Martin and Hilde entered Martin's apartment. Hilde looked around as he closed the door. "This the furniture you had when you had the condo?"

"Yes. Fortunately these rooms are large. There's only one suite of bedroom furniture and a big desk I didn't use much that I had to put in storage, plus a few odds and ends that I suppose everybody accumulates and nobody worries about." He watched as she looked around. "Aside from where it is, this apartment was exactly right, and was available at the right time."

"Lucky it's across from Leona and Aaron." She ran her fingers over a mahogany table. "This dining room furniture is beautiful, Martin. We'll have to ask Leona and Aaron over to have dinner with us as soon as we can arrange it."

"They'll be available, I'm sure. Leona knows people in the building and the neighborhood, but Aaron's sort of an orphan at loose ends like I am."

"Well, you're not an orphan at loose ends anymore," she went to him and put her arms around him, "You're spoken for."

"Oh, you're one of those who like to talk," he made a face at her. Something about his undeserved good luck made him throw in some discouragement when the chance rose. He remembered Aaron's reaction and couldn't quite understand his good luck himself.

"Well, yes," her arms loosed a little, "Guilty as charged. We haven't had very much time together, and I'm selfish enough to want that, yes. I wouldn't have been in such 'hot pursuit' as the paperbacks call it, of someone I didn't like." She stopped and looked up at him. "You do like me, don't you?"

Martin found it difficult to speak as he looked down at her, their arms around each other. He found her candor childlike and appealing and he liked having her around, even if she hadn't been what was to him a classical example of the aforementioned paperbacks' description of 'a desirable woman.' But he would never have had the courage to pursue her. No way. He was still having trouble believing she was pursuing him. "You ask the darnedest questions," was all he could manage. He kissed the end of her nose, then her lips.

"And you never answer them," she pointed out. "But you do like me, don't you?"

"Yes! Yes! Heaven help me," Martin laughed, "I'm falling in *like!*"

Hilde laughed too, "Well, I'll settle for that, for now. Whether you admit or not, you must have a pretty high opinion of me, or you wouldn't be trusting me with one of your little tadpoles."

"I knew you'd finally figure that out," Martin turned away to get out a can of coffee. "Go on in and get comfortable, I'm getting this out for in the morning —if you're still here," his eyes slid sideways at her.

"Oh, I'll be here, and so will you," Hilde paused at the door, tilting her head as she smiled a knowing smile, "The way you talk, you won't be able to *leave!*"

"Oh, you've done it now—I know a challenge when I hear one!"

***

The morning sun woke Hilde. She stretched and touched Martin, waking him. "I thought I dreamed all this," he mumbled. He rubbed his eyes and grinned at her, "Want to try again?"

"Tonight. It's breakfast time."

"Oh, you're getting me on schedule, are you?"

"Hilde chose to ignore him. "Got anything sweet?"

221

"Me. I'm sweet."

"Sure you are, but I want icing too, or toast and maybe some jelly on it. Anything sweet." Hilde got up and headed for the kitchen, "Something smells good."

"It's our coffee. Leona gave me the automatic pot, but there's nothing sweet, I'm afraid."

"I know where there is some. Back soon." Hilde hitched up Martin's robe to keep from tripping on it and went in pursuit of goodies.

Aaron answered the rap on Leona's door, looking like a hibernating bear aroused before spring.

Hilde pushed her hair out of her eyes and said, "About those cookies—"

Aaron squinted at her, taking in her touseled hair and Martin's paisley bathrobe. *"Leona!"*

The next six weeks were like a sabbatical in another world for Martin. Having a partner and friend and all the things they were for each other was what the diet called life was made of and they were both starved for it when they found each other.

"What do you want to do on your day off," he asked Hilde one night at dinner.

"I want to go to the zoo."

"The what? You want to go to the zoo? Is this some kind of trick answer?"

"No, it's not. I like to walk around and enjoy the scenery and the trees, and the peacocks, and all that fun in the sun stuff. People look at you strangely if you do things like that alone."

"The zoo." Martin turned it over on his tongue, he tried to remember the last time he and Mildred had taken a walk in the park. *I wonder if they still make that pineapple pudding Mildred and I used to like.*

"Unless you don't want to," Hilde amended, seeing his hesitation.

Martin grinned, "It's fine with me. I'd like to, it's been a long time since I was there in the park or at the zoo. Let's do it!"

The trip to the zoo and other things Hilde planned brought Martin happiness he had forgotten and Hilde possibilities she had passed up with regret, not wanting to do them alone. Their happiness was not lost on their friends. Not those at the clinic, or Aaron and Leona.

"I think Martin's remark Hilde told us about, when he said he was falling in like, has turned into something deeper," Aaron told Leona. "And Hilde is a pretty good cook, too. Have you been giving her lessons?"

"She didn't need lessons," Leona corrected him. "Just someone to cook for. We have swapped a few recipes. The fried corn cakes with peppers and onions in them that we had last night were one of her recipes."

"They were good," Aaron smiled. "I called it right, he's a Lucky Son of a Sea Bisquit."

***

Several weeks later, Martin stood at the phone in the clinic's waiting room waiting for Aaron to answer. As soon as he heard his voice, Martin asked, "Did you get any information on our donor?"

"Yes, have it right here. There's nothing on it but some petty thievery. He's no menace, according to his record."

"He would have had an assault and battery charge if we hadn't saved the court's time by making him do community service," Martin pointed out. "But you're right, he doesn't sound like any menace to the community and we've got blood from him four times now. I guess we should let him go. Beep Burke and Harry and tell them to put him on a slow freight or an outward bound cargo ship or whatever strikes their imagination. Anything safe and won't hurt him and where he can get back if he needs to, but not too soon."

"Okay, I'll take care of it." Martin could tell he was smiling, "His little stay with us may have straightened him out."

"Yeah, he's recycled," Martin laughed. "That's not all I wanted to talk about. I've got news. Hilde saw a gynecologist this morning. The little tadpole did his thing. Hilde's pregnant!"

"That is good news," Aaron agreed happily. "I'll tell Leona right now—and *congratulations!*"

"There's more. After the baby is born, I've got to look for a safer place for Hilde and the tadpole to live, while I'm still here to see to it."

"You're right. This place is only filling a temporary need. I miss having a pool to practice my fly casting. And didn't you say you're going to get married?"

"Yes, I told you, it was a condition I made to the deal when I agreed about the tadpole. And what about you and Leona? You're going to marry her, aren't you? Or has she wised up and turned you down?"

"No, don't get your hopes up," Aaron growled, then laughed. "We both know we're together for keeps this time. I've been waiting to see what Alton does. I saw in the paper Blanche has filed for divorce, but that's all. And I've also got a couple of business things I'm working on. Why do you ask?"

"How about the four of us going this weekend and tying both knots? We ran away from the old folks home together, we might as well commit social suicide together too."

"Is that what the younger generation is calling it these days, I'm a shade out of touch."

"I was judging by their attitudes. What do you think of the idea? We can find a resort somewhere over the state line where we won't have to wait—"

"I can beat that state line plan. I lease a private jet, it's better than buying one, taxwise. I'll put the pilot on standby for this weekend to go to Las Vegas. How about we leave Friday morning and come back Sunday evening, if you can both arrange it?"

"Sounds good to me. I'll check with Hilde and call you right back if she can't go. And I've got to go out and buy her rings—"

"You check with Hilde and if I don't hear from you in the next few minutes, I'll meet you at the side door to the parking lot as soon as I can get there. I'll get Leona's rings too."

Jackie Griffey

CHAPTER TWENTY-ONE

Honor emerged on the street, looking like the world had shifted and put her off in the wrong place as she left the medical building. She felt the breath from the heavy door behind her legs as if it was pushing her out onto the busy sidewalk. Her eyes stared, unseeing, at the people coming and going, swirling around her in an unconcerned human tide. No one seemed to be aware of her presence, much less her importance in the universal plan.

I might as well be invisible. Alone with my own little bag of troubles and worries.

She began walking slowly. She sighed, her feet seemed even heavier than her heart with its burden of uncertainties. One thought took priority, *I'll have to tell Alton. That's the first thing I've got to do, and I should tell him now, as soon as he comes home.* Home, the word held magic. She thought of Alton's face, smiling at her, his love showing in his eyes. She remembered when he had put the beautiful ring on her finger, he was excited as she was and proud of getting it for her. Her heart suddenly lightened with a joy that nothing negative could erase. She smiled to herself as she touched her stomach.

I'm with child. I knew it! I knew when I went in I was pregnant. I'm with child, her mind nearly sang it. *I knew and now it's official, I am pregnant with our child, my and Alton's first child!* She giggled, walking faster, *First—first child—how's that for optimism!* She pictured Alton's face again as he would look when she told him, happy and excited by her news.

In the parking lot now, her smile faded as she got into the six year old Chevrolet she had bought just last year.

I guess it's easy to lose track of reality when you're as happy as I've been with Alton. And he's happy too. I know he is. But, this old car reminds me, I'm not a teenager any more, I'm a school teacher who should have her feet on the ground and not chase after romantic notions—or take chances. If Alton—if he… She couldn't bring herself to think that he wouldn't be pleased about the baby. Her lips pressed together in a determined line. *I want our child, whether he does or not. I'll love our baby enough for both of us, if that's how it is,* she vowed to the little seed of love growing within her. *But he will be pleased, I know he will, he loves me and I love him,* she assured herself, remembering how happy they had been when they found each other again. She drove carefully, trying not to worry. To think nothing but good thoughts.

A tear rolled down her cheek. *No, I won't lie to myself, this is too important. Close as we are, I don't know how he will feel about this. We've been happy, but that house, that's what worries me. That house I thought was so perfect for Janetta and her family, it really is perfect. When I think how perfectly planned and decorated it is, and it is, after all, his house. He may not want anything as disrupting as a child can be. He told me he's been married almost ten years, and there were no children. That seems strange if they did want them. But, I'll have to tell him, even if I have to leave him. I'll not have him offer to marry me because he feels like he has to. Even if I have to leave him, I'll tell my baby about his father, I owe that to my child.* She loosened her hands on the steering wheel. They hurt from the death grip she held it, with desperation, as if her happy life was already slipping away from her. She wiped away her tears. *I'll wait and pick a good time, but I should tell him as soon as possible.*

***

Martin hurried to answer a page, feeling like a salmon fighting its way upstream in the crowded corridor.

Why do all the interruptions come when you're trying to get things squared away to leave for a weekend, he grumbled at fickle fate. *Whoever's calling must think it's important, to have me paged. Not that I can't do without another tuna fish sandwich!*

At the desk a nurse glanced up and handed him a phone. Martin took it, "Dr. Hammond."

"Martin, it's me." Aaron's voice sounded strange.

"Aaron? I'm trying to get everything caught up and covered before the weekend. I can barely hear you. What is it?"

"I don't want Leona to hear me," Aaron spoke slowly and distinctly, but no louder. "There's going to be a rumble near here. That's a gang war, like a real one, only smaller. Can you hear me?"

"Yes. I hear you. A gang war? Where?"

"I heard it was going to be the next street over from us, where the alley widens, there. But you never can tell about those things. That's all I know about it, except it's supposed to happen today, maybe late today, and I wanted to warn you and Hilde about it."

"Thanks." Martin smiled into the phone, "Your connections reach into some strange areas. Hilde gets off at three, so I'll leave then too. That's not long and at least we'll be together. We'll be leaving soon and we'll keep an eye out and get there as soon as we can. Thanks for calling to tell us, Aaron. You're surely staying close and keeping Leona inside?"

"Are you kidding? You know I wouldn't let her out at a time like this, it's just not knowing when in the afternoon it's going to start and not wanting to tell her and frighten her. Fortunately, she has this fixation about feeding me. I've had so many cookies and cups of coffee I slosh when I walk!"

Martin laughed, "We'll hurry—save us some cookies."

At two minutes till three Martin looked up at one of the big clocks behind the desk, his hand on Hilde's elbow as he hurried her along.

"It's not quite three," Hilde argued with him looking askance at him as he hurried her into a run.

"Yeah, yeah. How conscientious you are about that. Here's my car. We'll leave yours here."

"Leave it here? Martin, you rushed me out of the clinic so fast I was looking around for smoke! Tell me what's wrong? Where are we going?"

"We're going home, if we can get there. Fasten your seatbelt."

"What do you mean if we can get there?" Hilde grabbed the armrest as he turned a corner, then finished fastening her seatbelt, waiting for an answer.

Martin concentrated on his driving, taking the usual route home. He was watchful but fast. "Aaron called nearly an hour ago, we probably should have left then. He heard somehow there's going to be some trouble in our neighborhood near the apartment house."

"I knew there had to be something. What kind of trouble?"

"A gang fight. They call it a rumble."

"I've heard the word," Hilde nodded.

"We've got to get in before the trouble starts, if it hasn't already. I thought about arranging for you to stay at the clinic, but I knew you wouldn't go for that."

"You're right. I wouldn't. It's after three now, we'd better be careful, I've heard some pretty wild things about these so-called rumbles."

Martin nodded watching the street. They were getting nearer home. The first sign of trouble came a few blocks from the apartment house. Something hard hit the metal frame of the windshield.

Hilde instinctively ducked, then looked out her window. "I don't know what it was he threw, but there he goes!" she craned her neck, "See him? That tall, thin boy in the red shirt. He's going between those two buildings."

"Just be glad it didn't crack the windshield and we can still see."

A familiar looking van caught Martin's attention. *That's Burke and Harry,* he thought in surprise as he recognized it. *I wonder what they're doing in the middle of all this? Up to no good, I'd bet on it.* He kept it to himself.

Hilde watched the sidewalks as Martin drove, they were getting close to the block the apartment house was on.

"There are bloody fights everywhere, Martin. I'll bet they're coming into the clinic by now. There are two wearing gang colors breaking glass out of parked cars!"

"I saw, and you can bet there's not going to be a radio antenna left on a car by the time the sun goes down."

A siren's high wail cut through the noise, coming from behind them.

"It's about time," Martin gritted his teeth as a boy zig-zagged across the street in front of his car.

"Missed him," he breathed, "No fault of his own!"

"Martin!" Hilde stared out the back window in horror, "They're rocking the police car—*hard!"*

Martin jerked his eyes up to the rearview mirror just in time to see the police car go over.

Smoke billowed out from somewhere as Martin kept his eyes front, trying to cover all directions as well as ahead of them. They were now less than two blocks from the apartment house. "A couple more buildings to go. I'll get close enough for you to run in. There's Aaron and Leona at the basement door, you'll make it!"

"But—you—"

"Don't argue with me! Between those two parked cars! G*o!*"

Hilde jumped out as Aaron opened the basement door for her. He ran to the car and jumped into the passenger seat beside Martin as Leona slammed the door behind her and Hilde.

"What do you think you're doing?"

"Evening the odds—*scoot!*"

Martin didn't have to be told twice. They were already leaving the apartment house behind.

"There must be a parking place somewhere within running distance." Aaron clutched the armrest, not bothering with the seatbelt.

"Didn't see one. I did see Burke and Harry—Hey! There they are, up ahead of us!"

"I see them. They're carrying a kid with a red bandanna on his head. Putting him in their van."

"That's not a bandanna, Aaron, it's blood! If they're trying to help him, it's too late. And it's not like them to get mixed up in a mess like this unless there's something in it for them. I'm going to follow them."

"Why not? No sense leaving one more car to tear up. Anything to get away from here, you'd think we'd taken up residence in Bosnia!"

"You mean a big guy like you is getting shaky?"

"I'm just big, not stupid!"

"Were you really a golden gloves champion a millennium ago? And why didn't you stick with it? With boxing?"

"Yes, I was, but I've already told you, I'm not stupid. There wasn't enough money in it to pay the medical bills. I moved on to better things."

Martin stayed as far back from the van as he could without losing it as they left the neighborhood and the bloody chaos behind.

Aaron fastened his seat belt loosely, eyes watching the sidewalks and traffic in the area the van was leading them through. "They're heading into an industrial area," Martin observed. "I knew they weren't taking that gang member to any hospital or clinic."

Aaron scanned the signs on buildings they were passing. "Yeah, warehouses, fences, metal buildings—"

Martin slowed down. "They're turning in up there. Doesn't look like much of a plant, the best looking thing about it is that high chain link fence around it. They must have been here before, that man wearing a guard uniform is waving them in."

"Oh, *God,*" Aaron moaned. "Please, please, tell me that sign doesn't mean what I think it means!"

"Champion Chewables," Martin confirmed his fears. "No wonder the pervert never showed up anywhere. They're supplying an el cheapo dog food plant!"

"Let's get out of here," Aaron managed to voice his misery. "And go back to our own war!"

***

At his office, Alton was listening to something decidedly unpleasant. His bearing was more like a soldier on guard than a white collar worker. He clutched the phone as if he had his hand around a throat, his face contorted as the voice continued until his rage burst forth.

"Blanche wants what?"

Theo Jones held the phone away from his ear for a moment. "She wants the silver service and all the things, the punch bowl, platters and tray, and things that go with it." He was specific about the long list and spoke quietly. "Blanche thinks you should have got more for the house than you did, but she agreed and signed the papers. Also, she's not asking for any alimony, only half the community property, which as I believe you know, is customary—"

"All right. All right! I'll send the silver service and the other pieces to you and you can give them to her." His face was grim. "But that's it! After this, I don't expect to hear from her again, is that clear?"

"Yes," Theo Jones answered in a tired voice. "That's clear. You won't."

Alton slammed the phone down, not caring if he damaged the instrument or not. *It's a good thing I planned to leave early today because of the meeting tonight. I'm liable to bite somebody!*

He raked everything that was loose off the top of his desk into the top drawers before steaming out of the office.

Honor was in the kitchen when she heard Alton's key in the lock. Controlling her excitement, she ran to meet him. He returned her hug, didn't kiss her, and started up the stairs.

"You're home early today, going to take a little time to enjoy being home," she smiled hopefully.

"Not likely." Alton could have committed murder with less hate written on his face.

Honor slowly followed him as he entered the bedroom, not venturing any further remarks until he took a clean shirt out of the closet and started to change.

"Bad day at the office," she ventured.

"It's not the office." That was it, there was no explanation. He put his shirttail in and put his suit coat back on before turning to her. "I've got a meeting and I'll be late, so don't wait up for me."

When Honor started to speak he cut her off with, "I'll grab a sandwich somewhere."

"Alton?" Honor stopped, losing her nerve. She turned away.

Alton forced his angry voice into a civil tone. "Don't worry, Honor, I'm just a little on edge. Everything's going fine at work. It's just that I'm a little busy right now. And then Blanche's lawyer called just before I left. Now, she wants the silver service, even named the pieces she wants to go with it, so she'll be sure to have it all!"

Honor nodded, not making any answer as he straightened his coat. On the way out, he slapped the door facing with his hand, she jumped at the sound.

"Dealing with that woman is as bad as trying to deal with a two year old!"

Honor stood still, listening to his angry steps retreating down the stairs. She started again when the front door slammed, tears welling up in her eyes. They ran down both cheeks unheeded.

Bad. *Bad as trying to deal with a two year old! He doesn't want children to mess up his house or change his life.* Honor's lower lip quivered, *And he acted like spending more time at home is not what he wants either. Or maybe it's he doesn't care to spend any more time with me.*

Honor sat down on the bed and cried, her head in her hands. Her heartbroken sobs were the only sounds in the silent house.

Jackie Griffey

CHAPTER TWENTY-TWO

Aaron and Leona, Martin and Hilde, arrived at the airport and were met by Aaron's pilot, Jason Turner.

"Good morning, Mr. Willoughby, good day for a trip."

"Looks like it. These are my friends, Martin Hammond and Hilde—soon to be Hammond. And this is my beautiful bride-to-be, Leona Miller. This is Jason Turner, our pilot." He added, "And we can dispense with that 'kissing the brides business' since we've only got till Sunday morning."

"It won't take me that long!"

Jason, a laughing, youthful, fifty, defiantly kissed both brides' cheeks before turning to the men. "Glad to know you," he shook hands with Martin smiling broadly enough to take in both of them, "Congratulations to both of you!"

He quickly set about getting the portable stair in place and making it stable for them, then stepped back, waiting for them to board.

Aaron smiled affectionately at Leona, taking her hand to help her up the first step ahead of him. "Some people get awfully sure of themselves just because they have your lives in their hands," he hissed in a loud stage whisper to Martin, eyeing Jason with a twinkle in his eye. Jason grinned back, he had been with Aaron over ten years and had ample cause to celebrate the day he came to work. He pretended not to hear and put his hand on the metal rail in a protective gesture.

"It could have been worse," Martin soothed Aaron's feelings about his pilot's attitude.

"Humpf, how worse," Aaron grunted as he stepped into the plane ahead of Martin.

"He might have tried to kiss *me*!"

"I'd have fired him if we had to walk!" Aaron vowed as Martin held Hilde's arm.

"You notice I said tried—go on, or we'll never get there."

Hilde stifled the laugh rising in her throat at their fussing as Martin clung to her leaving the stair. "Feel free to give him a push," he told her.

"Everybody's giving me a tough time this morning," Aaron kept up his grumbling as he followed Leona.

On the plane and free of Martin's more restraining than helpful hand at last, Hilde placed her hand over her tummy. "You lucky little tadpole, I can't believe we're going on a private jet!" She looked at Martin, "Can he hear me, do you think, our little tadpole? I've heard they are aware of conversation and music and of course physical changes…"

"Oh sure, he's probably not paying much attention though. Thinking about more important things than listening to a lot of distant kinfolks."

Hilde got settled and Martin sat down beside her.

"Who's got more important things on his mind," Aaron raised his eyebrows.

"Our tadpole. He's growing fingers and toes and more than likely already thinking up ways to get around those two push-overs, his parents."

"What an imagination," Hilde giggled. "And to think, I was happy without the added bonus of a sense of humor!"

"I've heard the first twenty or thirty years are the hardest," Martin went on.

"Never had any first hand experiences of my own, I'll admit. But I've heard some pretty scary tales from other people who had teenagers. Shame we can't handle youth as efficiently as the butterflies. Some life forms have all the luck."

Leona shot an unbelieving glance at Aaron. "Don't encourage him," he advised solemnly.

"But I want to know," Leona insisted, "What do you mean handle youth like the butterflies? Tell me. No skeptics need to listen," she squeezed Aaron's hand.

Aaron closed his eyes, abandoning them to their fate.

"I want to know too, tell us, Martin."

"Don't tell me you haven't noticed, Martin assumed his innocent mask. "At a certain age, the little things simply weave themselves into a cocoon and stay out of trouble until they're old enough to handle whatever problems are thrown at them like adults while the human parents, about the time puberty strikes, are dealing with rebel-peer pressure and learners' permits to drive. They have to cope with their rising insurance rates and high blood pressure and the economy all at the same time. The butterflies have it made, all right."

Aaron opened one eye, "I tried to warn you."

"Never mind," Hilde patted Martin's knee. "I prefer the human way. It's more fun."

"I think so too," Leona agreed. "And if it worries Aaron, you sure can't tell it, I can't see a trace of worry on those closed eye lids."

Aaron opened the other eye, "I sacked out at about whopper number three."

When they landed at Las Vegas Jason had arranged for a rental car and began loading their luggage into it as Aaron and Martin watched. Hilde and Leona watched everything that moved, unwilling to miss a thing.

"Would you believe this is the first time I've thought about reservations," Martin mused as if talking to himself as he watched Jason handling the luggage.

"I'd believe that, yes," Aaron nodded.

"Did you make any," Martin pinned him down.

"Yes, do you want a map and particulars?"

"No, I quit worrying when you nixed the state line plan. All I want to do is get married, so the little tadpole will have my name."

"That's what I figured," Aaron's smile was kind, with an affection even occasional temper and impatience hadn't been able to dim. "Just play follow the leader and we'll get it done."

"Play it by ear," Martin grinned.

"You got it. But when we get to the hotel and drop Jason, I want you to drive."

"No problem. He's got everything in. Ready?"

They climbed into the Lincoln Jason had rented and he drove slowly, knowing the women were enjoying the ride and seeing all the sights. At the hotel he pulled up in front.

"Wait here, sir," Jason beckoned to a couple of bellhops. Before they finished loading the bags on the cart, Jason was back with card keys. "My room's on the same floor as your two suites, I'll be there, or you can page me if you want me for anything."

"Fine. You're a good man," Aaron handed him several bills, none of them small. "I guess 'page you' means you'll be in the casino. Here's some walking around money. Try not to lose the plane?"

"Yes, sir." Jason cheerfully saluted the rest of the party and promptly disappeared.

They followed the bellhops into the elevator. "It's early yet. Soon as we get settled in, we'll get in the car and go looking for a likely looking place to get married," Aaron told Martin.

"Good. I want to get that taken care of before Hilde thinks of some excuse to change her mind."

Hilde smiled, her hand over the tadpole again, she enjoyed touching him, knowing her feelings would surely penetrate as goodness and warmth if not words. "It's a little too late for that, isn't it? Oh, we're here."

She stopped in the hall with Martin as the other bellhop went on with Aaron and Leona's bags.

Inside their suite, Leona looked around at the luxurious furnishings; the well equipped bar; a cut flower arrangement in what looked like a crystal bowl and the bath with its own hot tub.

"They must think we're high rollers," Aaron smiled as he watched her reaction to the suite.

"It's really something, isn't it! Do you want to unpack?"

"No." Aaron opened the door. "Martin's ready, which is putting it mildly," he smiled. "Let's go, we can unpack later." He pushed the door almost shut first, and kissed her. "This is more important than unpacking."

"It's our wedding day," Leona beamed.

Martin's knuckles rapped smartly on the door before he stuck his head in. "Thought I saw you coming, Leona get a bad case of particular and back out on you?"

"No, you're not the only lucky fellow in this party, I was just letting her know I know that. We're ready to go."

Martin drove the car with Aaron sitting beside him, reading the signs on buildings and billboards as they went. Hilde and Leona tried to watch everything and still manage to look for a place they might want for the ceremony.

"Biggest gamble of them all," Aaron read, chuckling to himself, they got that right! Hey, over there—let's check that one out."

The place Aaron had spotted was a small building which looked like an old fashioned white frame chapel, with a small, well tended bit of lawn in front of it. It too had signs posted about their services.

"It seems to have everything the rest of them have," Martin observed tentatively.

CHAPTER TWENTY-THREE

There was a brief conference as Martin drove slowly by, then turned and came back to the little chapel.

"It looks like a church," Aaron pointed out.

"That's what I liked when you spotted it," Martin said. "All in favor of checking it out?" Everyone voted, liking the look of the little white chapel.

"Your luck's still with you, there's a parking place," Aaron pointed and Martin did an expert job of parking considering he was still eyeing the little chapel.

"Look at these pictures," Leona exclaimed when they stood in front of the place. "And it says they have dresses, flowers, and pictures," Leona stared at some of the sample pictures. "How can they do all that?"

"Let's find out," Hilde said, touching one of the pictures of a bride and groom.

"Interested in tying the knot?" A man appeared beside them. He looked like a member of a wedding in his white coat. "We've got the whole nine yards," he smiled around at the whole party.

"Can we get the licenses here, too," Aaron hedged.

"Sure can. The works, just like the sign says." The man held up an expensive looking camera.

"Hilde?" Martin hesitated.

"Yes, I like it. Better than any we've seen so far, and they do have everything."

"I like it, too," Leona agreed. "Aaron is right. It looks like a real little chapel."

"I'd like pictures too," Hilde eyed the camera.

Jackie Griffey

"Yes, that's a nice looking camera he's got," Leona agreed.

Aaron beckoned the man in the white coat closer. "Looks like this is the place. We want a double ceremony and the works. Pictures too, if that's not included in the works. And we'll want separate pictures and pictures together—"

"Yes, sir. I'll get things started. Just give your information to these two clerks, for the licenses. I'll be with you in a few minutes. You did want the dresses and the tux and the whole deluxe deal?"

"The works," Aaron confirmed.

"Now, Martin teased Hilde, "I'll find out what Hilde is short for."

"Hilde—that's it. But I cheated. I had it shortened from Hildegaard Hascholdsdottir."

Martin wiggled his finger in his ear as if cleaning the wax out, "That's an earful, all right. Hilde it is." It could have been Rumplestilzkinsdottir and not ruined his happiness.

Aaron's attention was on the young man with the expensive looking camera, he moved closer to him and spoke quietly. "I'm too old to do this again," he confided as the rest of them answered the clerks' questions, "So be sure to get plenty of pictures for the ladies. Of each pair, each bride, and all of us together."

Everything they did was accompanied by flash bulbs, the first pictures taken as they were handed their licenses.

"It's a good thing we won't have to move around very much," Leona whispered to Hilde in the dressing room. "These alterations are just basted."

"But they look good," Hilde tilted her head admiring Leona's gown. "You look beautiful, I'm just glad to be getting some pictures." They were interrupted by a girl with a camera who got a regal looking pose of Leona with something which looked like a long train on her arm; one of Hilde; and even pictures reflected in the dressing table mirror of them putting on their tiaras of flowers and veiling.

Before Hilde could get up the courage to ask, the photographer assured them there would be many more formal pictures taken after the ceremony and as they said their vows.

"Oh, this is wonderful, I didn't dream we would get so many pictures!"

"I didn't know what to expect either," Leona agreed happily, "It's all turning out even better than I hoped."

"And the little chapel is perfect, let's get one of the outside too, if they don't just do it, we'll ask?"

"Why not," Hilde laughed, giddy with happiness.

In the mens' dressng room, Aaron admired himself in the full length mirror, glad he didn't have to bend down to see in this one. "I'm all set, if I don't do anything reckless, like breathe!" He turned to Martin, "Why so quiet? Jealous?"

"Yeah, jealous," Martin's laugh was short. "I was remembering that old adage, 'marry in haste, repent at leisure'—remember that one?"

"This is what you wanted," Aaron reminded him.

"I know. It still is. I want my child to have my name and know I cared enough about him to be sure he gets a good start." His brows came together, deepening his worry lines, "But Hilde, she's the one—that's going to be here a lot longer than I am." He looked lost, helplessness was not a thing he was accustomed to. "I'm not going to be much help to her and the tadpole."

"Yes, you are. She was going to a sperm bank, what help do you think she was expecting from that kind of deal?" He put his hand on Martin's shoulder, "Don't sell that woman short, the tadpole will be in good hands." He smiled at Martin, his own happiness bursting at the seams, "And you're a—"

"I know," Martin's grin came back as he admired their reflection in the mirror, "I'm a Lucky Son of a Sea Biscuit!"

After the ceremony, Leona and Hilde sat in the waiting room admiring the pictures presented to them.

"These are beautiful," Leona dashed away a tear.

"They really are good, I like all of them." Hilde held one of her and Martin to her heart briefly before going on to others.

"Yeah, they're all right, considering what they had to work with," Aaron held up a picture of Martin balanced on one foot in the dressing room.

"You rat! You bribed him to take that picture of me changing with a hole in my sock!"

"Not guilty!" Aaron shouted indignantly. "I didn't know you had a hole in your sock," but it was hard to be indignant when a laugh was struggling to get out. He handed the picture over for Martin to look at better.

His grin was malicious, "That guy had some good ideas of his own. I only crossed his palm with a little reward," more laughter tumbled out.

"Sure! I can see the halo over your head! Oh, well," Martin got over it. "We can all admire ourselves later, let's go have some fun!"

***

Sunday morning the phone in Aaron's suite rang shrill and insistently. His hand fumbled for it on the bedside table. His eyes fluttered, then closed again as he relaxed under the warm covers. His hand holding the phone was the only member outside the drowsy warmth. He sighed, "Good morning, Martin."

"How did you know it was me?"

"Who else would call at the *unGodly* hour of—what time is it, anyway?"

"It's ten o'clock, Sleeping Beauty! Let's have breakfast and talk about when we're going to leave. Wouldn't want Hilde to get fired, now that I'm officially the Head of the House—I want that paycheck coming in!"

Aaron's eyes sought Leona. She was just coming out of the bathroom. "I think we've created a monster," he grumbled to her. "Martin wants to cut short my beauty rest with breakfast."

"Sounds good to me, I'm ready to eat. And I noticed we can play keno while we eat downstairs."

"Okay, I'm sold." He turned back to the phone, "Did you hear that? Leona says we can play keno while we eat downstairs."

"Throw on enough clothes to keep from getting arrested, Hilde and I will brush our teeth and still beat you down there!" Martin hung up.

"Show off," he smiled at Leona. "Well, you always look good and there's only so much I can do, so they won't beat us down by much."

Martin and Hilde, Aaron and Leona emerged in the hallway at the same time, to Aaron's delight, "I figured you were just bragging!"

Martin stepped quickly into the nearby elevator, *"Beat you!"*

"Will you two declare a truce or something? I'm ready to concentrate on *food!"* Hilde tickled Martin in the ribs. "Our little tadpole wants to eat!"

"Chip off the old block," Aaron commented in spite of Leona's warning look.

Downstairs they chose a table where Leona and Hilde could admire the fireplace which was part of the decor summer and winter, and where Aaron and Martin could see the keno results.

Hilde was lucky choosing one number. *I won! I won!"* She gleefully stuffed her winnings into her purse. "None of that 'let it ride' stuff for me, this may not be enough to get the tadpole through college, but it's a start," she announced.

Martin warned her, "By the time he gets to college, that will probably cover lab fees, if we're lucky."

Aaron asked for a phone and called Jason Turner's room. He answered promptly.

"Wanted to see if you were there or had lost the plane and started walking back by now," he told Jason. "We're finishing breakfast, have you eaten yet?" He listened a minute and raised his eyebrows, "It ought to be against the law to be that young!"

He held the phone out a little, "He's eaten and jogged around the hotel and has his duds packed. Shall I tell him he can expect us down here with our bags in an hour?"

Martin nodded, watching keno numbers. Hilde reached over to hold his hand. "I didn't bet again, I'm going to quit while I'm winning, her smile told him she meant more than the game of keno.

***

The four of them waited at the plane as Jason loaded the luggage, and prepared to take them home. Aaron stumbled slightly as he stepped off the stair into the plane but caught himself as Martin reached out to him. He whispered for Martin's ears only, "I don't think I can do this again next weekend."

"Don't feel like the lone ranger," Martin whispered back. "We're both more golden wedding age than honeymooners."

Hilde and Leona had both fallen asleep when Martin got up. "Got to get some water," he explained as Aaron looked up at him.

"What was that you took," Aaron asked when he returned. "I saw you take something before, when you seemed to be running on nerves and no one else was watching."

"You might as well know, this is why I knew I was right about the physical examination at St. Josephs being phony. I don't have Parkinson's. It's my heart that will take me out. Rob examined me at the clinic when I went to work there."

"Your heart," Aaron's concern for his friend showed in his eyes. "I guess he ran all those tests you're so fond of?"

"Yes." Martin glanced at Hilde and Leona as they napped. "I've put everything I've got in Hilde's name. She doesn't know about the examination, or about the lodge at Lake Tahoe."

"I'd not take any bets on Hilde not knowing or at least having an inkling about your heart. She's too good a nurse and too close to you not to have a clue."

"You may be right, but I haven't told her, or discussed it with her." He continued, his eyes holding Aaron's. "There's a folder with all the information on my accounts, insurance and everything else, in a bureau drawer at home. If there's any question about any of it, you'll see it handled for her, won't you?"

"Of course." Aaron's eyes were intent, "But, let's not bury you yet, how bad is it? And tell me the truth."

Martin gave it some thought. "Probably not any worse than any man my age in a stressful occupation should expect. It could have been Parkinson's, or cancer, or any number of things. If I'd had a choice, given the suffering some of the other things put you through, Id probably have picked this. But it is serious enough to set my house in order."

"Thanks for telling me. You did right to get things arranged for Hilde and your child. And I'll certainly stand by if they need help. Let's catch us a nap, while we can."

Jackie Griffey

CHAPTER TWENTY-FOUR

The small jet touched down, waking Hilde and Leona. Hilde stretched, smiling at Martin who was watching her as she woke.

"I guess the honeymoon's over—"

"No, it's just beginning," Martin corrected her. "You wouldn't want to stay in Las Vegas permanently would you?"

"No, I like our own rat race. Either that, or I'm just used to it," Hilde grinned.

"I think that's called addiction," Martin pronounced solemnly.

"Wait till you get back to the clinic to start practicing medicine, will you," Aaron grumbled, stretching.

He got up and led the way down the stair when Jason had it in place, followed by Leona, Martin, and Hilde last.

As they started to walk away from the plane, they had only gone halfway to the hangar when Martin gasped in pain.

"Oh, this one hurts."

Aaron stopped, touching Leona's arm as Hilde's arm went around Martin "It's your heart, isn't it," she gazed into his contorted face, holding onto him, willing her strength into him. "Hold onto your arm if that helps. Do you think you can make it to the car with Aaron's help? I'll call and tell the clinic we're coming, we're not going to wait for an ambulance."

Aaron answered for him, "We'll make it, go on and call." His strong arm took Hilde's place and she ran to find the nearest phone, her face as contorted as Martin's.

Jason had run to their help and they got Martin into the car. Aaron drove like he was alone on the planet, cutting in and out of traffic like a pro. He didn't start shaking until he pulled up at the emergency entrance.

Dr. Rob Payne, Jennie Graves, and plenty of help were there waiting for him as soon as the car stopped. A white, empty gurney stood ready for Martin. The team worked with swift efficiency.

In a matter of seconds, Aaron and Leona were watching them hurrying in with Martin. Someone had scotch taped a sticker on the lower part of the gurney, proclaiming, 'I BRAKE FOR TRANSPLANTS.'

A tear rolled down Aaron's face. "Appropriate, wouldn't you say," he tried to smile at Leona through his tears, but couldn't make it. She laid her head on his chest briefly then took his hand to follow their friends.

"I know he's getting the best of care, by people who love him."

Martin adamantly refused to take up space in the intensive care unit. Hilde sat beside his bed in the room assigned to him.

"There's no sense making such a fuss," Martin said. "There's nothing anyone can do." His eyes found Rob, who stood leaning against the door. "Anything as beat as your patient, Dr. Payne, can't be fixed except by jacking it up like an old car and running a new one in under it." He smiled, thinking about that, I can't believe how many people with good sense on other subjects think new parts are the answer. Putting in a new heart would be like putting a new motor in an old jalopy, the other parts couldn't stand the strain. So there's no sense in feeling that there's something you should be able to do. We're all intelligent and over twenty-one, and worn out is worn out."

"I'm always looking for a less painful way to say that, to explain to people," Rob said slowly. "But you always did get right to the bottom line, that's what made you such a good teacher," his eyes met Martins's. "And I'm grateful you came to help us out, and continue teaching us, while you were at it," he added.

"Prove it then, by getting on with your work." Martin raised his head as Rob reluctantly turned to leave, "And if you let Hilde work too hard before the tadpole gets here, I'll come back and *haunt you,"* he chuckled.

"I don't doubt that for a minute," Rob retorted emphatically, laughing and crying at the same time, ignoring the tears that fell. "I love you, you old perfectionist, and I'll go now and get on with my work like you told me to."

The door closed behind Rob, and Hilde laid her head down on the bed and gave way to her grief, sobbing her heart out at the brief time they had had together until she felt Martin's hand on her shoulder.

"Cut that out," Martin ordered quietly but sternly. "You've got to be strong enough for both of us. The tadpole's depending on you. Give me a kiss and send Aaron in here."

"All right," Hilde wiped her face and nose on the sheet, making Martin smile, and stepped out into the hall.

"Aaron, he wants to see you," Hilde sat down beside Leona, who put her arm around her shoulders, comfort speaking louder than words.

Pausing at the door, Aaron studied Martin, "Does this mean we're not going to be recycling humanity any more?" He sat down in the chair beside the bed as Martin chuckled like a mischievous child.

"Now, don't get your hospital gown in a wad trying to tell me what to do. I remember everything you told me about the lodge, the accounts and your insurance. I will see to it. And since I may not be very far behind you, I'll do it tomorrow. You can see now, why I don't go to doctors unless I have to, can't you? I don't want to know what's gaining on me. My affairs are in order at the end of each day."

"I still say you could have got something for the pain I know that arthritis caused you. And we did do a few people some good, didn't we?"

"We certainly did. There have been times I wish we'd met a little sooner in life, but I guess the world wasn't ready for a pair like us." Aaron grinned, remembering some of their exploits.

"I'm sure that's what Leona would say. You give that beautiful, sweet lady a hug for me. And thank you, for standing by in case Hilde needs you. Send her back in here, will you?" His face serious, Martin raised his arm as Aaron got to his feet.

Aaron reached out for it, not fighting tears he couldn't stop. Their hands clasped in a last strong grip of friendship and farewell as their eyes met.

Hilde returned, taking her seat beside Martin's bed. She sat beside him, talking about the tadpole and her plans for him.

"Or her," Martin reminded her with a smile. Hilde had not wanted to know the tadpole's sex, her old country faith praying only for good health and strength to see their tadpole through life.

"Or her," she smiled back, her heart in her eyes. She raised his hand to her lips and kissed it, pausing only briefly in painting him a happy picture of the tadpole's future. "I hope he's somewhere near the man his father is, but that's a tough act to follow."

"Or beautiful like her mother—who thought she was plain," he rolled his eyes at how foolish an idea that was. "And who's the best nurse I ever had." He stopped, "Of course if I live, I'll probably take that back!"

Outside in the hall, Leona clutched Aaron's hand when she heard Hilde's laughter, her heart too full for words.

A few minutes later Aaron and Leona stood when Hilde came slowly back to them. Seeming more at peace, she held out her hands to them and said simply, "Martin's gone."

Jackie Griffey

CHAPTER TWENTY-FIVE

Alton locked his desk and left the office in a good mood because his business meeting had gone so well. He was whistling softly under his breath by the time he got to the parking lot.

I'm certainly due some time off. I've been working my can off, keeping everything in good shape for when my transfer comes through. Honor must feel like a widow, and we haven't even made it to a preacher yet.

He smiled, picturing how pleased she would be that he came home early, her pretty face wreathed in smiles. *It was so late when the meeting was over I was too tired to think of anything but getting a room and my head on a pillow. It would be an awful fate to wreck the car and get killed on the way home just when I've finally got a reason to get there. I've only been gone a night and I feel like I've been gone a week! I was right, it makes a difference when you've got the right partner and you know where you belong. That answering machine I've cursed so much finally came in handy. I'll surprise her getting home this early. And I'll take her out to dinner tonight to thank her for all the good meals she's been cooking for me. Besides, I think it's time I showed her the diamond wedding band that goes with that engagement ring.* His happiness put the whistle back on his lips and hurried his step.

At home he left the car at the front of the house and let himself in with his key. He closed the door quietly, listening for sounds from the kitchen. There were none.

It was as depressingly quiet as the house had been before Honor came. Some of the pizzazz went out of his high spirits. He cast a puzzled glance around the spotless kitchen.

She's crazy about this kitchen, I figured this is where she would be.

Alton touched the oven, it was cold. A little disappointed nothing was baking, he rationalized that was good because he was taking her out.

She deserves a night out, she'll enjoy it and I'll show her the ring I got. She must be doing something upstairs. Maybe she waited up so late she's taking a nap. That's why everything's so quiet.

Leaving the kitchen, still thinking logical if not entirely comforting thoughts, he started up the stairs, listening, feeling a little haunted for some reason.

It was as quiet upstairs as the kitchen had been. His brows drew together, *I'm beginning to feel like I did when I came home from that last business trip when I couldn't find dad...*

At the top of the stairs he strained his ears. He didn't hear a thing. Nothing moved, not even a breath of air stirred in the silent house. He recognized all too well the fear rising from the pit of his stomach, the same feeling he had when he was looking for Aaron. The bone sure feeling something was terribly wrong.

He forgot quiet and ran the last few steps to the bedroom. The nightmare feeling intensified as he stepped inside.

She's not here!

He looked around the bedroom, as panicked as he had been when he looked in vain for his dad. He pictured the two of them standing together in some dark, enchanted place, unreachable as if a witch or a magician had stolen them away from him.

He clenched his fists and got a grip on himself, his eyes searching the room for a clue, no slippers beside the bed, no robe on the nearby chair. Then he saw the message light blinking.

He walked over and looked down at the phone and the blinking red light, the ache spreading from his stomach to his heart. *Maybe she didn't get my message when I called home. But, why wouldn't she? Or maybe this is something else.*

He pushed the playback button and listened to his own voice saying it was two o'clock in the morning and he would stay at the hotel they were meeting in and go to work from there. "I love you, I'll try to come home early tomorrow," he heard his tired voice promise. A promise that wasn't heard? But if not, why not?

Honor, he breathed, his voice coming out in a moan.

He went to the double doors of the closet, his feet not wanting to take him there. With a sickening dread, he opened the doors, folding them back.

Her clothes were gone. *Honor's left me!*

He stood there, trying to make sense of it. *But why? What happened? Where has she gone?* His eyes fell on the phone book on the writing desk. *Janetta! Her sister will know where she is.*

He fumbled through the phone book, willing his fingers to work. *Here it is, Tyson Long.* His chest hurt. He let out the breath he hadn't realized he was holding, and dialed the number. It took several eternitys to ring three times. At last, Janetta answered.

"Janetta! It's me, Alton—"

"Alton. Alton Willoughby, I don't want to talk to you." Janetta's voice was icy. "I don't hang up on people, so I'm saying goodbye."

"Wait! Wait, Janetta! What's going on? I just came home, came early to take Honor out to eat and she's not here—"

"She left you a note."

"A note? Oh!" Alton's eyes found the note, a small folded piece of paper on the bed. "I see it now, it's there on the bed—"

"Goodbye, Mr. Willoughby."

Alton winced as Janetta hung up. He looked in disbelief at the phone, feeling wounded when the dial tone buzzed. "Mr. Willoughby?" He asked it out loud.

He went to the bed and picked up the note. Something fell out as he unfolded the paper. It was her engagement ring. His eyes devoured the brief message.

Gone! She's really gone! She's pregnant and she thinks I don't want her or the baby either! My God! No! This can't be happening!

Shaking himself, he dialed Janetta's number again. It rang seven times before Janetta answered it, he counted them, willing her to pick up the phone.

"Janetta! Janetta, please, don't hang up. I didn't know Honor is pregnant. I haven't been around as much as I wanted to. That's beside the point. I love Honor and I *do* want her and the baby too. Please, Janetta, where is she? I love her, I was going to suggest we go on and get married here and not wait for my transfer. I came home early to take her out to dinner and show her the diamond wedding ring I got. Please, Janetta, tell me where she is. Is she there with you," he added hopefully.

"No, she's not here," Janetta said slowly.

"Janetta, please—"

"Alton, you love Honor? You're telling me the truth?"

"I am. It's the truth. The worst thing that could happen to me would be to lose her and our baby. I love her, Janetta, please tell me where she is."

"But, she left you a note, and she was here last night. She came here yesterday. And you didn't even call—" Janetta's voice was getting cold again.

"I was at a meeting and it lasted till the cows came home," Alton talked fast explaining. "The message was on the recorder when I got here, maybe she didn't get it."

"No, was it late?"

"Yes, about two o'clock in the morning. That's why I left a message instead of ringing again and waking her up. But she was there you said, she didn't get it, did she?"

"Alton, I guess not. She didn't know why you didn't try to call her, she thought you must be glad to get rid of her and the baby."

"Rid," came out in an anguished cry. "Janetta! Please, just tell me where she is!"

"May not do any good," Janetta sounded doubtful. "When you didn't call her—Alton, she's going back to Tennessee. To the farm. I don't know, there may not be time. The train leaves in about forty minutes—Alton?"

Alton dropped the phone and ran. He sped down the stairs touching about every third one and slammed through the door, not taking time to lock it or even make sure it was closed.

I'll make it! I'll make it! I've got to! He panted as he ran. *Oh, God help me, I've got to! I've got to!*

***

The cemetery where Martin was laid to rest beside Mildred was an old one. There were huge old trees and sections where the stones were weathered almost beyond reading, but it was well kept and beautiful.

The graveside service was brief but moving, the pastor of the church where Martin and Mildred were members remembered the kindness and generosity of the man he committed to eternal rest.

"I'm glad someone who knew Martin was available," Aaron said quietly to Leona.

"Yes, and it was like Martin to have prearranged everything when he buried his first wife so no one else would have the details to see to—so like him," Leona pressed a handkerchief to her eyes.

Aaron glanced at Hilde and at Donnie Albright who stood next to her. "I'm glad Hilde has friends here, too. That man there with her is the one he did the liver transplant on. And over there I see Dr. Payne and some of the others from the clinic"

"There are so many people here, Aaron. He must have helped a lot of people."

"Yes, he was one of a kind, touched a lot of lives."

***

Alton drove fast, wishing his car could take to the air, cutting in and out of the traffic in his way.

I've got to get there, got to! I'll take a short cut through the cemetery. He abruptly changed lanes, ignoring the horns and threats yelled at him, as he raced through the traffic without giving a signal and headed for the cemetery. Careening around the cemetery's narrow, curving lanes, he came upon a crowd, a funeral where people were just beginning to congregate into little groups before leaving. He slowed, watching the few people already coming toward their cars. A tall man in black caught his attention.

"Dad!"

The screech of his brakes drowned his cry. Alton veered to the right and left his car with one wheel at an angle, up on the concrete curbing. He ran to his father. "Dad," he called when he got closer.

Aaron heard him. He stopped, his hand in Leona's as his eyes found Alton. Alton was almost to them when he knew for sure it was really his son's face.

"Dad!" Alton took his arm and started pulling on him. "Dad, you've got to come with me!"

Aaron stood as if he'd taken root, wondering what could be wrong until Leona said, "Go with him, Aaron. I'll be fine. *Go with him!*"

Aaron let Alton pull him away from the crowd, and seeing the panic on his face, he began to run with him to the car.

As Aaron got into the passenger seat, Alton jumped behind the wheel and pulled away from the curb with a bump. He raced out of the cemetery before the rest of the crowd could get to their cars and clog the narrow road. Aaron hung onto the armrest, too winded by the running to ask questions.

As he pulled out of the cemetery into street traffic, Alton said, "Blanche and I are divorced, dad."

"I know, I saw it in the papers, where she had filed," he nodded.

"I've been looking all over for you!"

"I'll tell you about that—"

Attention to traffic interrupted.

"Why I've got to hurry—I've found the woman I should have married, I love her and she loves me."

Alton swerved and missed a large utility van by a thin coat of paint. "But it happened so fast. She's pregnant, dad, pregnant with my baby—our baby. And she's left me! She thinks I don't want her or the baby either!"

A pick-up truck honked angrily as it veered out of his way.

"Try your lights," Alton spat out the window.

"She's getting on a train, maybe right now. I've got to get there—"

Aaron's hand reached down, checking his seatbelt, his face set in determined lines. *"Drive son, I'll get the tickets!"*

Through sheer luck or devine intervention or a combination of both, they managed to arrive in the busy parking lot at the train station, not so much parking the car as abandoning it in a handicapped slot as heads turned to stare.

Alton jumped out and ran as hard as he could.

Aaron stared down an elderly white woman who glared at him and the handicapped sign.

"First things first," he muttered in her direction, not caring whether she heard him or not. He calmly shut the car door and hurried after Alton as fast as he could.

I'm doing good to keep him in sight, Aaron panted. *I'm too old for this, Martin would laugh his head off at the spectacle I'm making of myself!*

***

Honor waited her turn to get on the train. She kept her eyes down, moving slowly, the picture of forlorn desolation in the middle of the uncaring crowd of people who had their own little soap operas to direct or deal with.

He didn't even call. She fought back tears of self pity. *I thought I would be able to see through anything he said, that I'd know if he was telling me the truth or not. If he really does want the baby and not just saying so.* She bit her lower lip. *But he didn't even call. Didn't even care enough to tell me any lies…*

She didn't let the tear fall that trembled on her lashes, she looked stoically ahead as the line began to move slowly.

At last, she stepped up to board the train. She tried to tell herself she was glad to be leaving. Glad to be going to Tennessee. She turned slightly as she got on the train. *I thought I heard my name,* she thought. *But I don't guess I'm the only Honor in the world.*

She passed several windows as she made her way up the aisle, and noticed a man hurrying outside the train, making his way through the crowd.

"Honorrrrrrrrr!" It was faint, but it was her name. She bent to look out the window.

That man pushing his way through the crowd, he looks like Alton. It is Alton! He's running along looking into every face in the train windows like a lunatic! And he called my name! I heard him! Oh, it's Alton, it's Alton!

Honor leaned over an empty seat and knocked on the window and Alton saw her. His eyes lit up with hope, his lips formed her name. "Honor!"

He began making wild gestures. Honor watched as he waved his arms and pointed, trying to make out what he was saying.

The train, she realized, *It's moving! He's pointing to the back for some reason.* She moved along, looking out the windows as Alton hurried along trying to make her understand.

Oh! The back of the train! This is the last car, that's what he's trying to tell me!

She straightened up and ran, her suitcase knocking against the seats as she ran. She managed to open the heavy door at the back and stepped out on the platform into the wind.

"I love you!" Alton shouted.

Honor put her hand over her joyous heart that threatened to leap out of her chest in its happiness. Her other hand had a tight grip on the railing, her smile was radiant, his I love you echoing in every beat of her heart. She peered down at the two black iron steps, trying to keep her balance.

"Come down, I'll be here to catch you."

Honor stood, undecided, the train was gathering speed now.

"I love you and the baby too! I love you!"

Honor made up her mind. She threw the suitcase off the train and stepped down the first step.

Alton held out his arms, encouraging her. The train was still moving slow enough to make it safely, she moved toward the bottom step, but something held her fast.

"I can't move," Honor shouted, looking back, "My dress is caught!"

Honor pulled in vain at the material. Then a hand reached up from somewhere and slashed the cloth with a knife. She pulled free and half stepped, half jumped toward Alton's waiting arms.

"Alton," she screamed as her feet left the solid safety of the iron step. Then Alton's arms were around her, holding her safe and close to him.

"Oh, Alton," Honor's heart was still beating fast, but she was on solid ground now, watching the train picking up speed. "I—I thought you were tired of me, that you don't want to—to fool with children," tears ran down her cheeks.

"I'll never be tired of you, *never!* And I *do* want children," Alton vowed happily. "This one and a couple of brothers and sisters!"

Honor rested her head on his shoulder, feeling safe at last and loved, back where she belonged and wanted to be. She blinked the tears from her eyes and realized she was staring into an elderly face wearing an anxious expression. *But he has smile wrinkles, like a kindly person,* she thought, dreamily floating above any of earth's problems, safe in the arms of the man she loved.

"And I love you," the weathered, anxious face told her earnestly. "And I want you and the baby too!"

"Who—ah—" Honor drew back, looking from the elderly man to Alton.

"Honor," Alton said, still holding her close, his arm around her waist as she turned. "This is my father, Aaron Willoughby. Dad, this is the woman I love. Her name is Honor Dean."

"Soon to be Willoughby," Aaron said sternly.

"Yes, sir, soon to be Willoughby," Alton beamed.

CHAPTER TWENTY-SIX

Aaron led Honor toward the parking lot, walking slow enough for Aaron to keep up with them. "I hope the car's still there and hasn't been towed away."

"It'll be all right," Aaron confidently assured him., "There wasn't anybody around but a mean faced old woman looking for someone to scold and I scared her away."

"You're a man of action, aren't you?" Honor laughed, "It was you that cut my skirt material, wasn't it?"

"Had to do something," Aaron admitted complacently.

Alton, at peace with the world again, listened as he walked, smiling at his dad.

Aaron reached into his pocket, "I did it with my genuine super sized Swiss Army Knife," he chuckled as he held it up to be admired.

"I guess that knife collection of yours finally came in handy. We used to tease him about it," Alton explained to Honor."

"What do you say now?"

"Thank you."

"You're welcome," Aaron replaced the knife. "Where's the car? All I noticed when we got out was that handicapped sign."

"There it is, we're in luck. It wasn't towed, but I see something under wiper. Bet it's a ticket."

"We weren't in any position to bargain over the price of parking," Aaron reminded him. "I said I'd get the tickets, give it to me."

Aaron looked at the paper, "It's just a warning," he grinned. "We got lucky on that too." He stuck it in his pocket for a souvenir of the day.

Alton looked the car and tires over, then opened the door for Honor to get her safely seated. Aaron patted his pocket with the warning ticket in it and looked up at the heavens, thinking about Martin. *If he's looking down, he's making sure Honor and my grandchild are all right. You hear that, Martin? I finally made it—I'm a lucky son of a sea biscuit!*

Alton put Honor's suitcase in the trunk and opened the door for his dad, then got in behind the wheel, but he didn't start the car. "Now. You said you were going to tell me about why you left. I heard some of it from Blanche, but you know about how much I can depend on any of what she said being so."

"Alton's been looking for you," Honor added. "He even went down to the police station and looked at two dead bodies, trying to find you!"

"Humpf! I've been a lot busier than those two dead folks. I moved my office before you left on your business trip, Alton. I've been wheeling and dealing from pay phones and and—ah—had some other plans I've been working on."

"Would one of them have to do with that attractive woman who was holding your hand when I found you there at the cemetery?"

"An attractive woman, the plot thickens." Honor smiled, raising her eyebrows at Aaron.

Aaron hesitated, wondering where to start.

"And whose funeral was that you were attending, dad?"

"He was a friend of mine. It will take a long time to tell you about him. Martin's not a subject to be covered quickly. We'll get around to it."

"And the attractive lady," Honor pursued.

"The lady is someone I met a long time ago and just ran into after I left the nursing home. I thought you wanted to know about that. What did Blanche tell you?"

"At first, she only said you were gone. Then I finally got it out of her that she had taken you to Pleasant Hill nursing home. Then, and it was like pulling teeth, trying to find out what was going on, where you were. When I said I was going to get you, she said you had left there! That you had disappeared and they didn't know where you were."

Aaron nodded.

"Sounded like a fishy story to me. I asked her if she had reported you missing. I had to do that—"

"Did she hire a private detective?"

"Yes, she did, how did you know?"

"He came around a few places asking questions. I figured she was the one who sent him."

"Well, at least he was doing something then, but he didn't get anywhere. I made her call him and fired him. I've been looking for you ever since, had the police helping too. Where did you go?"

"The man I told you about, the friend whose funeral I was at, he was in the home, too. At Pleasant Hill. He was a doctor, a fine surgeon, and a good friend I'm glad I found. He helped a lot of people. When we left the nursing home together—"

"They got out through a window in the dark of night," Alton told Honor. "Like kids playing hooky. The private detective found out that much."

"Well, we got out. I looked up this lady I'd met a long time ago, and rented a room for us at her place."

"Why did you do that? Why didn't you just come on home?"

"Because Blanche was trying to find out about my business and investments and anything else she could. Taking me to that nursing home was the first step in her getting me declared incompetent so she could take over everything she was hoping I had. It griped her just not knowing, along with being greedy, is why she tried to go the incompetence route."

"She couldn't have done that," Alton stated positively.

"I know it and you know it. But I figured it was time she showed her true colors. As I said, I moved the office before you left, then after my and Martin's Great Escape, I left some dead ends for her to investigate and some other red herrings, and just waited."

Alton laughed, "You *planned* it! I should have known! You planned it, didn't you? That's why she agreed to the divorce so fast, she thought you were *broke!*"

Alton doubled over the steering wheel with laughter, "This ought to be on television! You moved the office, planted your 'clues' and made a game of it. When she put you in Pleasant Hill, you escaped like the hero in a B movie plot—dad, you're priceless!"

"Maybe so, maybe not." Aaron tried to smile mysteriously, not admitting a thing. "Can't help but feel sorry for the next poor fool to take the bait," Aaron intoned piously.

Alton started the car, "Don't waste your pity, Blanche has probably got her eye on that lawyer that handled our divorce."

"Lawyer, humm? You know what all the jokes say about them, he probably deserves her. You're right I won't waste any time worrying."

Alton sat back, happy and proud of himself, an expectant father as his eyes met Aaron's in the mirror.

"I want to know about the pretty lady," Honor insisted.

"And where are we going, dad?"

"I'll give you directions, and we'll go to her place now and you can meet her. 'I've found some happiness of my own, son."

"Are you going to marry her?"

"No. Already have. We eloped to Las Vegas, us and my friend and his bride."

"Las Vegas!"

Honor touched Alton's hand, seeing the brief sadness that touched Aaron's features when he mentioned his friend.

"Just tell me how to go, dad."

"Yes, we're happy for you, both of us."

"Dad. You can call me dad, too." Aaron's face was wreathed in smiles again, "I'm going to be a *grandpa!"*

Honor smiled at him in the rear view mirror.

"When we, my friend Martin and I, went out that window at Pleasant Hill—"

"Yeah," Alton chuckled, "I told you I got a little bit out of Blanche. Far as I know, that you went out the window is the only thing that private detective found out. His name is Holmes, but Sherlock, he's not!"

"I didn't mean to be found. But we needed a place to go. Somewhere nobody would find Martin and give him any more trouble, and where I could hide from Blanche until she had enough rope to hang herself and give up trying to find any information."

"Information must have been scarce as hen's teeth, to make somebody as set in her ways as Blanche is give up."

Aaron smiled to himself, "I helped that stony broke delusion along a little every chance I got. Seeing my office was gone and I was probably out of business was a good start. Then I left enough junk mail in my trash can to further the notion when she came looking for my secretary. I should have been giving that woman combat pay for the last year the way Blanche kept after her for information."

"Whatever you did, it worked. She didn't give me much trouble about the divorce, thinking any chance at big money had run out. I must have had my head in the sand not to have seen she was only interested in money."

Alton glanced at him in the mirror, "Dad, this lady?"

"This lady, yes. Her name is Leona Miller, Willoughby now. She's a good person and kind and we're lucky to have each other. You'll like her. When I told her I was in hiding, her first thought was for you, that you would worry."

"I did, I did!"

"I told her not to worry. That you would know I'd be all right," Aaron insisted. "You said you even went down and looked at two bodies at the police station. Some day when we're killing time, waiting for a fish to bite, I'll tell you something about those two bodies. One of them's pretty interesting."

Honor looked at Alton, wondering at that, Alton shook his head slightly.

Aaron leaned forward, "But we're getting close. Any place you can find to park along here will be fine."

Alton found a place to park and opened the doors for Aaron and Honor. Honor tugged at her skirt.

"This torn off piece is not big enough to be indecent, but it does look bad," she worried.

"Humpf! Looks like designer duds in this neighborhood. It was a safe place to hide from Blanche, but the scenery needs a little work. We're not going to stay here."

"That's something I want to talk to you about later," Alton told him.

"All right then, later. Here we are," he led the way up the steps.

At apartment three-oh-three, Leona looked at them through the small panel before opening the door wide.

She went into Aaron's arms, "I've been pacing the floor, but I knew you were all right." She turned, "And this must be your son," Leona smiled. "He's almost as handsome as you are," she teased Aaron.

"It will give him something to shoot for," Aaron appraised his son's appearance critically. "Leona, I want you to meet Alton, and his fiancee, Honor Dean." He put his arm around Leona. "Children, this is my wife, my bride, Leona Miller Willoughby."

Honor immediately threw her arms around Leona and kissed her on the cheek, "I'm so glad to know you, Mrs. Willoughby."

"Me too," Alton bent to kiss her other cheek.

Leona fought tears of happiness, "And I'm glad to know you, Aaron's family, and mine now. Please, call me Leona."

Ushering them into the living room, Leona said, "I've got fresh coffee made, or I've got cold drinks if you want them."

"I'll have a coke," Alton accepted.

"I will, too, or a diet drink if you have one," Honor said. "May I come and help you?"

"I'll go and help, you sit here and help Alton rest," Aaron volunteered.

"I am a little dehydrated," Alton admitted.

"Running after trains will do that to you," Aaron nodded to him as he followed Leona to the kitchen.

"Leona," Aaron reached for glasses as she opened the refrigerator, "I'm finally going to make Lucky Son of a Sea Biscuit like Martin!"

"Lucky Son of a Sea Biscuit?" Leona worked with the ice cubes, giving him a puzzled glance. "What are you talking about?"

"Honor's pregnant," he announced grandly. "I'm going to be a grandpa!"

Leona dropped the tray in the sink and threw her arms around him, "That's wonderful news, I'm so glad for you," she kissed his cheek. "And me, too—I'll be a grandmother!"

Alton spoke from the door, "I guess you beat us to the announcement," he accused Aaron.

"Grandpa's privilege," Aaron was undaunted. "Here, help me carry these things."

"Soon as we finish," Alton's eyes met Leona's, "I'll take Honor by home to change her clothes and we'll go out and have dinner to celebrate."

"Sounds good to me," Leona sipped her coke.

"Me too," Honor joined them, tugging at the rip again. "All I need is a skirt."

"Humpf, since I'm under new management, I'll just go along with what's been decided," Aaron tried in vain to find something to gripe about, gave it up, and beamed at them.

Jackie Griffey

CHAPTER TWENTY-SEVEN

Several days later, Leona called to Aaron, "Telephone call for you, it's Alton."

"Hello, son, everything all right?"

"Yes," Alton smothered a laugh, "Don't be so prepared for some kind of catastrophe. Everything's fine. Honor feels good, and I've got good news."

"About your wedding?"

"As a matter of fact, it is. If I wasn't already crazy in love with Honor I think I'd marry her just to get you off my back!"

"So, when's it going to *be?*"

"It's going to be a week from Saturday in the chapel of the church near our house."

"That's good. I approve."

"I didn't ask you," Alton pointed out.

"I approve anyway. I guess Leona will have to go out and spend her time and my money on a new dress and everything it needs to go with it."

"That's all right, it's one of the 'simple joys of maidenhood' you read about in books. And you don't mind a bit. I know you too well to take your complaints seriously, you just like to *gripe.* It's one of the things you're good at."

Aaron grinned into the phone, "Practice makes perfect."

Leona came to listen.

"Okay, you called my bluff," Aaron admitted, winking at Leona. "She will need a new dress for the wedding. For an occasion like this," Aaron graciously gave in, "I'll not even gripe any more. She'll get a new dress."

"So will you."

"Me? I don't need a new dress!"

"No, but you'll need to get or rent a tux. None of this college friends stuff at this wedding. You're going to be my best man!"

After a few seconds of silence, he asked, "So, will you? Dad?"

"I'm honored, son. I'll get one. I'll get a tux." Aaron found his tongue and returned to normal. "If you're not afraid I'll show you up?"

"I'll take a chance," Alton laughed. "There's more good news!"

"You'd have to strike oil in the swimming pool for the news to get any better!"

"You remember I put in for a transfer to Tennessee?"

"Yeah, you told me. And no way to tell when—"

"It's come through! That's why we can go on and make plans now. We'll get married a week from Saturday and go to Hawaii on our honeymoon, then I will report back to the Tennessee office to start work there."

"How are you going to manage to move, and what about the repairs to the farmhouse? How do you know—"

"Dad—dad—slow down. Give me credit for a little sense and know how—"

"I remember you haven't seen the place and Honor only had authorized repairs to the roof and floor, to make the house livable, she said."

"Everything will be packed up, and the things can be stored if we need to. I've got a call in to a van company right now, to work out some details. If we can, we will move into the house, if not, we'll leave most of the furniture and things in storage until we get the place the way we want it. And," he cut off Aaron's interruption. "I will find a safe and comfortable place for Honor. I know it's not *me* you're worried about." It was hard for Alton to sound aggravated in the midst of such good fortune and happiness, but being Aaron's offspring, he managed.

"You must have caught the gripes from me. You know you'll have to do a lot more practicing to compete with an old pro like me," he chuckled. "But you do seem to have everything under control. Guess that's in the genes, too."

"Determined to hog all the credit, aren't you?"

"And doing pretty good," Aaron retorted, grinning at Leona. "Now, you get off this phone, I've got to get out and find me a tux!"

Leona managed to keep Aaron busy looking at nursery furniture to keep him from interfering too much with the wedding plans since she could see Honor and Janetta were doing quite well unassisted.

The day of the wedding, Aaron stood before a full length mirror on Leona's closet door, admiring himself in the tux he had bought.

"You look like you're going to a movie premier or something," Leona's smiling face in the mirror admired his finery.

"Shame nobody's going to notice it, with you standing beside me," he managed to look chagrined and admiring at the same time.

"That's all right, maybe we'll just settle for 'handsome couple,'" she comforted him. "For two miserable old folks, we sure do make happy reflections in that mirror," she laughed.

Aaron laughed with her, their smiling faces side by side. "I have to practice my gripes and grumbles on somebody."

"That's all right, I can stand it. Long as I can see you're only practicing."

"Let's go then, and show everybody what a good looking family the bride and groom have!"

***

Janetta was Honor's matron of honor, her smile matching Aaron's in happiness and pride as Honor and Alton exchanged their vows. Aaron patiently posed every time he was directed, letting the professional photographer do things without his interference.

I hope, maybe, somehow, Martin knows about this. Aaron watched as Honor and Alton smiled happily for the camera, thinking about his grandchild. *Martin, I hope you can hear me, I wish you could have been here for this.* He quickly wiped away a tear and looked to make sure Leona hadn't noticed what a softy he was.

She was dabbing at her own eyes and looking as happy as he was.

Throughout the reception, Aaron's mind was busy. *I can't let Martin go without something to mark his passing. He won't be forgotten, I'll see to that…*

Back in apartment three-oh-three, Leona clutched her handkerchief, "The wedding was beautiful," she sniffed happily.

"Must have been, wasn't a dry eye in the house as the saying goes. How come you ladies always cry at weddings?"

Leona had her back to him, changing clothes, "Probably because of all the trouble it is breaking in new help," she giggled.

Aaron sat down, laughing at her response, "I can see living with me is going to rub off."

Leona turned, bending down to kiss his cheek. "I agree with Hilde. You remember what she said about having a sense of humor? And I feel so good about Alton and Honor, and the wedding was so beautiful."

"It was. The reception was nice too." Aaron paused, remembering it. "Sure was slick how Alton managed for them to sneak out in time to go by home and change. I didn't see them, and I was watching."

Leona turned to look at the clock, then out the dark window. "They're on the plane by now, headed for Hawaii," her eyes were dreamy.

"Good thing that transfer came through, since he likes his job. He will be at home more now."

"And able to enjoy his family," Leona smiled, stepping out of her pumps.

"His family," Aaron's face lit up, "My grandchildren."

"You'll have plenty of time with them too, since Alton said he'd send for us soon as they got settled."

"Honor said she liked the idea of having built in baby sitters. It's not every daughter-in-law would be happy as Honor is to have us build our house there on their farm. Looks like Alton picked a winner this time."

Leona put her arms around his neck, "Yes, I like Honor as much as you do. I'm glad he's got such a sweet girl."

Aaron continued sitting on the bed, thinking about Martin and some plans that were forming in the back of his mind. He looked down at his new shoes without seeing them.

Leona stifled a giggle, "Are you going to sleep in that tuxedo?"

"Haven't decided yet," he mumbled defiantly.

The next morning, Aaron hung up the phone and joined Leona in the kitchen for coffee and cookies. "What was that you were saying about Martin on the phone?"

"I was talking to Dr. Payne. I'm giving all that equipment in the basement to the clinic. They can use all of it, besides needing more room. I'm going to give them enough money to build another wing. It will be called the Dr. Martin Hammond Wing."

"Oh, Aaron, that's a wonderful thing to do." She got up and came to put her arms around him, smiling up at him. "I'm going to give you the Leona Miller Willoughby Award for thinking of that."

"And what's that," he eyed her suspiciously.

"Another cup of coffee and an IOU for another kiss, payable on demand any time you want it."

"I accept—both," Aaron deigned to nod his agreement complacently.

Ten days later Leona hurried to tell Aaron Alton was on the phone. He used what must have been his passing gear to get there. "I nearly spilled my coffee getting to the phone," he grumbled into that instrument. "What's the matter, Hawaii close up on you?"

"Nothing like that. We saw all the palm trees and coconuts we wanted to. I'm calling from Tennessee," Alton informed him. "We're at the farm. And dad, you're going to really like this place. You know it used to be a farm."

"I know, Honor referred to it as the farm. You're so excited, must have done a good job on the roof?"

"They did, but it's not that. It's the land. There's a hundred and fifty acres of it, and a branch of a river runs down one boundary of it. And the little plot with a rise Honor told you about where you and Leona might like to live? It's close enough to walk down to the water so you can fish—"

"We can? Listen, son. Get someone out there and see about building me a pier, not anything big, just enough to walk out on and fish from," he looked at Leona, "And sit and admire the sunset—"

"I will! I will!" Alton bubbled over with good humor. "The old house isn't much, but it's big and well built and got possibilities."

"And room for lots of grandkids?"

"Yes, it has lots of room. And an attic and a root cellar and—"

"And lots of fun stuff, I get the picture," Aaron grinned into the phone. "That's good, it sounds good, all of it."

"We're going to do some fixing and remodeling instead of starting from scratch and building another home. The place by the water has a little hut there, Honor said the children used to play in it when she was a little girl. Soon as we get the absolute necessities taken care of, we'll let you know. We can all stay here, or get a double wide or a place nearby, whatever's the quickest, until we can get you a place like you want built for you and Leona there by the water, whatever you want to do."

"Just go on like you've planned and get the needed things done and someone started on the pier, and let us know when you're ready for us. I've got everything I had to do about finished up here. I'll tell you about it when we get down there. But there's one thing I want you to do now, same as the pier."

"What's that?"

"That place you say is just an old hut, where the children used to play or camp out or other things—"

"Yes, sir?"

"Have whoever's doing your work on the house to look at it and fix it. Not renovate and take all the fun out of it, just make it structurally sound so it won't fall in and hurt the children. I want to keep that for another generation, they can play there when they come to see me." Aaron glowed with anticipation, "And you get started on that pier soon as you get off the phone. I've been missing my fly casting."

"I'll do it, soon as I can talk to them. Take this number, dad, and call any time you want to." Alton's voice dropped, as if talking about something distasteful. "I'm not having an answerphone installed. You just keep calling if you don't get an answer the first time. But there will usually be someone here."

"All right. With the experience you've had with recorders, I don't blame you a bit."

"I'm sorry it's going to take a little time to get things the way we want them. You can come on now, if you and Leona want to?"

"No," Aaron's answer came quickly. "There are some things, important things, I want to do here before we leave. We'll be along."

"Okay, I'll keep you posted on our progress."

"You do that, and take care of Honor and my grandchild."

Jackie Griffey

CHAPTER TWENTY-EIGHT

In less than a week of Aaron's conversation with Alton, the Lincoln Street Clinic had Martin's equipment picked up and stored in the clinic's basement to wait for the expanded lab and the new wing that was in the planning stages.

"Who was that on the phone," Leona asked two days later, "I didn't recognize the voice."

"It was someone from the construction firm. I'm to meet them in Dr. Payne's office to look over some of the plans for the new wing."

"None of your people are working on it?"

"Only some of it. I don't want to be accused of being partial, and not knowing I had a finger in the business they had already asked for bids. It'll work out, I've got my eye on it. I'll know more after I get a look at the plans."

"I don't know why I asked," Leona shook her head. "I know about as much about the construction business as I do what's under the hood of a car. I'll just stick to what I know a little about," she kissed him on the forehead. "How about some chocolate chips? My specialty?"

"Good choice, you're an expert in your field," Aaron grinned.

***

Aaron dialed a number and waited, "Ellen?" He smiled at the familiar young voice on the phone. "Let me speak to that man that pays your salary."

"Carl?" Aaron got right down to business, "I need you. What?" He smiled, "Fine, just fine. Yes. Thank you, the wedding was beautiful, you won't get any argument from me about that. As I said, I need you."

The rejoinder brought a grin back to his face, "To keep me honest, that's what for. And to keep me from showing my ignorance, as usual," he chuckled. "Meet me at the Lincoln Street Clinic tomorrow at three o'clock. Dr. Rob Payne's office." He made a few notes as he listened, "All right, see you there."

Several days later, Aaron checked to see if Hilde was home and called her in for coffee and cookies.

"Peanut butter? I'll take any of Leona's cookies any time I get the chance, but peanut butter's my favorite."

"That's what they are, come on."

"I just got home," Hilde greeted Leona. "Don't you sometimes get hungry for something you didn't cook and coffee you didn't brew?"

"I know exactly what you mean, and I've just taken these cookies out of the oven. Peanut butter," she smiled. "Come any time you're home, I've always got cookies."

"And I've got plans," Aaron turned from inspecting the coffee pot. "Let's get the plans out of the way first. It won't take long to tell you all I understand about them."

"Is this for the new wing?" Hilde watched as Aaron unrolled the papers. "You could tell me just about anything and I wouldn't know enough about them to argue with you."

"I'll show you what they told me, I'd not have known what I was looking at either, if I hadn't had some educated help."

"Oh, it's wonderful," Hilde's eyes glistened as Aaron finished showing her the plans. It's so good of you to do this, Aaron."

Aaron shook his head, "No, it's no more than should be done as a tribute to someone as dedicated as Martin was. The wing is needed, and it's a good thing to have his name remembered."

"You're right on both counts, of course. He was a good man and a good and dedicated doctor and surgeon." She looked up at Aaron, "A good person besides the sense of humor and all the other things I admired about him."

Her smile was sentimental and curious around the edges as Leona sat down with her coffee to join them. "I've—ah—heard just enough about some of your and Martin's wild escapades to make me curious," she hinted.

"Well," Aaron pressed his lips together, returning the look, "Whatever he told you, is all you're ever going to know!"

"Killjoy," Hilde laughed.

"I don't know all the things they got up to either," Leona confided, "But I've definitely got the feeling we're better off not knowing."

"Have you had any luck finding you another place to move," Aaron asked, changing the subject.

Hilde shook her head. "No, but I've got two places to look at this weekend, and one of them sounds promising. It's all the room we'll need, not too far from the clinic, and there are some nice schools nearby."

"Sounds good, about the schools nearby. I'd like to know you're settled in before Leona and I leave."

"When are you going to Tennessee?"

"It's not chiseled in stone yet, but probably in about two more weeks."

"I'll probably take the place I told you about, you needen't worry."

"Let us know if you need help with it or with anything else. There's one other thing."

"What's that," Hilde wondered at his serious expression.

"We won't be here when the new wing is dedicated, you will be Martin's representative there."

"I know. It's all right. The clinic staff will be there, all the people he worked with. And Donnie Albright is coming." She smiled at Aaron, "I know it's that river you're in a hurry to get to, I wouldn't want to keep all those scaly friends of yours waiting," Hilde and Leona shared a mischievous grin.

"You're right," Aaron admitted gleefully. "I've got a date with a couple of catfish and maybe a few crappie."

***

Preparations for the new wing and helping Hilde get settled sped the next two weeks along. Aaron and Leona sat sipping their after dinner coffee.

"Everything I had to do is about taken care of," Aaron nursed his cup, savoring the fragrant warmth. "With Hilde moved to her new place and the work started on the new wing, and the movers coming to pack us up tomorrow, I'm beginning to feel sort of useless."

"Well, you're not. Think of all you've done. And as you said, the new wing is started. Do you want to go over there and mix the concrete yourself? Be glad everything you had to do is taken care of."

"Not quite all." He looked at his watch and set his cup on the table beside him.

"What else is there?"

"Nothing major. I've got to meet some people in the basement. I'll go on down."

"What on earth for? The equipment is already gone, been picked up and stored at the clinic—"

"This is to pay for some work Martin and I had done. I won't be long."

***

Aaron stood alone in the shabby looking cab of the elevator. *Martin knew the minute he got in this thing I'd had the works fixed.* He was still smiling to himself when he entered the basement.

He looked sadly around the empty spaces. *Strange how this old place went back to being just a dull old basement so fast, after all the action it's seen. I remember standing there in that lab door, holding on hard enough to break my fingers when Martin tried to hand me that scrub suit.*

His mouth turned up at the corners, *Part of my spirit will probably haunt this place! I don't remember being so scared of anything in my life as I was of that scrub suit Martin was holding out to me, knowing what it meant.* He sighed, *Just an old door now.*

A rap on the outside door brought him back to the present. He opened it and ushered Burke and Harry in.

Burke's eyes traveled over everything, all the empty space, as if searching for something of value he could salvage. The night lights were on, and the lamp on the card table cast eerie shadows around them.

"You're right on time," Aaron commended them.

"You all by yourself," Burke's sharp features took on a speculative look.

"Yes. Since Dr. Hammond's gone, we won't be doing business down here anymore."

"I wondered about that."

"I beeped you to tell you your services, yours and Harry's, will be cut off officially as of tomorrow."

Burke laid their beeper on the card table. "Okay…"

"And to give you something in the way of severance pay."

Burke nodded, listening, still with a speculative air about him. "We wondered if you would be needing us now—for anything?"

Aaron tilted his head, he'd just told them—

Burke eyed the beeper on the card table, then looked boldly up at Aaron. "You remember when you hired us, me and Harry, what a fix you were in then. And there were other times we took care of some things for you," his glance at the lab door was menacing now. "We, Harry and me, we could still tell some things that wouldn't sound so good to the police."

Aaron stood silently, hearing him out.

Burke put on a comic attempt at innocence, "Of course we wouldn't do nothin' like that though. Not if you was to give us a good amount of, what was that you called it?"

"Severance pay," Aaron repeated, feeling too tired and depressed to deal with them and their demands, the implied threat rubbing him the wrong way. He stood there, silent, studying his shoes for a few seconds. When he looked up again, Harry had grabbed Burke's arm and Burke himself stood as if rooted to the floor, his mouth open, staring at something behind Aaron. Something strangely bright reflected in Burke's eyes.

Aaron felt the hairs on the back of his neck rise at the expression on Burke's face. He carefully placed a hand on the card table to steady himself as he slowly turned around.

"Ahhhhhhhhh," Aaron gasped. "M—Ma—Martin?"

A bright apparition stood before them, tossing off glints of light as Martin's ghost literally glowed with righteous indignation.

299

"Yes! Martin!" The apparition spat out the words in aggravation. "It's a good thing I managed to get back to check on things, too. *You!"* The angry apparition's arm raised and a glowing finger pointed at Burke and Harry, tilting it's glowing head at Aaron.

"This good man came down here in good faith, to help you, to put money in your pockets and give you papers to take to the bank. You will have a livable income so you can stop doing business with Champion Chewables—"

"You—you *know* about Champion Chewables," Burke began to shake as hard as Harry.

"Yes. We know. We followed you the day of the gang rumble. We saw you pick up that gang member and saw you take him there. *How dare you come here and make threats!"*

"No, no. We didn't—we never meant—"

"Here," Aaron held out the envelopes, resigned, anxious only to be rid of them. "Just take it and go!"

Burke grabbed the envelopes and ran, Harry behind him closer than a shadow at high noon. The outside door slammed shut behind them.

Aaron sighed, "Well, that's over. I want to tell you something, Martin." Aaron's face lit up again.

"I know," Martin smiled, "You finally made Lucky Son of a Sea Biscuit! I heard you in the parking lot at the train station. You did good with that Swiss army knife and got your future grandkid off that train," he laughed. "I saw you."

"Yeah," Aaron hugged himself, beaming, "I was hoping you'd know. I'm going to be a grandpa."

"That's great. And don't worry, you won't be bothered again by Burke or Harry or anything else."

"I wasn't worried about that, we're going to be moving soon. Hilde found her and the tadpole a place too, I've seen it. It's comfortable and safe. They will be all right now, but all of us miss you, Martin."

"I know Hilde and the tadpole will be all right, so will you and Leona, things will be fine," he smiled reassurance at Aaron. "And Aaron, Dengen Po and the pervert are here."

The bright glow began to fade and Martin spoke quickly. Aaron cupped a hand behind his ear to hear better. "What? You say Po and the pervert are *there*?"

"They are," Martin raised his voice, speaking faster as he faded. "They're in some sort of program I guess you'd call it." The affectionate grin Aaron knew so well surfaced, briefly brightening again, "You always said we were recycling humanity, But Aaron, *you ain't seen nothin' yet!"*

Jackie Griffey

HAPPILY EVER AFTER JAZZ

Aaron made it to Tennessee and was catching catfish and crappie from his custom built pier before either of the two homes were finished.

He lived to enjoy six fine grandchildren and to attend the ceremony when Martin and Hilde's son graduated from medical school with honors.

Young Martin was almost as good a boxer and martial arts expert as he was a surgeon, since the 'tadpole' nickname stuck, and he had to fight his way through school.

If you want to know what kind of recycling Martin and Aaron are into now, you'll just have to obey the ten commandments and follow them, won't you?

***

WELCOME TO LAZARUS

"Peril! Passion! A possible Pulitzer? Its all part of reporter Bob Smith's 24 hour memory gap."

Memphis Sci-Fi's Darrell Award Honorable Mention

Jackie Griffey's books are available on net pages from Barnes and Noble to Wal-Mart or at Booksurge and Bookman Publications. Go to her web page for other books in print and announcements of upcoming works. http://www.webspawner.com/users/webspawnerjacspromo. Happy Reading!

CHAPTER ONE

LORD!

Bob ran a finger around his collar and loosened his tie, watching the road signs along the freeway. The heat and the air conditioner seemed to be fighting it out, and the air conditioner was losing. He questioned his sanity for driving when he could have been sitting in an air-conditioned bus.

He had been freelancing, writing articles and anything else he could pick up in the way of work, when the chance at a job in Little Rock offered him enough permanence, if not money, to entice him into the unpredictable Arkansas weather.

There should be a better word for this than hot! This humidity is something else! He wiped his face with a handkerchief, catching sight of a distant road sign.

At least, having no one to notify and not much in the way of possessions, all I've got to do is get there, if this antique of mine will make it.

He smiled to himself, *Have heap, will leap!*

The sign turned out to be a state line marker and the exit sign just beyond promised fuel and food in a couple of miles.

I'm in Arkansas now, thank goodness for that next exit. I'm ready for a drink of damn near anything, as long as it's got plenty of ice in it.

He pulled into the right lane to exit and frowned, sucking in his breath. Wisps of smoke appeared, coming up over the hood of the car.

That looks like trouble. There's fuel at this next exit, maybe my luck will hold long enough to find a mechanic who knows what he's doing and not trying to make enough to retire on every deal.

The sign as he left the freeway read, *Welcome to Lazarus.*

Just beyond was a group of buildings. A neat and efficient looking post office nestled among large, old looking trees, a Dairy Delight centered in a big parking lot, and at a little distance up a hill, he saw the promised service station.

Eyeing the wisps of smoke he pulled into the Dairy Delight lot. He stood beside the car holding the door open, hoping the stop and cooling off would help whatever might be wrong.

As if anything could cool off in this heat, I feel like I'm done medium well, myself!

He rolled down the window and slammed the door. He pulled at the back of his shirt, which was already beginning to stick to him and headed for the Dairy Delight's service window.

A teenaged girl saw him and slid open the window. "Yes, sir?

Bob pointed, "Give me a biggee cola like that picture. Better make that two.

The heat wrapped around him again when the window closed, but he felt better for the brief respite and didn't see any more smoke coming from the car. He turned at the sound of the window opening again.

"That will be four dollars and twenty cents, sir."

Bob hunted for change, then peered inside as he handed the girl his money.

"Is there any place at all to sit in there," he asked hopefully.

"No, sir, I'm sorry. There's a couple of tables at the side of the building, and some benches across the street." The last was said as if she had memorized it.

"Okay, thanks."

The girl went through a door inside and Bob regarded the two concrete tables in the hot sun.

Probably raise blisters on your backside. He cringed at the thought, turning away.

The benches in front of the post office were in deep shade from the ancient looking trees. With the sack in one hand and one of his drinks in the other, Bob started across the street.

All the benches were occupied. He walked slowly, hoping someone would decide to get up and leave him one to himself. No one did.

Not having any choice, he approached the sole occupant of the shaded bench nearest him and stood looking down, feeling like an intruder.

"Mind if I sit here?"

"Nope, suit yourself."

Bob studied the man from the corner of his eye. He appeared to be about fifty-five or perhaps closer to sixty, was wearing sturdy boots in spite of the heat, and bib overalls which had faded to one of the blue shades in the sports shirt he was wearing.

Downing about a third of his drink, Bob managed a tentative smile and stuck out his hand.

"Bob Smith," he introduced himself. "Is it always this hot in Arkansas?"

The man shook hands, smile wrinkles deepening in the weathered face. "No, sometimes it's hotter. My name's Dale Carpenter. You visitin' kin hereabouts?"

"No," Bob unwrapped his sandwich as he answered. "I'm on my way to Little Rock. Going to take a reporting job on a newspaper there."

"Oh," His voice dropped a little. "Reporting job," his voice trailed off.

Bob wondered if he'd heard a little disappointment in the reaction to his only passing through, but put it down to wishful thinking.

With a little less drawl, his voice sounds like dad's. He looks like the uncle I might have had if I weren't the only child of only children. Now who's doing the wishful thinking? He wondered briefly if one could adopt family other than children, like perhaps an uncle, if you found one who seemed compatible?

A slight breeze rustled the leaves above them. Paper dry, the sound added to the deep shade's illusion of coolness.

As they talked, their conversation was punctuated by several local people passing by. Two of them wished Dale Carpenter a happy birthday.

His natural curiosity prompted Bob to ask, "This your birthday? Today?"

Dale looked away, "Yep."

Amused at the short answer, Bob prodded. "How old are you? Or shouldn't I ask?"

Still looking away as if making up his mind about something, Dale finally confided, "I'm a hundred and twenty-eight."

Bob smothered a snicker. "Not telling, huh?"

"Just did," was the curt reply. "Ain't no secret."

"Oh, come on, how old?"

Dale Carpenter was not amused. "A hundred and twenty-eight."

"Yeah?" Bob's expression was as scornful and skeptical as his voice, "Quick, what year were you born?"

"Eighteen sixty-seven," came without hesitation.

Bob did a little mental arithmetic as Dale continued, not as irritated, but still studying the dusty street.

"June it was. Maw was glad to have Paw back from the war with all his arms and legs, and have a couple of good crops behind them. I reckon that's why I got my invite to join the human race."

"The war," Bob echoed cautiously.

"Yes, the war." He treated Bob to a glimpse of impatience before his eyes returned to the road. "The war between the states, the one you Yankees call the civil war. Humpf! Ain't nothin' civil about a war!"

"Yeah, you're right about that," Bob was carefully neutral. "I don't know if I'd qualify for Yankee or not, being from St. Louis, but I sure can't argue with that. Nothing civil about a war."

309

Having carefully agreed with the obvious, he busily gathered up the scraps from his meal and crammed them into the sack to throw away.

He turned around at the trash can, "Well, have a good birthday."

"Thanks." Dale hesitated, giving him an oddly speculative look as if he wanted to say something else. He didn't. Turning to leave too, he added only, "Hope the reportin' job turns out good."

Back at his car, Bob looked back at the empty bench as he closed the door.

Takes all kinds to people a planet, I guess. He's got some kind of hang-up about his age, that's for sure.

He felt better after his lunch and the refreshing rest in the shade. He smiled to himself, remembering Dale sitting there with his thumbs hooked under the straps of his overalls. *He's a better straight faced con artist than I am when I'm working on a story. Must be a heck of a poker player!*

He chuckled to himself as he turned the key. His joy was short lived, the car wouldn't start. Several more tries resulted in only an ominous silence. There wasn't any more smoke, but the car was deader than last week's news.

Bob got out and stood looking at the uncooperative heap.

Great! Just great! And I don't see anything as helpful as a phone anywhere around here.

His eyes searched the Dairy delight lot as well as the area in front of the post office. He pictured himself being towed ignominiously into Little Rock. *Some grand entrance! As if I could afford a tow that far!*

He slammed the door with the thought that it was all that still worked, and started back toward the Dairy Delight's service window.

There was no one in sight inside. Bob knocked loudly on the glass window. "Miss? Miss?"

The girl hurried through the door from the back room. "Sorry, sir. I didn't hear a car, didn't know you were here."

"There was nothing to hear." Bob kept the sarcasm out of his voice. It wasn't her fault the car wouldn't start.

"Do you have a phone I can use, and is there a repair shop around here that you can recommend?"

"No," the answer was apologetic. "There's a coin phone around the back, but it's broke. Best mechanic around here is at that station up the hill there," she gestured.

"He's good, is he?" Bob was doubtful, she didn't look old enough to drive, to him, but she did seem sympathetic.

He tried to explain. "I don't know what's wrong with my car, has this guy been in business long? What I mean is, I need someone who knows what he's doing, who's got enough experience to find out what the trouble is and get it fixed."

"He's been up there as long as I can remember," was accompanied by a reassuring smile. "And he must be good, because everybody around here takes their cars to him when something needs to be fixed. That's where my daddy takes his truck when he needs help," she added by way of encouragement.

"That sounds pretty good to me, he must be good if he's got his neighbors' confidence." He grinned at her and raised his eyebrows, "Your daddy's truck still running?"

"Yes," she grinned back. "Runs good."

"Okay, I'll go and talk to him."

He turned and heard the window close behind him. With a last look at his car, he cut across the lot and started up the hill remembering when he'd made the decision to move.

Bob had stood in front of the weathered exterior of the old and respected newspaper's building. The sturdy facade looked as tough as the profession it housed. He glanced at the sign beside the door as he entered and went up the stairs to the editor's office.

The door was open and he was alone. Bob knocked on the door's facing, hoping he'd have better luck talking face to face than a phone call would afford him.

The editor, a balding man in shirt sleeves, beckoned him in.

"I was in the area and thought I'd check with you," Bob began, ignoring the tight feeling in his chest.

The editor shook his head, his expression dour. "We've hit a dry spell newswise," he smiled slightly. "The help, even clerical, is bored enough to drink that bad coffee in the breakroom, to give you an idea."

"Yeah, that's desperate, all right," Bob's smile didn't quite make it. "You mean there's nothing at all?"

"Nothing means nothing. Not even a storm anywhere. My top reporter is training the cub I lost my mind and hired in one of my optimistic fits."

He learned back in his chair. "Believe me, if I had anything, you'd have heard from me. Why don't you take this lull for personal business, or just rest, take some time off?"

Bob saw the boy sitting beside one of the desks in the newsroom and wondered briefly if he should go and warn him about this business. The lack of work always managed to come when he needed work the most. Murphy's law echoed between his ears. Anything that can go wrong will, and at the worst possible time. It summed up freelancing just right. The editor's advice taunted him.

Some time off. Yeah, like the next ninety years!

Aloud he'd said, "I'll think about it. I'll be in touch."

He had gone directly to the pay phone on the street in front of the building and called about the job that had been offered to him in Little Rock.

So, here I am, dead in the water and melting like a snowball in July. But I know I made the right decision. Now that I've given up my glamorous jock, unpredictable life for a job where I can pay my predictable bills, I'll get there, by George, if I have to push that Dodge!

He slowed his uphill trot to catch his breath as he neared the open shop doors beside the station. He stopped, letting his eyes adjust to the comparative dimness inside.

A light on a cord hung over an open hood and someone was moving around in the back of the shop.

"Yes, sir," someone called. "Be right with you."

A hood slammed down and Bob saw the mechanic moving toward him, wiping his hands on a shop cloth. He stopped in front of him, cramming the cloth into his back pocket, and looked past him at the empty drive.

"You got car trouble?" He eyed Bob's shirt and tie, "I'm not in the market to buy anything right now."

"Oh no, no, I'm not selling anything. I do have car trouble. The worst kind. It won't start."

"Uh-huh. Where's it at?"

"It's parked down there by the Dairy delight There was some smoke as I pulled off the freeway, and I was going to have it checked anyway, but it won't start."

"Did it turn over at all? Sound like it might start but couldn't make it?"

Bob shook his head. "No. Nothing. It's just - dead. And the battery's only a couple of months old, so I don't think it's that. But, like I said before, there was some smoke coming up over the hood before I stopped."

The mechanic nodded solemnly, "More'n likely steam, not smoke, 'ud be my guess. Come on, well go get her."

He shoved the shop cloth farther down in his pocket as he walked, and Bob followed him to the wrecker parked in front of the station.

He must be good as the Dairy delight clerk said, if he keeps this truck running. Wonder what year this thing is?

On the way down the hill, Bob's imagination tortured him with possibilities of what might be wrong with his car. He pictured himself standing in front of it as it cowered before him. He got out a gun, facing it in a Clint Eastwood stance as he gazed at it with a stone face. There was a loud, metallic twang as the fenders broke loose and the front ends shielded its lights like eyes. He raised the gun. His finger tightened on the trigger -

"Keep your seat," the mechanic's voice broke into his fantasy. He got out, looking a lot more cheerful than Bob felt.

"Won't take long to hook her up."

Bob cringed back against the truck's hard bench seat and squeezed his eyes shut, trying to block out the sounds as his only transportation was hoisted groaning, it seemed to him, to be towed. He pulled out his billfold and checked to make sure his credit card was there just to have something to do with his hands, and the mechanic was back.

"All set. I'll give her a look soon's we get back. There's no rush on the Chevy I'm workin' on."

"Thanks, I appreciate that."

Back at the station Bob got out and looked the other way as the mechanic backed the car into the shop. He was braced to hear breaking glass any minute, but there weren't any sounds except the door opening again. He paced like an expectant father as the wrecker was parked back out front. He followed the mechanic back in and stood by as he raised the hood.

I feel like he can fix it, and it's not like I've got much choice anyway.

"Now, lemme see where you hurt" The mechanic frowned down at the ailing insides and fanned a wisp away with his cloth.

Bob quickly stepped back, "Don't know why I'm trying to see anyway, I don't know any more than I did. My expertise stops at the accelerator. Or maybe the brakes."

"Oh, you majored in radio, did you?" The mechanic laughed.

He bent over, eyes and fingers busy. "Good news for me. Couldn't make a living if everybody could do his own mechanic work."

Looking around, he saw how worried Bob was and suggested kindly, "Why'nt you wait in the office? There's a fan and a few magazines in there. I'll holler when I find out what the trouble is."

Bob nodded and went, feeling like he'd done all he could and the heap was in good hands.

He got the feeling he'd stepped back in time as he looked around the small office. The magazines were old and the fan wasn't doing much good, moving the warm air around. He took off his tie, shook his head at being taken for a salesman, and paced the small office space until he heard the mechanic call to him.

"Mister?"

Bob hurried through the door. "Smith," he said, "My name's Bob Smith,"

"Mine's Silas Wilson," he pointed, "Like on the sign there. Mr. Smith, I checked the radiator first. A rock from one of our gravel trucks around here can do a lot of damage to one -"

Bob's heart sank. Radiators are expensive.

"But the radiator's all right. The rattling I know you've been hearing is the water pump. Bad bearing. It's a wonder that's not what went out. You're going to have to replace it soon's you can."

Bob's worry lines deepened, "Will it make it on into Little Rock? I'm on my way to take a job there."

Silas Wilson spoke cautiously. "It's in bad shape, but yeah, I think it will make it on into Little Rock. The water pump, that is. What caused the steam you thought was smoke was the lower radiator hose. It's old and cracked, and plumb wore out. It's got to be replaced. Now, It won't go without it."

"It won't." It was an admission, not a question. "You got one you can put on it?"

"No, I ain't. It's an eighty model Dodge and I don't have one that will do. Have to send to the next town to get one. But," he added on a brighter note, "I can get one here by in the morning and start on it soon's I get it. I can have you outta here by this time tomorrow."

"Tomorrow?"

"Yes, sir, it's the best I can do. There's not a parts house here. What I'll do is order it by bus and they'll bring it tomorrow. And as I said, I'll put it on soon's it gets here."

Bob sighed, resigned. "Well, as you pointed out, it won't go without it. But, do you think it will get me there? To Little Rock? Maybe I'd better go on and take the bus myself." He added regretfully, "But I need my car, that's why I decided to drive it."

"I know what you mean.," Silas sympathized. "That water pump needs to be replaced as soon as you get there and can, but I think putting the hose on it will get you on into Little Rock, all right."

"Okay, let's do it, then."

Silas nodded. "You want to call the people about your job you're going to?"

"No, it's all right. I don't have to be there till Monday."

"Oh," Silas's smile was friendly, "That's good. Who you goin' to work for?"

"The newspaper there. A friend of mine told me about the job opening. He's an investigative reporter in St. Louis and he told me about it when he found out I was looking for something."

Silas's expression had been getting progressively grimmer as he listened. "You mean," he asked as if hoping he'd heard wrong, "You're a reporter?" He made reporter sound like it might be contagious.

"Yeah," Bob grinned, almost laughing at the look on Silas's face, "Is that bad?"

"No! No," Silas was embarrassed. "I, I just ain't never met one before is all."

"Well, now you have. And if I'm going to have to stay here until tomorrow, is there a motel or hotel where I can stay near here?"

Silas perked up. "Yes, there is. A real nice motel on the other side of town where the by-pass ends. It's called The Local Gentry. Has a nice restaurant, too. If you want to call, there's a phone in the office and I'll take you over there soon's I close up. It won't be long now."

"All right, I'll go in and call. And I'll take you up on the offer of a ride," He turned at the door, already feeling better. "Thanks."

Silas looked up as he came back a little later, "Get a room?"

"Sure did. I'm all set. Got a room, read all your magazines, and there's a customer waiting to pay you for some gas."

He held the door open for Silas as he entered the office.

The customer was a boy of about twelve. He had filled up his plastic container with gas and stood waiting to pay for it.

"Tommy Joe," Silas's face lit up. "Just the gent I want to see, to save me a long distance call."

He waved at Bob, "This is my customer, Mr. Smith."

"Mr. Smith," Tommy Joe acknowledged and nodded solemnly.

"Hello," Bob smiled, noticing his bare, browned feet.

Tommy Joe held up the gas. "Come to get me some lawn mower gas."

"All right, but leave your gas here for now. I want you to take this envelope down to the bus driver before he leaves." Silas scribbled something quickly and held it out to him. "It's an order for a hose I've got to have."

"First bus. Okay." Tommy Joe scooted the full container farther over on the desk and put the envelope in his pocket. "Be back in a little bit."

Bob watched Tommy Joe hop on his bicycle as Silas started back to the shop.

"I'll be trying to persuade that hose to come off." He stopped, "When Tommy Joe comes back, tell him he can have the gas, but I want him to meet the bus in the morning and bring me that hose. I'll do a couple of things on the Chevy while I'm waiting."

"Okay, I'll tell him"

The noises from the shop were somehow comforting, and Bob continued exploring the small office. He examined the slightly shop-worn items beneath the cash register.

I guess that cash register came out about the same time as Silas's wrecker. He shook his head at a three year old calendar, admiring the pretty girl in a red bathing suit. *Must be keeping it for the art work.*

A movement caught his eye and he looked out the window to see Tommy Joe pumping his old bicycle up the hill.

"Hi," Bob greeted him, "Silas gave me a message for you."

"He did?" Tommy Joe wasn't all that trusting, in spite of his youth, "What's that?"

"He said you can have the gas, but he wants you to meet the bus and bring him that hose in the morning. I'd appreciate it, too."

"All right, I'll do that." Tommy Joe's answer was dead serious.

"Tell him I said thanks," he reached for the gas.

Bob beat him to the plastic container. "Here, I'll get that for you." He followed Tommy Joe out and watched as he picked up his bike. There was no basket.

"How are you going to carry this?"

"Pass the handle over the handlebars and I'll tie it on with this belt."

"Oh, okay. There you go." He watched as Tommy Joe finished securing the container. "You looking forward to going back to school?"

"Nope, outta school."

"I know. God knows, it's summer time, all right. I meant in September."

"No," Tommy Joe took hold of the handlebars, "Graduated years ago."

Surprised, Bob gazed into the hazel eyes above the freckled nose, "How old are you?"

Tommy Joe had one foot on a concrete block. He gave himself a good push off as he flung back his answer.

"Forty-two!"

CHAPTER TWO

Bob realized his mouth was open as he stared after the boy. He closed it with a snap and watched as Tommy Joe dodged a couple of chickens and sailed past the Dairy Delight.

Hick town's full of comedians, he grumbled to himself.

Silas appeared in the door behind him, "Did I hear Tommy Joe in here?"

"Yes, he just left. He said he would pick up the hose in the morning."

"Good. I got the old hose off, and thought I'd clean her up a little while I was at it. Get the stuff you want to take with you and put it in my truck while I get washed up. I'll be right there, if you're ready."

Why in the name of idiocy wouldn't I be ready? Bob ground his teeth before answering. "I'm ready," he managed without turning around,

He heard Silas's footsteps retreat and went back to his car, glad he would be leaving tomorrow. He got an old pajama bottom, underwear, and socks, and crammed them in on top his shaving things in his overnight case still wondering why he brought out such sarcasm in the local population. Silas was the only one who didn't seem to have any problems. His expression brightened, glad it wasn't the other way around and the only mechanic in town wasn't trying to be a stand-up comedian.

The old wrecker was functional if not beautiful, and familiar to everyone in town. The street they took wound through the town which was typical of all small towns except that the houses seemed to Bob to be roomier or older, and better kept than the ones in other small towns he had passed through on assignments for the Dispatch and others who had given him freelance assignments.

As they passed, most of the people were outside either caring for their lawns or sitting on wide front porches. They recognized Silas Wilson's truck and smiled or waved to him.

"Nice little town, more people here than I thought there would be."

He looked up as some of the street lights came on in the gathering dusk. "Those old fashioned street lights look like gas lamps. Cozy touch. They're not really gas, are they? It's hard to tell."

"No, they're not. But some of the fixtures are so old, they may have been, once. Truth is, electricity came here gradually, like everything else, and they just wired up what they had is what I 'spect happened. Why take them down if they can be used?"

"You're right. And they look good, too. Nice little town," Bob repeated.

"Yeah," Silas smiled. "It's home. Most of our families have been here so long, the ones who aren't related to each other feel like they are. At least kissin' cousins," he waved back at a boy crossing the street.

"Looks like a good place for a kid to grow up. That reminds me of something Tommy Joe said when he agreed to pick up the hose in the morning."

Bob paused, a little uncertain. "I asked him about school, and he told me he's graduated. I couldn't believe that and asked him how old he is. He said 'forty-two' and took off down the hill."

Silas looked straight ahead, either watching for children or pets which might dart out in front of him, or perhaps weighing his answer. Bob wasn't sure. He wondered uncomfortably if the boy was a nephew or might be one of those kissin' cousins, and he had been out of line with his remark.

Finally, Silas said as gravely as Tommy Joe, "He shouldn't have told you that."

Relieved, Bob shrugged. "Oh, it's all right, just took me a little by surprise is all. He's such a serious little fellow. But, every kid has to smart mouth a little, it's a natural part of growing up."

There was no further comment and Bob's attention was soon drawn to the motel they were approaching.

It was not only unexpectedly large and modern looking, it seemed to have a lot of business both in the motel and the restaurant, which had its own outside entrance.

"Something must be going on, there's so many cars, Silas commented. He jerked his head toward the parking lot, "You can tell when most folks get paid by checking the cars in front of it," he grinned at Bob.

"That's a good sign. I've skipped dinner when I'm working on something, but I like a good breakfast. I'll have a good one to start me out in the morning."

They slowed to a stop, the driveway ahead of them blocked by a couple waiting for someone to come out of a parking space.

"Just let me out here, Silas, and I'll walk on up. I've only got this little overnighter, no point in your sitting here waiting."

"Okay, then. I'll just back out. I don't know if they'll bring you back to the shop in the morning or not. I heard they've got a new van, so I think they will. But if they don't for some reason, give me a call and I'll come get you."

"Are there any cabs here, I don't remember passing any, come to think of it. But, how can you -"

"Don't worry about it. I can close up a few minutes, that's what I do when I get a wrecker call. It'll be no problem."

"Okay, see you tomorrow."

Bob watched until Silas got safely back on the road, his natural good nature restored by having a comfortable place to stay and a good breakfast to look forward to.

Thank goodness Silas will get my car fixed tomorrow. Nice, friendly little town, I might just stay if I was ready to retire like Dale Carpenter.

He frowned without realizing it. *Can't help but wonder why he told me that whopper about his age. Then Tommy Joe got into the act. Must be some kind of local humor.*

He walked slowly, busy with his thoughts, and stopped when a loud noise caught his attention. He stood watching in admiration as a beautiful young girl on a tractor sized mower came across the lawn toward the drive.

"Hey there," he called out to tease her, "You're going to need lights on that thing in a few minutes!"

The setting sun caressed the pretty face and made golden glints in her hair as he watched, fascinated by her looks and her expertise on the big machine. His smile faded as she came alarmingly close.

"That's not your problem, Sonny Boy," came the terse reply not softened by a smile or even a pleasant look as she concentrated on the machine, "I can handle it."

She swerved at the last minute, neatly, as if she'd done it before.

Bob looked down at the grass sprayed over his shoes as she wheeled the metal monster around to head back across the broad expanse of lawn, ignoring him.

Well! Excuse me! And Sonny? I've never been called Sonny before in my life - and by an old hag of what? Sixteen or seventeen?

He started walking again and smiled to himself. *Or maybe she's forty-two like Tommy Joe! Oh, well, good looking, anyway.*

He was now close enough to see through the glass doors and looked around as he went in. His whole body breathed in the refreshing coolness of the air conditioning as he made his way over to the chest high desk to register.

There were two other people ahead of him, giving him time to admire the place. He hadn't got over his surprise of finding a place like this in the little town of Lazarus.

Whoever runs this place must have the know-how and the money to do it right. No doubt being the only inn here helps. I'll use my credit card for this and my meals.

The clerk behind the desk was pointing to what looked like a restaurant sign. Bob moved closer to hear what she was saying.

"And we have excellent room service, too. You'll find a menu, both breakfast and dinner, in your room."

The customer nodded and left, and Bob stepped up, sporting the friendly smile he felt had already taken such a beating at the hands of the local wise crackers.

"I called this afternoon. My name's Bob Smith." As the clerk consulted the computer he added, "Paying by credit card."

"Yes, sir, here it is." She smiled back at him, "You're in room thirty-two. Will you be with us more than one night? We have a program which lets us give you a discount on the fourth night," she explained.

"No," he smiled again to soften the negative answer. "One night and a good breakfast will fix me up. I'm on my way to take a new job."

"Oh," the young clerk was politely interested, "Will you be working near here?"

"No, not too near. I'm going to work in Little Rock. For the newspaper there."

Her eyes widened, "You're a reporter?"

"You know, you're the second person who's asked me that. You must not get many reporters through here."

He raised his eyebrows and squinted at her, comically suspicious. Trying not to grin, he lowered his voice to an accented stage whisper, "Or iss there some terrible dark *zeecret* you are trying to hide from the *world?"*

"No," the clerk denied with a breathy little laugh, "Nothing as exciting as that. But we don't have many reporters staying with us, you're right about that."

She brightened, "Let us know if we can do anything to make your stay more enjoyable."

"Now, that's friendlier. More enjoyable?" Bob considered briefly, "How about a date with that yard person I saw on my way in?"

The clerk giggled, "You'd better reconsider that. She's married to a great big farmer, and besides that, she's probably too old for you!" She laughed, her eyes dancing.

Bob laughed with her. "Oh, well, then I'll just have to be a good boy and eat my dinner. I think I heard you say the restaurant entrance is on the other side of that sign down there and they open at seven in the morning?"

"Yes, sir." She handed him his key. "And the food is good, too. Enjoy your dinner."

Room thirty-two didn't disappoint Bob. It was comfortably and attractively decorated, and he approved the shampoo and lotions provided by the management as he brushed his teeth.

This is certainly a lot better than I was expecting. I'd class it somewhere between the better Holiday Inns and the more expensive chains. But that restaurant puts it way ahead if it lives up to what Silas said about it.

He rinsed his mouth and struck a pose in the mirror. *I don't kid myself I really look like a teeny-bopper Sonny, but the clerk saved my ego by flirting back with me and she said the yard smarty is probably too old for me, bless her generous heart.*

He chuckled at his reflection. *She must have been kidding about her being married.*

On the way out he checked to make sure he had his key, surveyed the room again, and felt good about his prospects. Not having a choice about staying, he was looking forward to a good meal in the restaurant. It served to remind him he would be getting a regular paycheck from now on and could keep his credit card for emergencies instead of meals.

The dining room was large as well as colorful and cozy, charmingly decorated in keeping with the turn of the century gas lamps. The pretty hostess approaching him fit the scene in her long dress and apron.

"Party of one," Bob murmured self-consciously, his eyes confirming he was the only one in sight dining alone.

As she seated him and handed him a menu, the light caught a gold pin on the bib of her apron.

"Is that a service pin?"

"Yes," she paused, regarding the gold ten. "What it means to me, is I get an extra week's vacation."

"You must have started when you were in kindergarten, "Bob commented, finding her more interesting than the menu.

"How long has the yard person been here? The one I saw mowing the grass as I came in this afternoon?"

"I'm not sure. I think she's been here almost as long as I have, but she only works in the summer and part-time in the winter. A waitress will be with you in just a few minutes" As she left she turned and added with a smile, "Enjoy your meal," then hurried toward a couple waiting to be seated.

Bob opened the menu and was scanning the prices and good selection of entrees when the sound of sudden laughter caught his attention. The door to a private dining room was open and several waitresses were carrying in food and beverages for what seemed to be a large party in progress.

That must be the 'something going on' Silas mentioned when we saw all those cars outside.

Through the door he could see a white haired, attractively groomed woman of sixty or sixty-five. She was seated at a long table with other people apparently around the same age. It seemed to be a festive and happy occasion, with people of both sexes in attendance. On the table in front of the woman was a very large and intricately decorated, double tiered cake. On the wide bottom layer, the number two hundred was done in elaborate pink rosettes.

Bob didn't realize he was staring until he looked up from the cake to find the woman's eyes on him.

Jackie Griffey

Her expression struck him like a physical blow. It was unpleasant to the point of a threat, surprisingly foreign to a party setting. And from a total stranger!

She looks as paranoid as the sick humor going around here, maybe I should get Silas out of here. He almost laughed, wondering if she thought he was going to ask for a piece of that wonderously decorated cake.

He simply returned the unsmiling stare. Then as suddenly as it had opened, the door closed, cutting off his view of the gathering.

The waitress appeared and took his order. He concentrated on the meal he had been looking forward to.

The door to the private room opened and closed as the party was served, but didn't stay open long enough for Bob to see any more or have a clue as to what the occasion was. He decided the group must be some local business to be so well attended.

He refused dessert and paid with his credit card on the way out, still puzzled at the woman's unfriendly expression. He dismissed the unpleasant face as he noticed the same friendly clerk was at the desk. He stopped.

"Excuse me?"

"Yes, sir?" The clerk smiled, recognizing him. "Did you enjoy your dinner?"

"Sure did. Excellent meal. What time is check out time tomorrow?"

"Eleven o'clock, sir."

"And I was told you have a van. I'm having some work done on my car, the shop owner brought me over here this afternoon. Will the van be available to take me back to the shop tomorrow?"

"Yes, sir. Just let us know when you want to leave in the morning."

"Oh, and one other thing -"

"Yes?"

"What business is it that's having the company celebration in the dining room tonight? Looks like it might be a retirement party?"

The clerk moved to her desk, "Just a minute and I can tell you."

She turned pages in a ledger, her finger moving quickly down the lines. "Here it is."

She looked up. "But it's not a business in there, the reservation was made by a private party."

"A private party," Bob recalled the stern face. "A woman?"

"Yes, sir," she smiled confidentially. "It says here it's her birthday."

"B - birthday –" Bob repeated the word softly. The knuckles of his hand gripping the edge of the desk showed white.

"Sir?" The clerk was alarmed at his pale face. "Sir, are you all right?"

"What?" Bob recovered from the shiver that shook him like ice water running down his spine. "Yes. Yes, I'm all right. I'm fine. Heat's getting to me, I guess. Thank you."

He backed away a bit. He smiled weakly by way of reassurance and moved toward the door, unaware of the hostile eyes that followed him.